'Precise and perceptive . . . Deeply satisfying . . . We may struggle to find hope, Hope tells us, but it is there in the landscape, in faith and memory and ritual, in the ancient unchanging silences that persist' *Guardian*

'Mesmerizing . . . Imaginative . . . Among its many impressive elements is Hope's handling of the past . . . Her greatest talent is in getting under the skin of her characters . . . There is a subtle plangency in this powerful portrait of human folly and ferocity' *Herald*

'Full of wisdom about the blink-and-you'll-miss-it nature of our lives' *Good Housekeeping*

'Lyrical and timely' *Stella*

'Mysterious and beautiful. It reminded me of *Cloud Atlas*, but it's very much itself: so bold and wild, but controlled and fierce. It's stunning writing and it has left me with hope that we can tell stories like these even as the carbon builds, and that imagination and ideas remain powerful and valid' Russell T. Davies, writer of *It's a Sin*

'Brilliant. A stunning book of extraordinary, audacious scale' Sadie Jones, author of *The Snakes*

'Poetic, philosophical and wildly captivating . . . Anna Hope captures the human condition and feeds it treats while you watch it shimmer. Her characters dance, crawl and blast off the page, like mystical beings who are at the same time solidly human. I swam in this book and didn't want to come up for air' Emma Jane Unsworth, author of *Animals* and *Adults*

'I loved it. I became invested in each of the different eras and was struck by the sense of unknowable forces outliving us all. It is full of wisdom, intricate and emotional, and it will linger in my head for a long time' Dave Haslam, author of *Sonic Youth Slept On My Floor*

'Anna Hope is such a generous and sensitive writer, and *The White Rock* is full of extraordinary voices and ideas. Absolutely a story for our times, and a fiercely important one, too' Clover Stroud, author of *The Red of my Blood*

'I loved the sparseness, the moments of poetry, the quiet brutality. The voice throughout is fierce and graceful and utterly compelling; each central character is rich and beautifully pinpointed. It is her strongest work yet' Melody Razak, author of *Moth*

'*The White Rock* is a sublime, poetic and visionary work of art' Ron Rash, author of *In the Valley*

The White Rock

ANNA HOPE

PENGUIN BOOKS

PENGUIN BOOKS

UK | USA | Canada | Ireland | Australia
India | New Zealand | South Africa

Penguin Books is part of the Penguin Random House group of companies
whose addresses can be found at global.penguinrandomhouse.com.

Penguin
Random House
UK

First published by Fig Tree 2022
Published in Penguin Books 2023
001

Copyright © Anna Hope, 2022
Illustrations by Josie Staveley Taylor

The moral right of the author has been asserted

Lyrics on p. 31, 'we've all gone to look for America', a variation on lyrics from the song
'America', written by Paul Simon and performed by Simon & Garfunkel; the song title on p. 39,
'Hello, I love you', written by The Doors; on p. 58, 'arms that are braceleted and white and bare',
from T. S. Eliot's poem 'The Love Song of J. Alfred Prufrock'; lyrics on p. 230, 'trouble on the way'
from 'Bad Moon Rising', written by John Fogerty and performed by Creedence Clearwater Revival.
Every effort has been made to obtain the necessary permissions with reference to copyright material.
We apologise for any omissions in this respect and will be pleased to make the appropriate
acknowledgements in any future edition.

Typeset by Jouve (UK), Milton Keynes
Printed and bound in Great Britain by Clays Ltd, Elcograf S.p.A.

The authorized representative in the EEA is Penguin Random House Ireland,
Morrison Chambers, 32 Nassau Street, Dublin D02 YH68

A CIP catalogue record for this book is available from the British Library

ISBN: 978–0–241–99549–5

www.greenpenguin.co.uk

For my father, Tony Hope (1945–2020)

Contents

The Writer
2020

Mumma,
Yes love?
Did you know?
What's that?
A billion is a lot more than tons.
It is. You're right.
Mumma?
Yes love?
Can I watch another cartoon?

*

It is very hot in the back of the van.

The writer's small daughter is sprawled uncomfortably in the seat beside her, headphones on, staring at the grubby screen of the laptop, watching a cartoon in which three children are dressed as superheroes. They have a totem pole with wings and a vehicle that flies. Their enemies are a young man with a grey streak in his hair and a girl on a hoverboard. They dress as a gecko, an owl and a cat. In this episode, the boy dressed as a gecko loses his voice, or finds it – the woman does not know which, despite the fact that she has half watched it many times. Five episodes of this cartoon downloaded hastily in an airless Mexico City hotel room ten days ago are all she has had – all her daughter has had, once the colouring books and food and juice and stories have lost their appeal – for distraction from the endless road.

The woman shifts in her seat and crumbs from saltine crackers fall from her lap onto the floor. Her back is stiff. Everything is stiff. Her skin is desert-weathered, her lips chapped. She spent the entirety of last night sitting, awake, alongside the other eleven occupants of this van, around a fire, several thousand feet up in the mountains of the Sierra Madre Occidental. Before it was dawn, they kicked earth over the embers, packed up their belongings, their sleeping bags and dusty blankets and coats and hats and bags, and carried them and their children down the side of the mountain. Now, after close to seven hours' driving, hugging the pines and the heights, the vegetation is changing, there are palm trees, there is bougainvillea, there are signs for Pacífico, the beer of the coast – jaunty, nautical; an anchor and the sea framed within a lifebelt – painted onto the sides of the little roadside tiendas.

She should really try to nap, but the episodes of the cartoon need changing manually, so if she were to sleep, she would need to wake again after eleven minutes. Which would likely be worse than not sleeping at all. Besides, soon, in a couple of hours, perhaps less, they will no longer be in this van, they will be in the town of their destination, a sleepy old colonial remnant, and when they have completed this last leg of the journey there will be a hotel room and a bed and air conditioning, a cold Pacífico, some food. And then, perhaps, sleep.

On the screen of the laptop, the credits roll. The woman presses pause and pulls her daughter over towards her. Her little girl wriggles. She feels hot to the touch. Her cheeks are red. There is the warm yeasty unbrushed-teeth smell of her breath.

Do you want something to eat?

The woman leans forward, rattles the seat pocket. Slim pickings: day-old crackers. An apple. Spicy crisps.

4

Her daughter shakes her head. Her glassy eyes slide back to the screen. Milk, says the little girl. Mi-ilk.

She seems only to want to drink milk. Not water. Oat milk if possible, almond milk if not. Three, four, five times a day, from a bottle. Which has necessitated frequent stops at roadside shops.

We don't have milk, poppet. We'll stop soon and I'll get some more. Promise.

Her daughter's face twists. She looks like she might be about to cry. Or hit something. I. Want. Mi-ilk, she says.

Most of the time, on this journey, here in this double seat they have shared across the miles and hours of Mexican highway, this is how her little daughter has looked. The writer doesn't blame her. Most of the time, on this journey, this is how she herself has felt.

I. Want. Mi-ilk. I.WANT. MY. MI-ILK.

Sweetheart. We don't have any milk. I just said. Story? the writer tries, reaching for her Kindle.

The writer went along to a parenting group once when her daughter was tiny, at which a need for statements was impressed upon the mothers who were gathered there.

Children, said the woman who was leading the group, *are presented with too much choice. Bamboozled with it. How are they supposed to know what they want for dinner? We think we are being good parents by giving them choices, by framing things as questions, but we are being quite the opposite.*

Tell them. Don't ask them. And everyone will be happier.

The writer has never quite got the hang of this.

No! her daughter says now, shaking her head. Not story. Another *car-toon*.

Her daughter, on the other hand, at three years old, has mastered the declarative statement. The woman shrugs. Right

5

now, at this stage in the game, she has passed the point of resistance and her daughter knows it.

Okay, she says, toggling at the keypad. Okay.

She finds the next episode and the superhero children are off, released from their digital slumber, streaking across the screen, leaving vapour trails in their wake. They seem to live in a French town, these superhero kids, leaping over higgledy grey houses with mansard roofs by the light of a cold northern moon. Her daughter sings along with the theme tune, drumming with her calves on the edge of the seat.

Inooo-e -night u aaave e day . . . oooaahh eees eroes oo owooo de way pJ masks duduPj MASKSdududu . . .

In the seat in front, the Senegalese woman half turns and smiles at the sound of the tuneless singing. Through the gap in the seats the writer can see the daughter of the Senegalese woman fast asleep and tucked in close to her mother, her face smooth and untroubled. Her lips gently parted.

There are many things the writer would like to learn about being a mother: she would like to learn, for instance, how this elegant Senegalese woman manages to keep her own daughter quiet and placid through all this gruelling journeying without the aid of a screen. How she manages to be strict without being mean. How she never seems to be on the verge of completely losing her shit. The writer would like to learn too how, every time they have arrived somewhere new, even the most improbable of places, the Senegalese woman has immediately managed to undertake the task of locating a pan, boiling water, pouring it into a bowl, and stripping then washing her daughter.

The first time she saw this happen, the writer was struck silent by the sight of the little girl knee-deep in the red plastic bowl in the middle of the desert. There was a leather rope knotted around her belly.

Is that for protection? the writer asked, shyly.

Yes, said the Senegalese woman, as she washed her daughter with her steady, sure hands, but said no more.

From what? the writer wanted to say but did not.

What she also wanted to say was – *Where might I get one? For my daughter, for myself?*

Instead, she asked to borrow the bowl when the Senegalese woman and her daughter were done.

After their baths, the daughter of the Senegalese woman was dressed in clean clothes, her skin massaged with sweet-smelling oil, while the writer's daughter went straight back out to play in the dirt – the thick desert dirt that wasn't really dirt, more sand and earth, but which coated everything: your hair, your clothes, your lungs. Her daughter loves this dirt – has insisted, when they make their fires at night, that she wishes to sleep on the ground, not tucked up safely in the blankets and sleeping bags of her parents. If she has not been given her way she has protested, has shouted and cried and lamented. And so, a strange little theatre has ensued, watched by all, as the writer and her husband have attempted to cajole their little girl back to the safety of the sleeping bags, away from the flames.

Throughout these scenes, the Senegalese woman and her daughter have invariably been sound asleep, tucked up together on a blanket on the ground, where they have stayed, without moving, throughout the night.

Outside the van, the sun is fierce. The corn crops are throwing shade in the heat-struck fields. The road they are on is a straight one now – for a long time this morning they were following the course of a looping river, the Grande de Santiago – but at the last town they crossed it and now they have left it to its courses further north.

They should, perhaps, have stopped and tried to get milk in

that last little town, but her daughter was sleeping then; everyone was sleeping then except the writer in the back and her husband and the two men – a Mexican man and a Colombian man – beside him in the front. They were talking, the men, and because there was no music playing, she was able to hear them – speaking about something that happened close to the quiet little town not so very long before, when the members of the Cartel Jalisco Nueva had, apparently, downed a police helicopter with a rocket launcher. The men spoke about this in hushed, sober voices as the van passed slowly through the plaza, past the church, past the small children in uniform hand in hand on their way home from school, their backpacks bumping on their backs.

La violencia, the Mexican man in the front said, shaking his head, as they passed out onto the road. It was too much – too much in the schools, too much in the streets. He was considering leaving Guadalajara, the town of his birth, with his Senegalese wife and child, for Spain.

But that was an hour or so ago. Now they are playing music up there in the front and the mood is different, festive. Her husband is talking, telling a story, gesticulating while he drives the van.

The writer leans forward, calling to him. If you see an OXXO, can you stop? We need milk.

Her husband doesn't hear: they are all laughing at his story. The Mexican man is laughing. Laughing too is the young French woman sitting in the seat behind the writer's husband. She has recently joined them, this young French woman, has only had a place in the van for twenty-four hours or so. She met them all up in the mountains, where she was travelling alone, researching traditional medicine for a book to be published in France. They invited her to travel with them. It might have been her, actually – the writer – that extended the

8

invitation, she can't quite remember how it happened, but the young French woman accepted easily, throwing her enviably light backpack into the back of the van, taking her place in the front where the breezes are cool.

The writer studies her husband's back: the set of his shoulders, the hook of his arm over the edge of the van window. He has taken up smoking again on this trip, a cigarette dangling constantly from his fingers. She knows this version of him well. This was the one she first met, twenty years ago, half-crazed and un-slept, right at the edge of everything, smoking as if his life depended on it.

They are separating, she and her husband, after two decades together.

This fact is new.

Only really a fact for a few weeks or so. Before that it was a possibility – one potential outcome among many. But now it appears to be, unequivocally, the case.

There are many ways of telling the tale.

One might be that they are separating because one day last autumn, back in England, he sent her a text – *we need to talk*. And when she got that text, the woman immediately knew two things – that he was going to tell her something she did not want to hear and that she would already know the thing he had to tell.

And so it had proved.

She remembers the way her body reacted, the breath fast and high, almost panting. *Okay*, she said. *Who?*

When he had finished with his inventory she remembers not moving, just sitting as still as she could, taking stock. Her first thought was *it could be worse*. There were not so many really. He was not in love with any of them. None of them were her close friends. No one was pregnant. She didn't, as she had once thought

9

she might, ask him for details. That could come later. She believed, even then, that things were salvageable.

But that, of course, is only one way of telling the tale. There are many more. You could tell the story from the point of view of the young woman who fucked her husband in a small university town in England – her own loves and desires and wants and needs. If you were feeling daring, you could try to tell it from the point of view of their bed – a bed made for them by a furniture-maker friend when he knew they were trying to conceive a child. You could have the bed speak – talk about all the different nights, all the different forms of love and sadness or anger or grief and absence that it had seen.

Or you could simply admit that it is complicated. That there are many different sides to every story, and leave it at that.

The writer leans forward and taps the Senegalese woman on the shoulder. Can you pass the message to my husband please? We need milk.

The Senegalese woman nods, leans forward, taps the shoulder of the French woman in front of her, gesturing towards the husband, and the French woman in turn leans forward and touches the husband on the back. He half turns, grinning at the French woman, happy to be touched. The French woman gestures to the back of the van and the husband's face changes, clouding as it assumes the mask of parental responsibility.

You okay back there?

Milk, the writer calls. If you see an OXXO store, please can you stop? We need milk.

Sure.

And can we try the air con? It's hot back here.

Her husband fiddles with the air conditioning. A cool trickle of air just about reaches the back.

Thanks.

Her husband starts talking again, picking up where he left off, gathering the threads of whatever story he is telling together, jabbering away, giving it his best Neal Cassady, holding court while driving the bus.

When they first met, twenty years ago, in a light-strafed jungle in Mexico, they got around to talking about books. He told her he loved Kerouac – *that bit in* On the Road *where they get into Mexico and everything just . . . opens up.*

He had been in Mexico for three months then, a young psychology lecturer studying shamanism, which took the form of steadily making his way through every sort of psychedelic plant he could find. Improbably, perhaps, this youthful pursuit of her husband's, in the years they have been together, has transformed into a career. He holds a conference every other year at his university, at which scientists and academics gather and chatter in earnest groups about the potential of psychedelic plants for western science and medicine.

They are serious people, these scientists and academics, slick young men and women with research chairs at world-leading universities. They walk through the quadrangles and talk about their research into psilocybin and depression. Into ayahuasca and intergenerational trauma. Into MDMA and PTSD for Israeli and US army veterans. These scientists have plenty of data; they have research laboratories and fMRI scanners and acronyms to spare. And they are backed by serious money – by Silicon Valley tech bros and ex-Goldman bankers.

A new renaissance, they say, *after the failed experiments of the '60s. A gold rush*, they say. *A new frontier.*

Two years ago, her husband was part of a team that gave scientists LSD in a research hospital in north London; their subjects were Oxford PhD candidates and eminent mycologists and young researchers who worked at the CERN particle accelerator. A partial replication of a study that was originally conducted in the 1960s: the participants were given a low dose of LSD, eye masks and headphones, and encouraged to focus on the deepest theoretical problems of their research. They emerged – most of them – with very interesting things to say.

But the writer finds it troubling, this influx of the moneyed, this seemingly unquestioned invoking of frontiers. They like to call in the Greeks too, these men: naming their companies after ancient mystery cults, initiation rites.

At present, her husband is on a sabbatical from his academic work, partly funded by an English billionaire with an interest in the numinous. The writer went along to his house once: a fifty-bedroom mansion with its own deer park and a temple designed by Lutyens in the garden. The billionaire had invited some of the world's leading anthropologists, cultural historians, neuro-psychopharmacologists, ethnobotanists and psychiatrists to a symposium to discuss the ontological status of entheogenic entity encounters.

She was sixteen weeks pregnant by then, and soon tired of the presentations, and hid in her bedroom during the evenings, reading Jane Austen while the other guests drank wine and whisky and wandered around the grounds.

But she had forgotten this conversation about Kerouac until recently, when she was listening to an episode of a podcast in which two sexy-voiced, smart young women sit in a studio in east London and debate the relative literary merits of certain books. In this particular episode the two young women discussed whether you should ever trust a man who liked Kerouac.

No. They decided. *Definitely not.* And then laughed together as though to say *surely that much is obvious?*

The writer had felt somehow exposed, hearing this, as though everything that she was feeling, all the terrible heartbreak she was trying to contain, might somehow have been obviated if she'd had better taste in literary men.

But the truth is the writer doesn't mind Kerouac. Or she didn't use to. When she was a teenager, she even had a post-card with a quote from *On the Road* on her wall:

The only people for me are the mad ones, the ones who are mad to live, mad to talk, mad to be saved . . . the ones who . . . burn, burn, burn, like fabulous yellow roman candles exploding like spiders across the stars . . .

On the screen, the children are back in their beds. They have saved the day, or the night, or both, and are tucked up in their pyjamas.

Mumma?

Yep?

Can I watch another cartoon?

Yep.

The writer brings up the next episode – 'Catboy and Master Fang'.

But I don't want to watch this one. I already watched *this* one, Mumma.

It's all we've got, sweetheart.

MI-ILK, shouts her daughter. I WANT MILK!

Across the aisle the sleeping man stirs, opens one eye.

Lo siento, the woman says to him. I'm sorry.

The man says nothing, just looks out of the window, gauging the route – a highway now, pylons moving across the landscape.

Cerca, he says. Una hora. Más o menos.

Sí, cerca, the writer agrees.

The man closes his eye again and appears to go back to sleep.

This man is in his seventies, although he looks twenty years younger. He has a large, full-lipped mouth, slightly turned down at the edges, which lends him an expression of constant wry amusement. His skin is unlined. He wears a black down jacket over a white cotton shirt and trousers. The trousers are embroidered with deer in vibrant shades of pink and purple and the deer are leaping across the hems. On his feet he wears huaraches – leather sandals made with car-tyre soles. He is, in the language of his people – the Wixárika – a mara'akame. A shaman. He is not what one might expect, though, this man. He is not in the business of making anyone feel comfortable. He is fond of jokes – the cruder the better. During daylight hours his tongue is firmly in his cheek. He is not available on any website. He is not seeking any five-star reviews.

This man also stayed up around the fire. Several generations of his family were there alongside him: his son, his son's wife, four of their seven children. He sang five songs to mark the passing of the night, his voice broken in all the right places – low then high, low then high again – and in between the songs those present, Mexican, French, Swedish, German, Senegalese, British, Colombian, sat close to the fire, drew closer to the flames, spoke prayers out loud or silently, sang their own songs, gave offerings of chocolate or tobacco, asked for healing, offered thanks. Behaved, generally, as though five hundred years of modernity and the scientific method and iPhones and aeroplanes had failed to occur, or had been cast out, in the fire-light and the starlight high in this sheltered bowl of these mountains of the Sierra Madre Occidental.

The last song this man sang was just before the dawn, and at the end of his singing he walked slowly around the circle of people and passed feathers over their skin and the skin of their children, drawing them slowly across their cheeks – feathers that smelled of animals and sweat and grease. He sucked along the length of them, extracting small crystals, which were offered to the fire. Then, while it was still dark, this man gathered up his few things and led his family down the mountain, ready for the journey to the coast. His son and his son's wife and their children are way ahead somewhere now, travelling in a pickup truck, the kids hunkered down in the back.

They have been doing the same thing, this man and his ancestors, this singing and offering to the fire, if carbon dating of the ash in their ceremonial hearths is to be believed, for many thousands of years. The indigenous group to which they belong was one of the very few unconquered by the Spanish – desert nomads who retreated to the high Sierra to escape the colonizers' gunpowder and torture and coercion. And the route they have taken in this white van, these last ten days, across central and northern and western Mexico, from Zacatecas to the desert of San Luis Potosí, to the high Sierra Madre Occidental and down to the sea, is an ancient pilgrimage route. Although they never used to do it with a ragtag bunch from three continents in white vans hired in Guadalajara; they used to walk.

The writer is aware of the improbability of it all. This journeying. This pilgrimage. The temptation to put it all in inverted commas. Aware of the risk of it appearing ridiculous, a postmodern conundrum, the beginning of a joke:

What brings a Mexican man, a Colombian man, a Senegalese woman, a French woman, a German woman, an English woman and two English men, a Swedish man, two children and a seventy-year-old shaman to a van on a highway in the state of Nayarit in Mexico in the early afternoon on a day at the beginning of spring, at the beginning of the third decade of the twenty-first century?

The writer has gleaned snippets of other stories, fragments, guesses as to why each of the other travellers is here. The Swedish man who works in an office in Stockholm and who has spoken of a depression so bad he wanted to kill himself. The German woman, in her late forties, who looks much older, her face ravaged by a thousand sorts of pain. The Senegalese woman who speaks hardly at all in the company of men, but who came alive while cooking the other night, telling the writer the tale of how she came to be here, how she met her Mexican husband by the side of the road in Senegal, how she fell in love with him and left everything she knew, her family compound and mother and cousins and her aunties, for a life in a small house on the edge of a Mexican city. How, despite the long days travelling, the lack of comfort, the lack of sleep, she is here on this journey for her daughter. To give the offerings. To ask for protection.

Yes, the writer agreed. That was why she was here too. To give the offerings. To ask for protection. Yes. Yes.

There are many ways of explaining her own presence in the back of the van, many places the story could start.

You could tell the truth, hands up; say the woman is a writer. That she is here in Mexico to research and write a novel – a novel she is struggling to know quite how to begin.

But even that would not be the whole truth – the real story starts many years before.

If you were to tell it in the briefest, most linear way, you could say that the writer and her husband tried to have a child for seven years. In those seven years they tried everything, charts and diets and drugs and apps and needles, but nothing worked. Then, one day, the husband was contacted by the young Mexican man in the front of the van. He was working with an indigenous group from northern Mexico. They wanted to come to the UK. He had been told that her husband was the sort of person who might be able to write a letter of introduction on special headed university paper, the sort which would help usher a Wixárika shaman through UK immigration. Might her husband help?

And so it was that the writer found herself, several years ago now, sitting around a fire, praying for a child.

This act, this *prayer*, was not something that came easily – not at all. How on earth were you supposed to pray? Who on earth, after two thousand years of Christianity and patriarchy, were you supposed to be praying to? Who was supposed to be listening? God? The fire? The blue deer which was sacred to the Wixárika but had nothing to do with her cultural heritage at all? And what right had she at this late stage in the game of colonialism and violence and dispossession to sit by fires with indigenous shamans and ask for what she wanted?

Nonetheless, all else having failed, she did as she was instructed. She tried to pray. Later, after the ceremony was done, the shaman laid her down in a small room, burned charcoal, then bent towards her, sucked along the length of a feather and extracted what appeared to be small crystals from her womb. He looked at the crystals, speaking quietly to himself.

A year ago, the writer visited the high Sierra for the first time. This visit was non-negotiable. Having prayed for a child, their child having come, there was another side of the bargain. It did not involve money, or not directly. It involved sacrifice. It involved taking their daughter to Mexico to give thanks.

Soon after they arrived in the mountain village, she and her husband were told to buy a sheep. When she first heard this, the writer laughed – *you're kidding, right?* But the shaman and his family were far from kidding. They were as serious as could be.

The animal was killed in a small ceremony at the wooden cross in the village square. Her daughter was unselfconsciously curious, sitting on her father's shoulders, wearing her pink fireman's sunhat, watching as the sheep twitched with the last of its life. Its blood was collected in a small gourd bowl, and the men dipped their feathers into the thick red liquid, dabbing it onto coins, onto their skin, onto anything they wished to bless. Watching the sheep die, its big black eye rolling to the sky, the woman was surprised. She had always thought of sacrifice as something abstract, something immaterial – but there were few things more material than watching an animal die.

The sheep was taken back to the compound where the women of the family butchered it quietly, efficiently, placing it in a large pot with vegetables and water, sealing it with dough and cooking it for hours over the fire. Later that evening many more people appeared, carrying plastic plates, sitting with huge bottles of Coke and Fanta and Sprite and piles of tortillas, waiting to be doled out some mutton stew – waiting to eat the flesh of the sheep that was killed to give thanks for their daughter's life.

Despite their down jackets and pickup trucks and mobile phones, the Wixárika live entwined in older, wilder logics: reciprocity, sacrifice. A sun which does not rise by right. A sun you must sing to. A sun you must thank.

In the side pocket of the woman's bag are several small gourd bowls: xukuri, each the size of an adult palm. On the inside of these bowls are beeswax figures – they were told to make them, yesterday afternoon, sitting in the thatched shade of a hut. Told to shape the beeswax into a deer, a sheaf of corn, into figures made to represent their family. The writer fretted over hers: it wasn't neat enough, clear enough – her deer looked wonky. She wasn't even totally sure what a corn sheaf looked like. But she did her best to form the images, pressing them against the husked skin of the gourd.

They are to release them, she knows, these votive offerings, onto the water: when they reach the white rock, in a few hours' time.

In his own bag her husband carries a candle – stitched carefully with a blue ribbon: the third of three. The first was left in the desert, a week ago now, the second at the summit of a sacred mountain, El Quemado, the third, the only one remaining now, will be offered to the sea.

The van is slowing, turning off the highway into a petrol station. On the other side of a forecourt there is a store. Not an OXXO, but it might do.

Her husband pulls up at a pump, leans out of the window and asks the attendant to fill it up.

The mara'akame opens one eye, and stares out at the bare concrete forecourt. Muy bonito, he says, drily, before shutting his eye again.

The woman's husband appears at their window. He leans in through the open glass, pulls a face at their daughter, and she looks up, delighted, putting her little hands out to press her father's cheeks.

Dada!!

It is as though they have not seen each other for months, for years, this giddy fizzing forcefield of their mutual physical delight.

You two okay back here? he says.

Hot.

Yeah. Did the air con help?

Sort of. Can you come and keep an eye while I go and look for milk?

Sure.

The writer scrabbles in the seat pocket for her wallet, then picks her way past feet and bags and dusty blankets to the tarmac outside. The sun is searing, bouncing off the petrol pumps, the oil pooled on the ground. The heat is intense. Her husband has come over to the passenger side. He stretches, and she can see the edge of his torso. The pale flesh where it disappears into his jeans. He is wearing jeans, boots, a bandana tied around his neck – a black shirt with embroidery on it like a cowboy might wear. A baseball cap. Comedy sunglasses bought at a roadside stall somewhere on the journey – ridiculous, unfeasible, the sort of mirrored sunglasses a woman in the 1980s might have worn. Somehow, just about, he pulls it off.

Not far now, he says, from the edge of his yawn.

Yeah. You want anything from the shop?

He shrugs. Water?

Sure.

They have taken to talking like this. Like characters in a play. Minimalist. Self-conscious. In a way, precise.

She hesitates – she used to put her hands on his cheeks. She used to put her hands on his neck. She used to put her hands on the place where his torso dives into his jeans. They would kiss sometimes, for hours and hours. The almost-delirium of his touch. Now they just nod at each other, as though they are distant, cordial, acquaintances.

She makes her way across the forecourt to the toilet. She is still wearing the clothes she sat up in last night: leggings for warmth, a long skirt, a long-sleeved thermal vest. In the stall she peels off the thick leggings, then the vest, prickly with static and sweat. She uses the toilet and goes to wash her hands in the sink. Her face in the little mirror looks startled – eyes wary, hair thick with dirt, lips chapped and cracked almost to bleeding.

A small smear of lurid green soap is released by the dispenser. In her head, as she washes her hands, the face of the British prime minister appears – his clown face – telling her to sing Happy Birthday twice. Being a good girl, she does so.

Last time she was near Wi-Fi, three days ago, she managed to look at the news. It was clear that what had seemed, before they left Mexico City a week before, to be something that

20

might easily be contained, was rapidly morphing into something else: empty supermarket shelves across England, intensive care units overwhelmed in Italy. No toilet paper or hand sanitizer left in the shops. A British prime minister addressing the nation on the need for washing hands for twenty seconds – *the length of time it takes to sing Happy Birthday twice.*

Happy Birthday to you.

Happy Birthday to you.

Happy Birthday to yo-ou. Happy Birthday to you.

She was forty-five a few months ago. More than halfway through her life.

If she is lucky.

This plague, though, this *novel coronavirus*, is not the particular horseman the writer has been preparing for.

Not since the summer before last, when, in the middle of a heatwave, she read a paper by an English academic which predicted ice-free Arctic summers in the next decade – multiple breadbasket failure, the likelihood of *near-term societal collapse*.

Not since, soon after that, she watched a YouTube video of a middle-aged woman in her living room, giving a talk entitled 'Heading for Extinction and What to Do About It'. The woman had a PhD in molecular biophysics. She spoke calmly about the recent data – how there was more carbon in the air than at any point since the Permian period, when 97 per cent of life on earth became extinct, gassed by hydrogen sulphide. How the earth was already well into the sixth mass extinction, and how this biological annihilation was accelerating. How the precautionary principle had been abandoned by those who governed in favour of capitulation to fossil fuel lobbies and short-term gain. This woman spoke of hedge fund managers, CEOs of brokerage houses, who were putting the finishing touches to their underground bunkers and wondering how they might maintain authority over their security forces when society had collapsed and money was worthless.

The woman then spoke equally calmly about how the only logical response to the criminal inaction of governments in the face of these threats was to engage in non-violent civil disobedience. She spoke about sacrificial action. Of the need to be a good ancestor. Of the need for courage, not hope. How courage was the resolve to do well, without the assurance of a happy ending.

She spoke of the suffragettes, of Gandhi, of Martin Luther King, of the need for people who would be willing to get arrested in mass, disruptive actions. To go to prison.

The writer had the same reaction, when reading this paper and watching this video, as she'd had when her husband told her about his multiple infidelities, a shallow breath that was almost a pant, almost comical. The sweat that broke on the palms of her hands. The sense of looking at herself from a slight distance, noticing this breath, these hands, this body, registering this feeling, which in both instances felt like a shock and an affirmation of something she had known for a very long time.

She would lie awake, night after night, checking her Twitter feed, reading article after article; the differing consequences of 2 degrees of warming, of 3, of 4.

It was the non-linear that terrified her: the idea of locked-in tipping points, after which the world could heat rapidly, devastatingly, the Amazon turning to savannah. The polar ice, which in its whiteness threw back the sun's rays – the albedo effect – gone: the dark water only absorbing more and more carbon. Everything twisted, turned upside down; carbon sinks becoming carbon spouts.

She walked the dusty summer lanes around her village with her daughter, picking blackberries, teaching her to name the things she saw: hawthorn, hazel, acorn, blackbird, oak.

She took her daughter along to that parent and child group, watched as she celebrated the season in crafts and in ring time with the other children, but inside she was scrabbling for purchase: soon there would be no more seasons, no more planting or blossoming or fruiting or harvest; no more of the rhythms that had sustained humanity for over eleven thousand years, since the ice melted at the beginning of the Holocene.

We need new stories, people said, *we need new stories, to navigate us out of this mess.*

But as the summer grew hotter and hotter and then autumn gave way to winter, with only more terrifying news (the insects were gone, apparently, from car windshields and jungles, 75 per cent of them, disappeared, no one knew where), the only stories the writer could think of in those small hours of the night were nightmares. She kept thinking of *The Road*, the moment when the mother understands she doesn't have the strength to go on and slashes herself with an obsidian shard.

She goes over to the paper dispenser, but it is empty, so she dries her hands on her skirt and makes her way outside, shading her eyes as she walks back across the forecourt to the shop.

The writer is aware that later today, or tomorrow, when they have finished this journey, when they have eaten and slept, she and her husband will have to log on with their laptops and assess the situation. Make decisions. Attempt to call airline companies that may or may not be able to accommodate them. If they manage to secure flights they will leave Mexico for England, fly back into a grey spring and empty shelves and – who knows? – possible societal collapse.

There is no milk in the fridges, no oat milk or almond milk or cow's milk, only water and beer. She selects the largest bottle of water from the fridge and heads to the counter to pay.

Last April, on a day that was over 25 degrees in the shade, the writer joined several thousand people in blocking off Oxford Circus in central London. She was sitting right at the front of the crowd beside a pink boat named after a murdered Honduran activist, when four members of the Metropolitan Police came and informed her that she was in contravention of Section 14 of the Public Order Act and invited her to move to another location. When she did not move, they reached down, one police officer for each of her limbs, and carried her away.

She was taken to a police station somewhere near Victoria where she spent the night in a cell, staring at the number for a drug rehab unit spray-painted onto the ceiling. Every half hour someone came to check on her. They gave her a blanket and some microwaved potatoes and beans.

There were more than a thousand people arrested over those few days in April. She was tried in the autumn with two other women – a grandmother from Swansea, and a gardener from Oswestry. The grandmother cried in the dock. The gardener spoke about how she saw the impacts of climate change in her work every day, how her daughters were refusing to have children themselves. How this shift, in her own relatively short lifetime, broke her heart.

As for herself, the writer dressed in her best dress and pled not guilty. She claimed that her actions were proportionate to the threat. She told the judge she had done it for her daughter. So there might be a world for her to live in.

She was aware, standing in that dock, of something performative, something dramatic, in the proceedings. The clerk, a woman in her fifties, cried. The judge listened and nodded and gave her a fine. As she left the courtroom she had the surging, heady feeling of being on the right side of history.

But sometimes the writer imagines a different sort of

court – a future court, an intergenerational Nuremberg where her generation is asked to answer for crimes against the future. Taking her turn in the dock.

What did you do when you knew that the world was burning?

I protested. I got arrested, I spent the night in a cell.

And why did you do that?

I did it for my daughter. I wanted to give her a future. It seemed like the only way.

The only way to what?

To call attention to the scale and urgency of the threat.

And then?

I took a long-haul flight to Mexico.

I see. Can you explain why?

I had to give thanks. To give offerings. To ask for protection. For my daughter. To research my book.

By flying across the world? By torching the bones of your daughter's animal ancestors at thirty-five thousand feet?

She pays for the water, and heads back to where the van is waiting. The tank filled with the bones of dinosaurs taken from beneath the deserts of Syria, or Kuwait, or the oil fields of Venezuela.

Around the time she was arrested, a leading black writer had posted a tweet wondering whether those activists in police cells would have been so keen to offer themselves up if people like themselves had a history of dying in police custody.

At the time, reading this, the writer had felt defensive; surely that was the point – that these mostly white middle-class people, these grandmothers and vicars and doctors and rabbis, were using that privilege by putting themselves up for arrest.

But in the time since, she has grown less sure, or, at least, more aware of her own desire to be at the centre of the story. To be *saving*, somehow, the planet.

She knows full well she was a tourist in that police cell.

Lately, she has felt caught in an Escher-like landscape – every move doomed to complication, to hypocrisy and implication.

Is it better, then, not to act at all?

Ready? says her husband.

Yep.

She climbs back to her seat. Her daughter looks up at her. Milk? she says hopefully.

No milk. Only water, love.

Her daughter's hot face crumples. I. Want. My. Milk!!

Sweetheart, I'm sorry. There was no milk.

I. WANT. MY. MIIIIILK.

I'm sorry. I'm just . . . we are nearly there, I promise. Just – please – hold on.

Her husband starts the van, the music comes on in the front, a playlist from the Colombian man. *Cuuumbiaaaa!*

She pours some water into her daughter's bottle, her daughter takes a sip, pushes it away. The woman whips open the computer. Places the headphones back on her daughter's head. The superhero children leap across the roofs. This time, her daughter does not sing.

As the van pulls back onto the highway, she opens the window wide. The breeze barrels in. The red earth is giving way to scrub, a fine dusting of sand. Tall palm trees. Not far now, not far. They are all awake now: the three men in the front, the French woman and the German woman, the Senegalese woman and her daughter, chirruping, sucking on an orange, the mara'akame, the two men in the back. The music is turned up further. They can all sense it – ozone, the ocean, the end of the journey at last.

The travellers' phones find reception, buzz with messages – they check them, faces puckered as they stare at the screens.

The Senegalese woman listens to a long looping voice note from a woman who might be her mother.

They look up, trade stories from their newsfeeds – the WHO has declared the coronavirus a pandemic, Trump has declared a national emergency.

They're closing borders, they say – and confer nervously as to which ones.

How would it have been, the writer wonders, if everything had collapsed while they were up there in the high Sierra Madre, miles from the nearest town or Wi-Fi signal? Like one of those zombie films where the virus rips through the world in hours, leaving chaos in its wake and only a few islands of humanity to remake the world? How would they have fared?

She rates them in her mind – the Apocalypse Top Trumps. The Mexican man would do well, he knows how to butcher, how to wield a knife. The other men are less skilful. Some of them carry machetes but they have no real idea of how to use them, and they are little more than props. Her money is on the Senegalese woman. She can cook on charcoal and rustle up a meal from meagre pickings. She can sleep soundly on a blanket on the ground. She can keep her child clean. She would find ways to thrive. She would win on all counts. The writer herself would come way down the list. Her need for solitude. Her terrible, crippling desire for comfort, for a bed. Besides – no one needs a writer in a crisis.

Her husband would likely do well though.

She has often thought that this man she married, with his capable, wide-palmed hands and his constitutional lack of anxiety, would be a good man to have around in case of plague or fire or flood. Often, during the last year, when her fear of the future started to spike, she would go into his study, sit on the floor.

We need to buy land, she'd say. *Sell up. Wales, Connemara, somewhere with a well. Learn to farm. Bore holes. All of that.*

And he would answer with his steady voice: *We have always lived in uncertain times.*

But now it is here, getting closer – an unravelling, one of the horsemen pulling away from the pack; they are unravelling too. Soon the fabric of their family life will be unspooled, the thread lying prone on the floor, with only the memory of the shape that it once held.

She reaches down and pulls her daughter's arm onto hers, splays her sticky hand open. Blows on her neck. Her palms are wide, like her father's. She is not yet four, but she already knows the names of all the tools in her father's toolbox. *Socket wrench*, she will say. *Spanner. Spirit level.* The woman is glad of this. This capacity to name things of use.

Now it is her own phone's turn to find a signal; it begins buzzing in the seat pocket in front of her, a jumbled round-up of her family's messages bumping up against each other in their insistence to be read:

I've got dad addicted to Schitts creek!

YES!!

Oh BRILLIANT

City's game tonight has been postponed.

Oh gosh

Morning

Work yesterday was a nightmare. No one is allowed to even put their own salt and pepper on their food unless it's in sachets which we don't have

It's creating so much wastage.

It all seems a bit over the top

It's going to get much worse I think

Oh dear. Yes and airlines collapsing

80% of us will get it

Between 250k and 500k Britons will die from it

Glastonbury will be cancelled

London Marathon will be cancelled

Blimey doom mongers

I'm not doom mongering Mum

This is the reality

Gosh it's too much to take in

So it's back to deliveries for me.

One good thing though. The free party scene will start again.
Illegal raves in the woods

Count me in

Although this is happening in Italy kids are sneaking out to
rave and coming back and infecting people.

Are you able to go to Tesco for Dad's prescription?

They are sleeping tablets

Cheap gin o clock

TOM HANKS HAS COVID 19!!

He also probably holds the cure

I'm now less worried because he will save us all

Jesus I hope I don't have to be quarantined with my kids in this house

I'm mostly concerned with them getting back from Mexico.

They should all return

I hope they don't think it's all hype.

She moves to her email. There are several from her mum:

Your Dads enjoying the audio books again which is good. At least his brain is being kept interested even if he's not able to get out walking. It's too difficult for me to push him so he sometimes manages to sit outside for a while, well wrapped up. We joke that he's in Marienbad

Hi honeybunch . . . we are all very concerned about the coronavirus outbreak. It is actually very serious. Airports might even close .. dad's dr said yesterday that hospitals won't cope.
   We all think you should consider coming home as soon as possible . . . all of you. The situation is escalating daily. The government is having a cobra meeting today.
   I thought you should read this as soon as possible ..
   Really think seriously . . . it's serious xxxx

Just wondering if you are okay and if you have wifi yet? Things are escalating here chicken . . . jet 2 stopping flights . . . check with tui!

Dad wants you to ring Aeromexico to find prices ..he's driving me potty

She puts her phone back in her lap.

In Manchester, in a house on the edge of the city, her father is ill. He is a little older than the vigorous man in the seat across from them, but not by much – born in August 1945, the end of a war.

It was her father who first brought her west: forty-two years ago, when she was three years old.

She has a photo of her father from that time: somewhere in Nevada, hands on hips, chin lifted, as though he has fully answered a question posed by his younger self, growing up in poverty in Yorkshire, reading Hemingway and Kesey and John Dos Passos, listening to Dylan and the Byrds and Simon and Garfunkel: *We've all gone to look for America.*

And so he went.

He was a lecturer in Manchester then, who gathered up his young family and swapped their northern moorland village for New Orleans and a year's teaching at Tulane, then travelled all over: Louisiana, Mexico City, Morelia, California, Oregon. There are yellowing pictures in albums in that house in Manchester, of them by slot machines in Reno, by the lip of the Grand Canyon, riding horses on Colorado ranches.

And then, when she was eight, he took them west again, to Tucson, Arizona, where they lived on the edge of the city, by the foothills of the Santa Catalina Mountains, where the grid of houses gave way to the canyons and creeks.

There was beauty there: the electric storms that laced the sky above the mountains but whose thunder never seemed to sound. The way her little sisters would run out naked into the desert rain. But there was fear too: every morning a new face of a missing child displayed on the milk cartons on the breakfast table. The rattlesnakes in the yard.

It was then she started counting things, checking under the bed and in the closet and round the back of the door. Started rubbing the desert dirt from the soles of her feet onto the palms of her hands.

Last December, three months ago, just before she left for this trip, her father could still walk, just – still manage to haul himself round the house with the aid of grab bars. Now, she knows, he is wheeled from room to room, from bed to chair and back again. He can no longer feed himself.

The writer knows the frame of a story, an old one, one of the oldest: the story of a dying king and the wasteland around him. The old king could be saved by the right question. The land, too, could be saved by the right question. The right questioner. They have asked lots of questions, these last years, as her father has become more and more feeble, and they have struggled to find a diagnosis. In the end there was an answer – progressive supranuclear palsy – a neurodegenerative disorder that lays waste to the middle part of the brain.

Her father has always been fond of questions too – they are his primary mode of communication. *What are you reading?* he asks of her, at the beginning of every phone call, and she will answer it – not usually to his satisfaction. Too limited. Too unambitious. Has she not read the new Samanta Schweblin? Or Laurent Binet? Has she really never read *Under the Volcano*? Jesus Christ! He has read it twice.

She has, actually, been reading *Under the Volcano* on this trip. Partly for her father. Partly for herself. On her last call with her dad, three weeks ago, she told him she was more than halfway through.

What was strange was, when she finally started reading it, she remembered something – a memory from the beginning of her relationship with her husband which had lain undisturbed for twenty years.

They didn't become a couple, she and her husband, not properly, that first meeting in that Mexican jungle; they met, then went their separate ways – she back to London to study, and he to teach English in Mexico City. But then, nine months later, she flew out from London to see him. He had given up his teaching job and was staying in a little village in Morelos, not far from Cuernavaca, near the hacienda of a man she knew slightly, an elderly German engineer. She wrote to the German man and asked if she might stay with him first. It felt proper somehow. A sort of chaperoning. A buffer zone.

She bought the cheapest flight she could find, one which brought her into Cancún, a thousand miles from the capital, then took a night bus across Mexico. She was tired and travel-weary when she arrived in Morelos, but the elderly German man was courtly, welcoming. He made her dinner and served her coffee and showed her around his beautiful home. Off the central courtyard was a large, dim salon, filled with books and artefacts. On the walls were photographs – one in particular caught her eye, it was of a man behind a film camera, light splashing onto the cobbled street around him. He was holding up his hand, measuring something between his fingers and thumb.

Who is that? she asked her host.

John Huston, the German man said – with a note of pride. He stayed here while he was filming *Under the Volcano* with Albert Finney.

She looked back at the photograph, at the lined, bearded face of the director – the angle of his hands, held as though navigating by the stars.

Have you read it? the German man asked her.

No.

You should. It's a wonderful book.

After dinner the elderly German man went to bed, and she went outside. It was quiet in the courtyard, and she sat in the scented dusk and listened to the sounds of the small town as it settled for the night, and as she waited there, for a man she thought she might love, she could feel the coiled promise of the future inside her.

The van reaches a fork in the road: a small tienda selling inflatable beach toys, banana bread; a restaurant advertising fresh fish.

They take the right fork, and now the road is smaller, closer, the vegetation thicker, mangroves and swamp: a crocodile sanctuary, the wide mouth of a river. Billboards with mosquitoes painted on them – cartoon insects with comedy evil faces, exhorting you to always wear spray to evade Zika and dengue. The bugs are vicious here – mosquitoes and jejenes, little biting insects that live in the sand. This part of the coast, wetland and swampland all the way up to Sonora, is notorious for them.

Her phone buzzes, a message directly from her mother: *Sweetheart. You need to come home soon. Find a flight today. Come home.*

I will, she types, *I promise.*

She presses send. She will. She'll look tonight. As soon as she gets a decent signal. She will, she knows, because it is the right thing to do. Because in a situation like this it is the right thing to be back in the land of your birth, close to family.

Although, it is tempting, of course, to stay – here where the trees are full of mangoes and the honey-light of the afternoon sun; where the tiendas are piled with avocados – while the rest

34

of the world goes to hell in a handcart, scrapping over the last bits of toilet paper left in the shops.

Hey.

She turns, sees the English man in the seat behind is leaning forward, addressing her.

Could I have a sip of your water, please?

Sure. She lifts the bottle by her feet and passes it back.

Something about this English man makes her shy. Some quietness. Some self-possession. Of all the occupants of the van his wounds are perhaps the most concealed. He is a music producer, living alone in the Mojave Desert in California, off-grid, on a plot of land miles from the nearest road, where he scores movies and works with bands in LA. This much she has gleaned from conversations overheard; he and her husband have become friends on this trip. Both seem to know many of the same people – people who occupy a liminal zone somewhere between Burning Man and Silicon Valley. Old psychedelic heads from the '60s. Internet utopians who used to write lyrics for the Grateful Dead and went on to have research posts at Harvard. That kind of thing.

She has only really spoken to this English man once. It was at the beginning of the journey, when none of the travellers really knew each other. They had stopped in a tiny town in the middle of the desert for eggs and coffee and tortillas. Her husband was with their daughter, letting her play and stretch her legs outside. The writer was at a table with the music producer and the Swedish man, and they were talking about their destination – the sleepy town on the Pacific where they would finish their pilgrimage. She told them she had been there before – had seen the white rock in the ocean, the place that the Wixárika call Tatéi Haramara, our Mother Ocean, the origin of life.

It was the first time she had spoken, and they turned to her as though surprised.

She told them she was a writer, that she was here in Mexico, in part, to research and begin writing a novel, the idea for which had arrived whole, one morning, a year before. That they had been staying in a fishing village then, she and her husband and daughter, waiting to hear from their Mexican friend – the same man who was with them now – about when they would be able to visit the Sierra. Eventually he got in touch and told them the arrangements were all made, that they were expected in the next few days, and that as part of their trip they would be taken to the town of the white rock.

The writer told the listening men that she had not known of this town before, and that, as preparation for the journey, she had read about it. Had learned that, as well as being a place sacred to the Wixárika, the town was also a crucial outpost of the Spanish colonial forces in the eighteenth century, the port from which their ships sailed to explore and claim northern California and the Pacific Northwest. That the ship that took the first Europeans into San Francisco Bay in 1775 had left from there.

That she had found the digitized versions of the logs of those sailors, and read that, in March 1775, while anchored by the white rock, readying to depart for California, one of the leading lieutenants of the Spanish line had allegedly lost his mind, locking himself in his cabin with four pistols, one for each of the men who were commanding the expedition. That the young man had been tried by junta that same night, an event from which there was no record of his words other than the fact that he was 'incoherent', and suffering from an 'unfortunate loss of his faculties', but after which he was stripped of his post, and never heard of again.

She had become fascinated by this incident – what had the young lieutenant said during that junta? And why had he been consigned to silence ever since?

She told them how she had learned too that the town had been the arrival port for thousands of Yoeme people, deported from Sonora in the first years of the twentieth century, under the regime of Porfirio Díaz. People who had been forcibly removed from their homes and villages because of their resistance to the opening of their ancestral land – the largest, most fertile river valley in Mexico – to make way for Mexican and American venture capitalists.

How thousands of men, women, children and the elderly were packed onto boats from Guaymas for a three-day journey south to Nayarit, docking in sight of the white rock and beginning a forced march two hundred miles over the mountains to a railway station – a march that would kill many of them – before boarding cattle cars that would carry them to Mexico City, where they were sold into slavery and taken to the henequen fields in Yucatán, thousands of miles to the east. That they had died there, in their tens of thousands, in those fields, most of them within a year. How many people considered this to have been nothing less than genocide.

And how, in the middle of last century, the port had become a seaside resort for the wealthy and famous. That a young singer had spent a weekend there in 1969, when he was twenty-five, two years before he was found dead in a bathtub in Paris in 1971, on the run from himself, from the law, and from an America that was growing ever darker and more disturbing as the Vietnam War intensified. A war his father, the youngest admiral in the US Navy, had had a heavy hand in accelerating, when he sailed his ship into the Gulf of Tonkin in August 1964.

How, after that first visit to the Sierra, she and her family had indeed visited the town – had seen the white rock, and the remains of the old Spanish fort and counting house, the Contaduría, on the volcanic hill that overlooks the town; an eerie place, and close by it a church whose rafters were long gone.

How she and her husband had borrowed bikes and cycled down the long strip of beach, their daughter perched on the crossbar of her husband's cycle, until they found the hotel the singer had stayed in, Playa Hermosa, right at the end of the beach. A ruin now, being reclaimed by the jungle, the pool drained of all but graffiti, the track that led to the beach littered with used condoms and plastic bottles and crisp packets. But how the view when you walked out to the beach – the mountains touching the water to the south, the white rock in the far distance – was out of this world.

It made sense to her, she said to them – being there, that this was a place the singer might have come. How she had come to see him as a sort of broken transistor, attuned to the frequencies of revolution and revolt, there on the far west coast, gazing upon the Pacific and contemplating his fate.

Her husband reappeared in the café then, their daughter in tow; it was time to climb back into the van. So – the conversion over – the writer took her place at the back, consigned to silence once more.

The next evening, though, the producer came to speak to her. They were staying in a string of adobe houses in the desert. Her husband was over by the fire, talking with the Mexican man. Her daughter was asleep inside. The writer was sitting alone on a bench. It was cold in the way that deserts are cold at night, the wind whipping and finding every crevice it could.

I wanted to say, said the producer, I liked what you said. About the singer, in 1969. That thing you said, about him being a broken transistor.

Oh?

Yeah. Also – it's weird. Weird that you talked about him.

Why?

Because I was given one of his songs to remix. A few years ago. By his record company.

Seriously?

Would you like to hear it? I thought you might. I have it here.

He reached into his backpack, brought out his iPad and headphones, moved to hand them to her, and then paused.

When the record company sent me the masters, and I listened to them for the first time, there was this . . . screaming at the end of the take. The guy was just screaming. And they didn't use it on the single. The original I mean. But the guy was really letting rip. It was wild. And it hadn't been heard for forty years. That scream. So I took the scream and used it. I let it roll.

Then he handed her the headphones and his iPad, queued up the track, and left her to it, wandering over to where the men were standing on the other side of the fire.

In the far distance were the ridged outlines of the mountains; beneath them, two miles or so away, the light of a freight train, on its way to the capital from the north. The men's voices came from the fire, low then louder. Laughter. Inside the house, there was the soft sound of the Senegalese woman singing her child to sleep.

The writer put the headphones on her head, and pressed play. The track started slowly; a solid electro beat.

Du duh du-du duh. Du du du-du duh. Du duh du-du duh. Du du du-du duh.

Then the vocal – recognizable, but twisted, a little bit distorted:

Hello, I love you . . .

The singer was addressing a woman, a woman he hardly

39

knew. But as the song went on, and she didn't answer, it seemed to become less about a particular person than an existential howl. By the end he was screaming, just as the producer had said – right at the ragged edge of his voice: *Hello hello HeELLOooo????* And then the sirens came in – police sirens – drowning out the scream, as though they were coming to take him away, lock him up; a madman, shouting too loud at the gods. And then the sirens faded and when it came back – the *hello* – it sounded resigned, as though the singer had been defeated somehow, put back in his box.

When the track had finished, she listened to it again. And again. Something about the singer's anger. Something about his scream. As though he were screaming for her, for all of them. After she had listened to it three times in a row, she carried the iPad over to the fire.

The wind, which had been blowing relentlessly for days, had dropped. Thanks, she said, as she handed it back to the producer. I liked that a lot.

She came down on her haunches by the fire and watched the way it burned – the slow blue lick of it. The whiteness of the ash.

Outside the window of the van, the woman sees that they are on the outskirts of the town: concrete houses line the road, small-windowed against the sun, and they drive through a white arch then into the town itself, down its wide colonial streets, past the bus station, into a pretty plaza lined with trees, their trunks painted white. The screech of hundreds of birds. Children holding candy, chasing each other in circles. A twin-towered church.

They turn left, past a little park where a small craft market is set up, then right past a low red hacienda-hotel with a Mexican flag outside, the van trundling over the badly paved ground. The woman has stayed in that red-walled hotel, its gracious courtyard with the terracotta tiles, and the palm trees and fountains, the leather rocking chairs and the family photos from the 1930s. She has shopped for gifts in the little craft market opposite, where Wixárika and Cora girls sell their distinctive beadwork jewellery and woven bags.

Just next to the market is a large stone building, framed by an elegant arched portico: the old customs house. Was it here that the Yoeme prisoners were counted and held, before beginning their two-hundred-mile walk over the mountains? It seems likely: there are no other similar buildings – and this one is right next to the dock.

Last month, she and her husband and daughter travelled to Sonora to visit the ancestral lands of the Yoeme; she had wanted to see where they had come from, to understand what they had left behind.

Driving along the highway from the airport, they had passed mile upon mile of grain elevators, marking the most productive land in Mexico, but when they reached the place where Google Maps said the river should be, there was nothing but a dusty, toxic-looking trickle. The river – that great, fertile river that the first Spaniards had compared to the Nile – had been dammed long ago, diverted by a huge aqueduct to the factories in Hermosillo and Ciudad Obregón, and all that remained in the traditional villages was polluted, unsafe for irrigation or to drink.

Heading north on Highway 15, the desert beside them, the cholla and saguaro and the petrol trucks and the freight trains and the mountains, they had been held up by a roadblock in Vícam Switch by men and women in bandanas, holding battered cardboard signs. They were handing slips of paper into each vehicle window, paper that said that they were fighting, still, for their rights to their river, that they had been abandoned by the federal government – that they desperately needed funds. Her husband handed over some money, and they were waved on.

They visited Guaymas, a rickety old port, its heyday long past, went inside the stone Palacio Municipal: its courtyard alive with the chatter of small birds, its roof open to the sky. She went down to the dock and stood, hand in hand with her daughter at the place where the Yoemem would have embarked for their journey south.

They stayed in a hotel that night that was named after Cortés, where the ballroom was called the Conquistador Suite. They ate club sandwiches in the empty restaurant beneath a wooden cut-out depicting the seeming rape of an indigenous woman by rabid soldiers. Outside the windows, young Mexican students in graduation robes posed against the fountains with their families. A woman approached their table and politely asked what they were doing there – she told them the beaches in San Carlos, on the other side of the bay, were magnificent. How they had appeared in *National Geographic* magazine.

Mumma?

A sticky hand lands on the writer's knee.

What, poppet?

Ineedawee.

We're nearly there, sweetheart. We're going to get out soon. You can have a wee then. I promise.

The van pulls up at a small dock. The travellers gather their belongings, and pile in an ungainly group out of the van and stand, new-shucked, blinking in the sunlight. It is late afternoon, and they have been travelling since before dawn.

The writer takes her daughter to a nearby piece of scrubby ground, pulls down her shorts and lifts her so she can have her wee. Parked next to them is the pickup with the mara'akame's family – his son and daughter-in-law and their four kids. The two youngest kids are grinning, waving at her daughter, who flaps a hand back shyly. Her husband claps the son of the mara'akame on the back. The son jokes about the slowness of the husband's driving – how long he and his family have been waiting for them to arrive.

The Mexican man makes his way over to the edge of the dock, starts up a negotiation with one of the skippers, haggling over the price of a boat to take them all over to the island. The sun is low in the sky. They bring out their phones and check their newsfeeds again – frowning at their screens. They slap their skin. It is the hour of the mosquitoes, the jejenes, and they are already biting. Hurrying now, they search out bug spray from their washbags, share it around, rub it on every exposed piece of skin. The writer chases her daughter, grabs her by the wrist, sprays onto her shins and ankles and arms.

Her husband is talking to the young French woman. She is laughing again. The writer notices the perfectly placed mole on the side of her mouth. The Senegalese woman is talking to her Mexican husband, telling him the bugs are too vicious, too much for their daughter, that she doesn't want to go to the island, and he is soothing her, nodding, saying she doesn't have to – that he will rent her a room in a nearby hotel. The writer watches them walk quickly across the cobbled street, disappear into the cool lobby of a small hotel opposite. She could follow them – do the same. Rent a room. Turn up the air con. Close the curtains and sleep.

Or read – finish *Under the Volcano* at last.

She knows exactly what they must do next: take the boat over a small strip of water to the island and walk across it until

43

they can see the white rock. Give their offerings to the ocean: these wooden gourds, these candles they have carried now for days. Ask for protection. Give thanks.

It won't take long. And then it will be done.

It is not much. It is the least, really, she can do. But somehow, standing here, her husband flirting with a young French woman with a perfectly placed mole, her daughter fractious and exhausted, it is too much.

Ahead is the dock and the strip of sea and the island. A lighthouse on a hill. Buzzards in the updraughts.

Here it was that the ships sailed to San Francisco and further north.

Here the Yoeme prisoners would have disembarked.

Here the singer may have stood.

Here she stands.

She should never have come.

She is a tourist. They are all fucking tourists.

Worse than tourists – they are miners, here to extract what they can from this ancient culture, this mara'akame and his family; to mine their pristine seam of connection to their songs and stories going back, back, thousands and thousands of years.

But they are not their stories, not their songs, not the songs of the Swedish man or the German woman or the young French woman or even the Mexican man from Guadalajara with his Senegalese wife.

And she herself – what is she here for if not to mine too? To take the raw matter of history, the pain and the trouble and the incalculable loss – to shape it into story, the hope of profit. No less venal. No less extractive than those who came this way three, four, five hundred years ago, searching for gold.

Standing here, waiting to get into this little boat, waiting to put the life jacket on, to be taken across the water to the island and the white rock, she feels like the singer at the end of that track – that existential howl.

Who is listening? Who the fuck cares as you call out into the void?

Hello?

Hello??

HELL-O??????

The Singer
1969

He dives deep into broken light, hits the water cleanly, and for a green-gold moment the world is weightless, silent. A slow underwater length until his lungs give out and then he surfaces, gasping, turns on his back and hooks his arms over the edge of the pool. Head resting on the concrete, eyes closed against the sun. Sounds: low chatter, the suck and slap of the water against the side of the pool, the harsh call of birds, the low ocean boom, his heart. Footsteps, coming close.

Buenos días, señor.

He squints – sees a young man, upside down. White shirt, bright smile.

Something to drink? Jugo? Cerveza?

He turns on his stomach, beard dripping onto the tiles. You got Tecate?

Tecate, no. Pacífico? Es muy bueno.

Pacífico. Sure. Bring me a couple.

Mande?

Dos. Por favor.

The kid heads off and the singer hauls himself out of the water and heads back to the lounger where he left his stuff. He towels off, sucking in his gut. Still a surprise, the size of him, still new, this walrus bulk. He used to be slender. He is a different sort of mammal now.

He wraps the towel around his waist, tucks it in, lights a cigarette and takes stock. Behind him and to the right is the hotel, a low, long three-storey building. Last night when the taxi pulled up and the soft call of the driver woke him there was only the sandy end of a track in the headlights, the thick smell of vegetation in the cicada-filled dark. The crash of the ocean somewhere not too far. The driver waved him towards the lights of the reception and drove away, back to the airport three hours to the south.

A tired-looking man came out when he rang the bell, and scratched his cheek as he checked the guest book, before showing him to a small room at the top. Not the best room (not the best room in the best hotel in Mexico City, in a compound guarded by a guy with a rifle in its own rain-jacket; not a white limo ready to drive him wherever he wants to go), just an ordinary room for an ordinary man because no one did this for him – no one made the booking, no one sent him his itinerary, no one called the taxi or hustled him onto the plane. No one sat beside him and counted his drinks and suggested that, perhaps, he should stop. He said, yeah, sure I'll take it, then fell asleep like a stone, still in his jeans, and when he woke this morning the light was strong and he was sweating and he had no fucking idea where he was.

The sun is hot. The pool coming back to cerulean stillness now. Beyond it a small rise with palms and scrub, and then the beach, a dun-brown strip beyond.

Cerveza.

The kid is back with two sweating beers, the first of which he pours with some ceremony into a frozen glass.

What time is it? You got the time?

Um . . . Como a las tres.

Tres? Sun's over the yardarm then.

I'm sorry?

Over the yardarm. Time for a drink. Hey – just give me the bottle next time.

Sorry?

I like the beer, not the glass. Just the bottle is fine.

Okay.

He drinks and the boy stays where he is.

Where you from, sir – America?

Yeah.

América del Norte?

Del Norte. Sure. Yeah.

He likes that. Del Norte. Puts it in its place.

Many Americans here. Last month Liz Taylor. Muy famoso. Y Ricardo Burton.

Liz Taylor? Ricardo Burton? Wow.

Sí. Many famous Americans here.

He waits, for the movement that says the kid has clocked who he is (he has grown expert in this now, in the moments when he is sober – can sense when he is being watched, when the person at the periphery of his vision is going to approach and ask for something: an autograph, a kiss, a fuck), but the boy is just looking at him the way a waiter looks at a full-bearded hippie who turned up sometime in the middle of last night and likes beer for breakfast.

Sure. Famous Americans. The singer shrugs. Well, they gotta go someplace for vacation I suppose.

Mostly in the winter though, says the kid. Summer is full of bugs and rain. The kid squints at the sky, as though it might hurl both, but it is only, completely, blue. Would you like breakfast? Sandwich? Fruta?

He probably should, though breakfasts have not been his friend lately.

Sure, a sandwich. Whatever you think. And another beer. Just the bottle though.

Okay.

The rest of the poolside is fairly quiet – a white couple sit over on the other side, facing out to sea. Americans? Late-middle age. Their clothes say they are wealthy, the woman in one of those large hats with the brims and a swimsuit that looks as though it has never been wet. Her husband beside her – both reading books with lurid covers, held away from the face so as not to interfere with the tan. A Mexican family over to the right – two small kids. The mother fussing, the father reading the newspaper. The father looks up and the singer raises his beer in salute. The guy looks away in distaste. It must be the hair. The beard.

They told the band about the way they treated hippies in Mexico soon after they arrived in the country, at a meeting with the promoters. She was there – Eva – alongside the two guys who ran the club, standing to the side with her clipboard, dark and small and serious.

We must all be careful to travel together. Do not walk out into the city on your own. They grab people in the street, cut their hair, shave their beards.

Who?

The police.

The rest of the guys in the band laughed about it, turned to him. *Can't we get them to do that to you?* They were joking then, but when they had all been down to the club and seen the kitschy fifteen-foot-high mural the Mexicans had painted on the wall – of the young god with the blow-dried hair, taken from a photo that was shot three years ago – they came back and, over dinner that first night, in the big dining room with the gilt chairs that looked like something a queen of France might eat her cake in, they asked him, seriously, to shave his face.

They were all there: the band, their girls, the journalists, the managers, the roadies, the promoters, all sipping Corona and wine and eating their lobster.

You're serious?

It doesn't fit. The image, you know. It's not who they expect.

Jesus fuck. When have we ever given them what they expect?

The band looked at each other, shuffled their feet. He threw a bread roll across the table. It hit the guitarist's girlfriend on the cheek. She screamed and he laughed. The room fell silent. He let the thunder-beats roll: one thousand, two thousand, three thousand.

Then, fuck you, he said – real slow. Fuck. You. All.

Over on the other side of the pool the woman shifts slowly in her chair, hooks one leg over the other. He watches her. The place where the swimsuit meets the crotch. She must be – what? Fifty? She has the body of a fifteen-year-old girl.

Three o'clock. Which means an hour to go until the band meeting. He knows this because he got today's itinerary on a piece of paper yesterday morning. The band and the manager had already gone, but they had left it for him, folded into a crisp white envelope, along with five one-hundred-dollar bills, all typed out neatly along with the flight numbers of three planes leaving Mexico for LAX that day –

4 p.m. – Band Meeting.
6 p.m. – Interview. Garden of Self-Realization, Pacific Palisades.

The interview is a Big One. They've been pitching it to him for weeks, a New York journalist flying out to meet them. *Serious guy, writes for the* Village Voice. *Loves our music, loves you. A chance to tell your side of the story. Put the record straight.*

A new face to show the world after their enforced three-month lay-off. After he – allegedly – showed his dick to two thousand kids in an aircraft hangar in Miami in March. After he became Public Enemy No. 1 and the President himself backed the decency rallies that brought thirty thousand little God-fearing roaches out of their Southern Gothic holes, baying for his blood. After the promoters got scared and their twenty-five-date tour was cancelled. After radio stations refused to play their songs. After their collective bank balances shrank.

We thought we'd go do the interview in the Garden of Self-Realization. Gandhi's ashes are there! No booze. Calm. Peaceful, dig? Show the world we're back.

Two p.m. What are the rest of the band doing now? Meditating and drinking their juice and turning up at the office ready for their big old meeting and their big old fucking interview and realizing he, their prize calf, is not there. Fretting over his whereabouts. Making phone calls, wondering whether he left the hotel yesterday, wondering whether he made the plane, whether he made it back to LA, and if so, where he spent the night. Sending their little spies out across the city to find him: Topanga, the Phone Booth, the benches on Sunset, the Alta Cienega, the bedrooms of various women whose numbers and addresses they keep on file. He knows full well they keep their lists of his trysts. His whereabouts is no longer his private concern. They are all in the business of business now.

Well, fuck them. He is still over a thousand miles away.

He knows what they've got planned – they are going to tell him that he has to quit: the booze, the drugs. Especially the booze. That it has all got out of hand. And they are going to look nervous because they have no leverage, not really, in this conversation; they know that they depend on him for their livelihoods, for their marriages and their houses and their cars and their clothes and their food – depend on him standing in front of them singing the hits that he (mostly) wrote. Have depended on him for three years, for the charisma, the magic, for the pure Dionysian hit of it, for the union of all opposites; have depended on him to bring them closer to God. And now they can feel him slipping away, fucking it up. They want him ready for market: for hair and make-up and lights. They don't want him covered in blubber and lawsuits and arrest warrants and chaos and dissent. They want Adonis, not Caliban. And they really, *really* want him to shave his beard and lose the weight.

They have been limping along together, the four of them, bound by finances and contracts and dependants, like the brittle husk of a marriage when the sex is long gone. Mexico was supposed to put the cojones back into the operation: a forty-thousand-seater bullring booked for three nights; tickets at a dollar each. But it never happened. Only a Las Vegas-style supper club in Mexico City happened, playing four nights to the President's son and the children of the rich.

The kid is making his way back towards him, a tray balanced on his upturned hand. He must be eighteen, nineteen, no more, torso tapering into black trousers. The perfection of the ratio of the shoulder to the waist. He used to be like that – half-starved and Vitruvian and twenty-two, sleeping on the rooftops of Venice Beach. The moon a woman's face. The dawn birds waking him with their messages and the ocean cleaning him and the avocado and the mango trees generous with their fruit. Two hundred mics of Owsley acid every morning for breakfast. If you caught the power of the dawn, you could surf it right down to the evening. It filled you, that power. It was you.

That was before everything. Before anyone knew who he was. Before they hit number one. Before he became the singer of the biggest band in the country, with all its attendant clamour: the managers and the agents and the record companies and the roadies and the concert promoters and the wives and the girls in their suburban bedrooms – the weight of their collective need.

Before it changed them. Slowly estranged them.

What the guys in the band don't understand though, when they are asking him to lose the weight, is that the skinny young god of three years ago was only a half-starved acid dream.

He was always a fat kid.

The sandwich is thin white bread and ham and mayonnaise. He takes a bite and the bread sticks to the roof of his mouth.

Uh . . . you got anything Mexican? Mexican food?

Ah. Yes – huevos? Eggs?

Yeah. Huevos. That's cool. Tortillas?

The kid shakes his head. No tortillas.

Shit. Why no tortillas?

The kid shrugs. They don't like them. The Americans.

Shit, man. I love tortillas. Well, bring me some eggs and some more of this shitty bread. And another beer. Two. And a whisky chaser. Two whiskies. Or, no – you got mescal?

The kid nods.

Bring me a couple of shots. No – wait. Bring me the bottle.

The kid nods, readies to head back to the kitchen.

A shimmer on the pool. A slight shift in the soundscape and he remembers – the peyote. He took it in his room an hour ago, had found he was wearing it still: several small air-dried balls of mescaline, threaded to make a necklace.

It was handed to him when he was on the way to the gig, the last night in Mexico City. One of the President's son's entourage: *This is the best stuff. Peyote. From the desert. Reeeeeeally gets you high.*

This morning, just after he woke up, he put a ball between his back teeth and bit. It split neatly. He swallowed one, then another. Then put the rest round his neck. He fingers it now, lifts the necklace to his mouth, bites off another ball. It tastes earthy, and bitter. Not bad. Not bad at all. He swallows it with his beer.

Over on the other side of the pool, the husband stands up, adjusts his shorts and bends down to kiss his wife on the lips before walking to the edge of the water and diving in. He starts to swim, brown and slick and fierce. Something about the man reminds the singer of his father – his height, the way he moves. Even in his forties his father would jump up on the monkey bars and execute a perfect kip. Hold still on the rings. How old is his father now? Forty-nine? Fifty? Has news reached the Admiral (the youngest admiral in the US Navy, out there on an aircraft carrier on the other side of the Pacific, patrolling the waters just off Vietnam) that his eldest son is facing nine months in Raiford Penitentiary for showing his dick to a hangar full of thousands of screaming kids on the edge of a swamp?

But the thing is, Dad, I'd been to see the Living Theatre, dig? You heard of them? They just came from Paris – the occupation of the Odéon. They played five nights straight at UCLA: the Plague, Paradise Now. *Those guys, honestly, what they're doing – that's the real revolution right there. It's Artaud. That's the real fucking rock and roll. And so I thought I'd give a little back. A little inoculation into the bloodstream of America. Hold the mirror up, show them themselves.*

And did you?

Did I what?

Expose yourself?

Awwww, shit, man. You know what? I honestly can't remember.

So, son. You were drunk again?

The last time he saw his father was three years ago. The last words they spoke were angry ones. He remembers the look on his father's face. The incomprehension, the dismay. As though, in his son, in his leathers and long hair, and his lyrics of chaos and dissolution, he had birthed his own demonic id.

The woman on the lounger takes a camera from her bag, walks several paces away from the chairs and lifts it. The glass of its eye catches the sun and he flinches – caught in the line of her shot, holds his hand up to cover his face and she inclines her head and moves for a different angle, one that doesn't include him.

The lenses. They metastasize. Are everywhere he goes. It is karma, he knows, for all the times he trained his binoculars on girls and women: in his teenage-sweat-filled Airstream down in Tallahassee, or on those Venice Beach rooftops. Peeping Tom. The voyeur. He made it his vocation, his religion, all those gentle arms that reached around to unhook the hooks that held those breasts, *arms that are braceleted and white and bare* – watching, writing, jerking off. Now the lenses are trained on him. Now the hot young breath of America is panting down his neck. What's behind those lenses? He knows the FBI have a fattening file on him, knows he is in Hoover's sights. Everyone is paranoid. Everyone is scared. You can feel it in the hot streets of the city. It is like the final scene of a western – all the guns are trained on each other: the police and the FBI and the kids on Haight Street, and the kids hiding out in the haunted canyons and the kids at the Democratic Convention and the kids in the jungle and the Viet Cong.

Something happened, out there on the west coast of America, sometime between '65 and '67 – a portal appeared somewhere above the ocean, the westward march was over and there was no more continent left to burn, and the grandchildren of the doctrine of Manifest Destiny, the children of the atom bomb, dropped acid and stared at the Pacific with a wild surmise.

For a while, standing out there in front of them, he felt it: Pan, Dionysus, roaring the hot sylvan spunk into their faces. The stakes were nothing less than the nation's soul. And there were nights when he could feel it – all of it moving through him – the thousands watching spellbound, not by him, by the more-than-him, by his porousness, his capacity to make room for the great mystery, for the ancient and the dead. But though the doors opened, they were not cleansed, and when it came to it, despite the satyrs and the piping and the mad dancing on the hillside, they could not lead the people through. Now the children in the crowd are ever younger and they grow crass and coarse and want only the performance of dissent and not its ragged disruptive truth.

They handed him a live lamb, in Miami, and he wondered which one of them was here for the sacrifice.

You're all a bunch of slaves, he had screamed back at the crowd. *You're all a bunch of fucking slaves.*

On the other side of the pool the kid sets a margarita glass down beside the woman, a juice before the man. Something perfect about the drink, the glass sweating in the heat – the woman's long fingers reaching for it, the flash of her rings in the sun. The kid makes his way to him, two more beers, the bottle of mescal. A plate of eggs. He hands him a beer with a little flourish. Puts the other one on the table beside him, along with the bottle of mescal.

The singer reaches for the mescal. Takes a draught. Feels it do its thing in his blood. The world resolves itself. Lately, this has been the only relief from any of it – a bottle of spirits a day.

Spirits for the spirits.

Hey – kid?

Yeah?

I'm looking for a rock. A white rock. In the ocean. You know it?

The kid frowns, then – Ah yes! he says. El roca de la Virgen. You walk to the beach, and then look all the way that way when you get there – he gestures to the right – and you will see it for sure. Or you take a boat. From the dock. They will take you closer.

Cool. Thanks.

He lies back on the lounger, lets the sun tighten his skin.

There is a white rock there, in the ocean, where the Indians say the world was born.

It was left there for him to find, when he woke up in that Mexico City hotel room alone. A neatly written note. Wrapped around a blade of black glass. An invitation? A dare?

Here is a gift: use it to cut yourself free.

Eva.

She had not recognized him, standing there, in the arrivals lounge, clipboard in her hand. He had flown solo from LA to Mexico, arrived before the band. He did not want the circus and the lenses and the interviews at the airport. He was tired, hadn't slept well for weeks. A small slight woman was watching him as he lit his first cigarette in the arrivals hall. She looked, looked away then looked again, then approached him slowly.

Excuse me, but are you –?

She put a *Mr* before his name. She sounded unsure.

Sure, he said. Who wants to know?

My name is Eva. I'm here to take you to your hotel.

She looked Mexican but sounded French. Dressed demure. Classy. Not like a hippie, none of that peacock-feather crap, just a skirt and a shirt and some shoes. Dark hair caught at the nape of her neck.

60

You only have this one bag?

Yeah.

She picked it up and carried it for him and he let her, following at a small distance, watching her from behind. In the back of the limo she sat way over on the other side of the seat. The air conditioning was up too high. He opened the window, leaned his head out: a four-lane highway, the smell of petrol and heat and animals and shit and steel.

You got any water? His hangover was setting in.

At the hotel, she said. It won't take long. He saw her signal to the driver to turn the air con off.

Have you been to Mexico before? She turned to him.

Ah, sure . . . Ensenada.

Two days across the border with his kid brother, the first time they had hung out in years. He paid for as much tequila and whoring as a seventeen-year-old could take. He caught the clap, started pissing green pus when he got back home.

Ensenada? She said it back to him in her French accent and smiled. Well, hopefully you will find a little more culture on this trip. The rest of the band arrive this afternoon?

I believe so.

It will be a circus, yes?

Sure.

This is why you travel alone like this? To escape the circus?

Yeah.

I think they would not recognize you anyway. I almost did not. You look different.

Different to what?

To your photograph.

Thin lips. Small breasts. He could see the edge of her bra beneath her shirt. Small damp patches of sweat. The faint trace of a moustache on her upper lip. She was older than him, late

61

twenties, maybe thirty? Maybe more? She did not wear a wedding ring.

I am sorry about the bullring, she said. The cancellation. Everyone is very sorry.

Yeah. We're sorry too. Sorry you didn't tell us in time.

She frowned. We only found out two days ago. The permits. The President refused. The government here . . . after the . . . difficulties last year. In October.

Yeah, they shot a load of students, right? How many?

She flinched, turned to look out of the window. They do not know how many. Several hundred? More? They took the bodies. No one knows where. Perhaps they threw them into the ocean.

Jesus.

My cousin is one of the disappeared.

Oh, I'm sorry, ma'am.

She looked down and brushed ash from her skirt. It is very bad. This is why they don't let you play for the – how do you say it – for the masses? They do not want the young people to gather at all. They are afraid.

Of what?

Of the young. Of revolution. Of you.

Her eyes were amber. Amber flecked with green.

They did similar, he said. In Chicago. They turned on the kids. They beat the crap out of them.

Yes. Yes, I'm sorry. I know.

Not murder though. Not yet.

They were silent then, for the rest of the journey, as the limo passed through the wide streets of the city and then into a low-rise gated neighbourhood, a palatial hotel. She checked in for him, rode with him up to his room, a suite on the first floor.

Will anyone be joining you? she said quietly. I know the rest of the band travel with their –

Their wives? Sure. No. Not me. Just me.

She held his gaze. Of course. Well. I'll leave you to settle in. I am your guide while you are here. I can show you things.

What sort of things?

Things of interest. What interests you? Mexico is full of interesting things.

He thought: *You interest me. I would be interested in you stripping off for me, lying back on the bed. You cursing me in your beautiful accent. I would be interested in licking your cunt while you curse.*

But – the club is nice. Her tone was brighter. You will like it, I hope. We hope that you can perform in the Alameda too. The park in the centre of the city. We hope the trip will be worth it, even so. Everyone is very happy you are here.

Sure.

She turned to go.

Are you French? he asked, when she had reached the door.

Half, she said, turning back to him. I was born in Paris. My father is French. I grew up there. But my mother is Mexican, and I have lived in Mexico for years.

She was there often: at the hotel, showing them into the limos that took them the short ride to the club; there at the lunchtime meetings with her clipboard, telling them the bad news – TV was not secured yet, the National Auditorium was looking less likely, the cover charge for the gigs that were happening was set at sixteen dollars so no students could attend. And she was there in the evening too, watching the first show from the back of the room, when he dressed in a Hawaiian shirt and old jeans, beard and hair fully in place, listening when he introduced the band in halting Spanish. And there, in a short dress with flowers embroidered on the hem, in the dressing

63

room after the show. He watched her move around the room, touching the other members of the band on their arms, thanking them. Somehow, though, she never came close to him, never looked his way, until he looked up and saw her, coat on, ready to leave. As she passed he grabbed her arm.

Hey. Have a drink. You tried this? Try it. He poured her a glass from a bottle he was already halfway down.

I am sorry. I have to go.

Where?

I have children.

Oh. Where are they? Are they here? He pretended to look under the table. He was drunk.

No, they are at home.

Alone?

With a babysitter. I have to go to them now.

He saw she was suddenly tired. And bored by him.

He watched her go and when he turned back another woman was already there in her place. Red-headed and willing. They went on to a club. He woke up at 5 a.m., sitting on the toilet seat. His jeans were unzipped. He still had the bottle in his hand. It looked like someone had recently sucked his cock.

Eva was back though the next day, at breakfast, which they were served in the dining room at two o'clock. She read out the reviews for them, translating them into English.

El Heraldo says you are a pirate. A red-bearded mixture of Fidel Castro with . . .

She read ahead, paused.

With what? he said.

The Hunchback of Notre-Dame.

They all laughed. He did too. But when she said *Notre-Dame* her accent was purely French, and he could hear Parisian streets and cobbles and something pitiless and scouring and cold. And he knew he was hungry for it, that scouring in a cold northern light.

Also, they say that you were . . . trastornado . . .

What does that mean?

Out of your skull.

The next day, she suggested an outing to the pyramids. Teotihuacán, an hour north of the city. He dozed in the back of the limo, seated directly behind her. They were playing US rock. The band's song came on and he opened his eyes – saw dead donkeys, stomachs bloated with flies, kids in packs crowding round the windows of the car, the searing sun.

They hired an official guide, who walked ahead, speaking loudly. The largest city in the Americas . . . one of the largest in the world. The name means Birthplace of the Gods . . . This is not a metaphor. They believed this was the birthplace of the universe . . . And then . . . collapse. We don't exactly know why . . . Environmental. Changing climate. This is the Avenue of Death.

He dropped back. He did not want the guide, did not want to be close to the rest of the band and their girlfriends. He fell into step beside her. His head was thick from the night before. He had no hat or sunglasses, and the sun was blinding. She was wearing an embroidered blouse, loose. Sandals. Jeans. Her hair caught up in a scarf. Sunglasses. A small camera around her neck.

They hardly spoke, but it was comfortable between them, as though they had agreed upon silence.

She took a photograph of him climbing up the Pyramid of the Sun. He was wearing his Frye boots. Black jeans. A white T-shirt. He remembered to suck in his gut. He put his hand in the mouth of the feathered serpent. She took a photo of that too.

That afternoon they went to the anthropological museum. A private visit. The President's son had been at the gig and so palms were greased and doors opened. By then their entourage had swelled to thirty or so – the red-headed girl who would not leave him alone, the President's son, with his bag of marijuana and cocaine, offering it around in the back of the limo. The singer watched the way Eva was with him: this young man whose father was responsible for the deaths of hundreds of kids his own age – and her cousin perhaps. He saw her politeness, but he knew that underneath it was a scream.

The others peeled off quickly, the band filming themselves, goofing it up for the camera. But he walked slowly, room to room. He had never been anywhere like it. Finally, he reached the Aztec room. He made his way slowly around: the astonishing circular calendar stone, three times the height of a man. Quetzalcoatl, Xochipilli – the Prince of Flowers.

Tucked away at the back of the room was a small plinth – the figurine of a god, a band of black across his nose and cheeks.

There was a noise behind him. He turned and she was there, standing close.

Tezcatlipoca, she said. Smoking Mirror. You know about him?

He could smell her – a gentle perfume, the light musk of her sweat. He kept his eyes on the statue.

Tell me.

He was the god most associated with human sacrifice.

Go on.

Each year, she said. A young man was chosen to represent the god. He had to be the most beautiful of all. He was lodged in the temple, taught to play the flute, denied nothing, given everything: the finest food, the finest women, the finest jewels.

He was carried through the city. His feet were not allowed to touch the earth. The people threw themselves before him when he passed.

And then?

Then, when the time came, he died alone, at a small temple. He had to climb the stairs, and at each stair he would break one of the flutes he had played upon. At the top the priest was waiting, holding an obsidian blade. Ready to offer the young man's heart to the sun.

A silence between them. The others were elsewhere – their laughter distant, as though rising from a memory. The sound of the fountain in the courtyard. The beat of his heart.

He could feel something forming in the silence between them, something whose shape was not yet clear.

How old are you?

I'm thirty-two.

Where's your husband?

Gone.

Say something to me in French.

What?

Anything. He stepped towards her. Tell me I'm a piece of shit.

Tu es un morceau de merde.

Tell me I'm a monster.

Tu es un monstre.

A hunchback.

Un bossu.

Tell me to go fuck myself.

Va te faire foutre.

Let's go to Paris.

Why?

I want to escape.

Then why don't you? You are your own man. You are free.

I am not free.

Then you must cut yourself free.

He laughed at that. How?

What are you afraid of?

Kidnap.

Murder.

Incarceration.

A small temple. The priest at the top.

The scapegoat.

The sacrifice.

The eyes behind the lenses.

Myself.

Let me touch you. He reached out his hand, undid the small thin buttons of her blouse, put his hand inside, felt the hard nub of her nipple. With his other hand he lifted her skirt, his hand sliding her underwear to the side. The unmasked pleasure on her face.

They were interrupted. The cars were leaving – they were out of time. She pushed his hand away, and he put his fingers in his mouth. She straightened herself out, laughed at them both, shook her head.

He sang to her, that night. Sang to where she stood at the back of the room, her yellow dress luminous in the low light. When he wanted to he could croon, could make his voice Sinatra-sweet.

He looked for her everywhere after the show. But she was not there. She had gone home to her kids, and when he woke the next morning, the light was strong at the window, and he was alone. Under the door was a note from the tour manager telling him to get the first flight back to LA – a timetable copied out on the bottom showing the schedule of the flights

from Benito Juárez to LAX. He threw his things into his suit-
case, pulled on his jacket, patted the pocket for money and
passport. That was when he found it – an obsidian blade.
Small, serrated, and wrapped around it, held in place with an
elastic band, a note –

You said you needed to escape, and I thought of this place.

*There is a white rock there, in the ocean, where the Indians say the
world was born. They make their pilgrimages there. It's a beautiful
place. A wild place. I think you would like it.*

Here is a gift: use it to cut yourself free.

And then a neatly written set of directions: *Take a plane to
Puerto Vallarta and then a taxi north around 3 hours. Ask for Playa
Hermosa. They will know it – it's right at the end of the beach.*

When he got to the airport, he had both – the instructions
from the tour manager and the directions from her – and he
stood in the middle of the departures hall and he took out a
coin and he tossed it, let it land. Then he paid for his flight and
turned the other way and took a little plane down here and
drank mescal at the airport and saw the volcano as they took
off – Popocatépetl – all red in the evening sun except for the
white on its peak and during the flight he drank another half-
bottle of the smoky medicine and the water below the plane
was dark as they banked and landed on the coast. He walked
straight out into the warm embrace of the Pacific night and
found a taxi driver and showed him the paper she had given
him, and the driver read it and nodded. Playa Hermosa?
Nayarit?

And when he woke up, how many hours later? Three? Four?
He was here.

A cloud across the sun. He sees the woman on the lounger
look up in irritation. She shivers a little, although it is still
hot.

He finishes his beer. A healthy chaser of the mescal – two-thirds of the bottle still left. He stands, a little unsteady. Holds himself against the glass table to wrap a towel around his waist and manoeuvre himself out of his shorts, pull on his old jeans.

On the back of the lounger is the Hawaiian shirt with the red flowers – the same shirt he has been wearing for days now. What day is it, even? Wednesday? Tuesday? When did he leave Mexico City? Yesterday, right? The last gig was on Monday night, and he remembers wearing this shirt then, wearing it on stage, this shirt that is splashed all over with flowers – what would you call them? Lilies? Gardenias? Lilydenias which are moving now, breathing a little on the fabric. He reaches for them, pulls the shirt over his head. It reeks. How has he not known how much it stinks? Did it stink this bad yesterday on the plane out here? He will have to buy some new clothes in town.

Okay. Dressed. Ready.

Darker now. More clouds massing. Where did they come from so quickly?

Now. Where is he going?

The rock.

The white rock. That's what she said. He lifts the bottle of mescal, takes another draught. Walks barefoot along the concrete, the bottle dangling from his hand.

Good afternoon, ma'am, he says as he passes the woman – his best Southern style.

She is gathering her things, wrapping herself in a zebra robe, silver and gold, her rings flashing in the compressed light.

Good afternoon – she angles her face towards him and smiles. East Coast accent, a flicker in the eyes. Does she recognize him? Does her daughter have a picture of him on her wall?

He walks out, away from the pool, follows a small rise in the land, to where he can see the ocean, a band of light – two, maybe three hundred metres away. He heads towards it, up a set of stone steps, out over grass and scrub, picking his way between spines and rocks. The path ends at the beach and the beach is huge – empty as far as he can see to his left and to his right. The ocean coming in, creaming gently onto the hard-packed sand. Three pelicans skimming the waves.

He shades his eyes – to his left, to what must be the south, the mountains appear to touch the water. To his right, to the north, lies a long low spit of land and there in the distance, sitting in the ocean, is a rock, quite small, quite squat from here, strangely shaped, like a collapsing wedding cake. Its whiteness unmistakable even from here.

He sits on the sand and stares at it: at the water between them, the tangled skein of light.

El Pacífico.

He is out there, somewhere, on the other side of the ocean, his father. On the aircraft carrier USS *Hancock*. Probably inspecting his troops. Almost 4 p.m. So what's the time in Vietnam?

How do you do, Father? You who sailed your ship into the Gulf of Tonkin five years ago. Did you know what you were doing? Did you have your orders? Did you know you were beginning this unholy war?

His face placid, easy. His father never got angry. Not really. That was the thing that used to bug him the most.

What does it take to become an admiral? How many deaths? What and who do you have to murder to move up the ranks?

Where are his father's corpses buried?

He remembers when he was a kid, visiting his father's ship. His mother insisting he cut his hair. His father teaching him to fire a gun.

Hey! he yells to the horizon. Hey motherfucker!

71

His father half turns at the call. A ghost call. The ghost of a son he once knew. Then he turns back to the massed ranks of young men in uniform before him. The righteous ones. His true sons. This placid admiral, on this Pacific Ocean, rising up the ranks on the tide of their blood.

He reaches into his back pocket – takes out the blade and turns it in his hand.

Then it arrives in him – the knowledge. If he goes back to LA and to the journalist from New York who will wait for him till tomorrow, if he goes back to the band, it will kill him. He will surely die.

He can feel it, invisible to the eye and yet stronger than any force he has ever known. He summoned it, after all. It was there on the faces of the people at the decency rally. It is there on his father's ship. It will be there, he knows, at his trial in Miami, in the papers, on the faces of the Florida jury – the machinery of state; they want him neutered, castrated. Punished.

Did he think he could outrun them, the powers that he summoned? He thought he was a god, but he is only a man, and withered now are the garlands that he wore. This is where it has all been headed, all along: the money and the women and the adoration – for him to be bent backwards over a stone and have his heart cut out. He thought it was a metaphor. The joke was on him.

Death – he has always felt it near. Has courted it on countless ledges outside countless hotel rooms above countless highways, in canyons which are said to be cursed, where the hot, dry desert winds blow. But now he feels he might not die the death of a holy fool. If he goes back now it's a long straight road to a trial and a Dade County jail. And he knows what they are capable of – those good old Florida boys with their buzz cuts and their gum and their guns and their gator-eyes. He grew up amongst them. And he does not want to die.

Not yet.

And he does not want to die for them: the baying kids, the money-men.

He starts to shiver. His teeth are rattling. Why are his teeth rattling?

He puts his arms around himself to stop the shivering, but it only gets worse.

Out.

He needs to get the fuck out.

Could they find him, down here? Unlikely, unless someone here recognizes him. And he does not look like he did.

There's nothing to leave anyway, nothing that means anything. He has not spoken to his family for years. His long-time woman has gone – for good this time, or so it seems – out of the country, consorting with aristocratic dope dealers in their Moroccan castles, taken her band of leeches with her, all fat on bleeding him dry. He has no home, no possessions. Has never lusted for those things. Has only the clothes he stands up in, his credit card and driver's licence, and he has those in the pocket of his jeans.

He holds the obsidian blade to the sun.

Cut yourself free.

Kill the god.

Give birth to the man.

So.

Yes.

The shivering stops – a sign.

He reaches for the bottle of mescal. Warm. Welcome. Grace.

Okay.

If yes, then how?

Fake it.

Walk into town now. Buy some more clothes. Come back out here and leave the stinking shirt and jeans by the shoreline. Take a taxi back to Puerto Vallarta, a plane back to Mexico City, go and find her. Tell her he has killed the god. That he is getting out. Out to be scoured by northern light. Tell her that she can come find him there.

Paris.

He can see it – a book-lined study. A different life. Her in his bed. The cold pure light of a November dawn.

See, Dad? You just watch me.

He coughs deep and spits. Tar brown. He stares at it for a long while, then he stands up.

The rock is there. The white rock. The place the world was born.

A good place to start again.

He starts to walk towards the rock, making his way onto the hard-packed sand at the water's edge, the water that is coming closer now, the breakers getting bigger, lifting and curling and smacking themselves down. The clouds massing, the light now gunmetal grey. He shivers. He walks, heading in the direction of the rock.

A call. A sound. A name. His name on the wind. Surely not his name? No one knows he is here.

He turns. Heart thudding. Mouth dry.

Wait!

Someone is running towards him.

It is the kid who brought him the drinks, running towards him, a loping run, but fast, like an animal. Like an animal that knows how to run. And he is holding something, something flapping in the wind.

Wait for me!

The singer wants to run himself. Knows somehow that he should run from this kid. Run into the dunes. Run into the sea. Run for his life.

Knows he can't outrun him.

The kid is gaining on him. Easy. Hardly even out of breath.

Okay, it's okay. He's just a kid. Just a waiter. Just a nice Mexican kid running towards him in the middle of the afternoon.

A kid who has somehow learned his name.

Hola, says the kid. He is smiling.

The sun is low in the sky. Behind the kid's head lie the dunes, and behind them the jungle breathes, massy and green. The light melting like molasses on the trunks of the trees.

It's you, says the kid.

Who?

The kid lifts the thing that he is carrying, and the singer sees it is a piece ripped from a newspaper. He opens it, holds it up. A large photograph of the singer, on stage in Mexico City. He is wearing the Hawaiian shirt. The lilies and the gardenias. The lilydenias moving on the page, on the stage. A microphone held tight to his face, as he leans out over the crowd.

He takes the piece of paper. His fingers are large and clumsy, the skin rubbery, as though they have been steeped in water. He peers at it.

Oh yeah, he says, yeah, it sure looks like me.

He tries a grin.

I knew it! The shirt!

Uh-huh.

It is the same shirt!

I guess it is.

You are a rock star.

I guess I am.

You are number one!

Is that right?

The kid sings a snatch of their latest hit.

That's pretty good, he says. Yeah.

You are famous! The kid is moving from foot to foot as though he needs to pee. You are very very famous! More famous than Liz Taylor!!!

Ah . . . hell . . . I don't know about that.

You are!

His heart. The pounding of his heart. He takes a draught of mescal. Feels the fire. Feels a little stronger. Slaps around his shirt pockets for his cigarettes, lights one up. Only a little tremble in the hand. He slaps a mosquito onto his arm and stares down at the bloodied pulp.

How much peyote did he eat?

Reeeeeallly gets you high.

Hey. The kid looks from right to left then leans in. You are hiding? he says, in a stage whisper. You are hiding here?

Um . . . The smoke from his cigarette hangs heavy in the air between them.

The kid steps back. You looked scared, the kid says. And the smile has gone. A flash of something in his eyes. A calculation. A price on his head.

His lungs are sore. Everything is sore.

Hey, the kid says. You want to come to town?

Town? He squints.

With me. I have finished work. I go into town now. You want to come? I can show you some places. Bars. Music. Girls. Places you will like. Come now, quickly, before the mosquitoes. Los jejenes. Pinches cabrones. He slaps his neck. I can show you the white rock.

He needs to think. He can't think with the kid all up in his face like this.

76

The kid leans in again. Don't worry, he says, in that hammy stage whisper. Your secret's safe with me. Then he takes the piece of paper, folds it with deliberate care and puts it in his back pocket, where he pats it gently.

The singer closes his eyes. Counts to five. Opens them again.

The kid is still there.

Okay, he says. Okay.

The Girl
1907

She is awake before the dawn, listening to the ship as it churns through the waves, watching the colours of the sky change above her head, and the stars disappearing, one by one.

Only one is left now – Machiwa Choki, the brightest, hanging in the sky by the thinning moon. He is still here, in his usual place, even when everything else is different: when the land has become a strange green tangle of trees and shrubs all the way down to the water, and the mountains are grey and blue and distant.

The sky is lightening now, above those mountains, and the girl huddles further into her shawl. The dawn is chill, and her shawl is damp with the sticky sea air, but it will be hot soon – the sun is beginning to rise, the first bright bar of its light hitting the metal of the ship's railings close to where the girl sits. She is stiff, there is nowhere to stretch – people are packed in front of her and to the side: the humped shapes of hundreds of sleeping forms. In Guaymas where they joined this boat, there were so many of them they took up the whole of the dock.

How many dawns, since then? It is hard to count. Her mind does not seem to work the way it once did, but she thinks four: four days in which this ship has not stopped moving, not stopped churning the water into white and yellow spray, nor ceased its low sound, thudthudthud; this beast that never tires, that does not need to stop or eat or rest or sleep, with each beat of its cold metal heart taking them further away from home.

Four days on this ship. Five days, then, since the day of the gun.

She turns to her sister, who sleeps on beside her, head lolling

81

on her neck. The light is growing stronger, and the girl can see the cut beneath Maria-Luisa's right eye, the white flecks of thirst at the edges of her mouth, her shawl still crusted brown with Carlos's blood. But it is her sister's foot that troubles her most – that keeps her awake like this; the bone is broken and should have been set days ago, and the wound is turning bad. The middle is scabbed and crusted, but the edge is swollen, a deep red swelling that is moving over her sister's leg. She can smell it from where she sits, a lingering sweetness. It is here, in this sweetness, the girl knows, that the danger lies.

She has been listening, in the chill of this morning, for her grandmother's voice:

For the fever – says her grandmother – *we need kovanao. Come.*

She has been following her grandmother, out into the dawn: the way her grandmother's feet make the dew melt, the way her skirt moves around her ankles, the way she pauses when she finds the right bush, the one covered with yellow flowers, and kneels beside it before touching it, asking the plant to help her cure.

She has been watching as her grandmother dries the leaves on the packed earth of the rama, then makes a strong tea for Maria-Luisa to drink.

This will cool the fever, her grandmother says.

She mixes the boiled leaves with ground deer bones and saliva to make a poultice. The girl has been able to hear her spitting into the bowl, the scrape of her knife, feel the cool paste as it is packed gently onto the wound. Her grandmother has bound the foot with deer hide and held it with carrizo cane to keep the ankle straight. She has lit a bundle of mesquite twigs and tended the small fire in a bowl. And she has been keeping watch: three days and three nights for the cure to take effect.

Beside the girl, Maria-Luisa mutters, then shouts in her sleep.

The girl touches her sister's cheek with the back of her hand. Her fever is higher this morning, and her skin is clammy. In this growing light, she can see a rash on the skin of her cheeks. This is new.

And her grandmother is not here. She is still in the village. And there are no herbs, no poultice, nothing to help Maria-Luisa at all. And their father is in Arizona, and their mother is in Hermosillo, and they are scattered, all of them, like seeds on the wind.

More people are waking now, faces emerging from blankets all over the deck: people coughing and spitting and scratching themselves into the day. Men and boys are taking it in turns to clamber over their fellow prisoners and do their business over the side. There is a hole, below deck, for the women, but by the end of the second day it was full to overflowing, so nobody uses it now. Since then, they have had to manage as best they can. The soldiers watch them all the time.

It will be a while yet before the sun comes over the middle of the ship. Till then, those on this side will be in shade, but soon enough the heat will scorch them, and they will beg for water. Often, because they are young, and sit so far from the middle where the soldiers and the water are, the girl and Maria-Luisa have not received anything to drink. The girl's tongue is fat and cracked, and squats in her mouth like a toad waiting for rain. She closes her eyes, pictures the clay water-pot at home, the way it sweats with moisture. The green mass gathered on its outside. The trough beneath where the chickens drink. The water inside is always cool, even on the hottest days. In her mind, she dips the gourd, brings the cool water to her mouth.

A cry comes from the family close by – the baby girl, her hands flailing for her mother's breast. The baby's mother brings it to her, shushing her, singing to her. The baby's father is already awake, staring out at the lightening sky. Like the girl, he is often awake before everyone else, looking to the sky, or the dark water below, keeping his secrets close. Two boys lie between their parents, curled around each other like braided rope. The man tucks blankets around his wife and children now, finding and covering the places where the cold gets in.

Something about the way he does this makes the girl feel better.

She has been glad to be close to this family, the way you are glad to draw towards the fire on a cold night. At the beginning of the voyage they had plenty of food – the mother carried it in a basket: tamales filled with meat, flour tortillas, water and milk. They had blankets for warmth and hats for the sun. They had laughter even: their father would play a trick sometimes with his two boys, hiding and finding kernels of corn behind their ears. Or the boys played with each other, a game of teeham: throwing small pebbles into a circle of stones, then counting up their score.

Sometimes, those first days, the mother passed the girl and Maria-Luisa a little something, a tamale to share, water to drink. The food was good, it tasted like home. But it has been four days, and the food is all gone. The boys' shirts, which were white when they joined the boat, are filthy now.

The two boys have woken now too. The littlest sits, yawns and rubs his eyes. 'I'm hungry,' he says. 'Mama. My tummy hurts.' Usually this boy has a smiling, jolly face, but this morning he is drawn, and pale.

His mother gathers him to her, takes out her other breast, offers it, and he feeds as the older boy looks on. The girl knows what that older boy is thinking: how hungry he is. How much he, too, would like the comfort of his mother's breast, but how he must be strong. His father reaches into his bag and brings out a piece of agave, which he slices with his pocketknife and hands to his son. The boy sucks on the cactus, eyes wary in the morning light.

The family have come from a hacienda in the north of Yoeme country, close to the border with Arizona. The girl knows this because, in the evenings, when the sun is going down, people have begun to speak with each other, trading their tales of how they came to be here, on this ship. The father has told of how a government agent came to the hacienda and ordered the bosses to give a list of all their Yoeme workers. How, a few days later, the soldiers came. How they were taken from the fields in the middle of the harvest: women and children and all. How the hacienda owners begged the soldiers to let their workers stay, but the soldiers did not listen, and brought them south to Guaymas to join this boat. The father still has the red dust of the fields on the cuffs of his trousers.

The tall father has secrets. From where the girl sits she can sometimes see the roll of money he keeps strapped to his shin, hidden beneath his trouser leg. The other secret is his guilt.

His guilt is strongest in the mornings, when he sits, awake like her, and stares at the water and the sky. She has heard him, whispering to his wife when their children sleep on: he should have taken them over the border to Arizona, to his brother's house, when he had the chance. He knew things were changing – they all did – that Yoemem were being rounded up indiscriminately now. He should have heeded the warnings. They would have been safe.

His wife comforts him: there was danger in crossing the desert. At least they are all here together and are well. He nods and agrees, but his face changes when he looks away. Arizona, he thinks, as he stares at the dawn. Arizona.

On the other side of Maria-Luisa the praying woman is awake now too, hands on her rosary, whispering her list of names:

'JosefaPedroDomingaChepaRosalioCruz.'

This woman has a wide face and sharp, watchful eyes.

She has also told her story: how, last week, her husband was lined up in the Sunday sessions in Hermosillo, which every male Yoeme in the area is forced to attend. How there were three lines there: one for the men who were to be shot, one for the deportation boats, and one line for the men who would be left to work another week. How Izabal, the Governor of Sonora, presided over these sessions, sitting high in a chair, smoking his cigar, like a god. El Segundo Dios. How there were Yoemem there who helped Izabal, in this task of sorting men into lines – torocoyori, who covered their faces with red bandanas so they might not be known.

But everyone knows who they are.

How, when it was this woman's husband's turn before Izabal, these torocoyoris nodded – yes, he was a bronco, his brother was fighting in the Sierra with the rebels. Yes, he should be shot.

So, her husband was taken to the Rincón del Burro, where he was killed by six soldiers that afternoon.

When she reached this part of the story, where her husband was shot before her eyes, the woman's hands flew to her face. She gasped for breath.

After he was shot, she said, they hung her husband from a tree.

Why? Why when he was already dead?

She had to wait until darkness to cut him down, to save him from the birds. Then, the next day, they arrested her too, came for her and her children in her home, and brought them to the jail in Hermosillo.

There were so many children, the woman said, *in that jail. Hundreds of them. Held in cages like beasts.*

The smell of those cages, she said, crossing herself.

They dragged her from her children and brought her to this boat. And her children are there still, in those cages.

Sometimes she opens her bundle, takes out her children's clothes, and holds them to her, but mostly she speaks her children's names, over and over, as though they themselves have become the prayer.

JosefaPedroDomingaChepaRosalioCruz.

Who will care for them now?

She is afraid, this woman, for her children, for herself, her fear leaking around her, puddling onto the deck. The girl wants to pull Maria-Luisa away from this woman's fear, but there is no space to move. Her sister must sit in it, just as others must sit in the puddles that their children make, because there is nowhere else to go – only the sun dries them. But the sun does not dry the fear, it only stretches it tight.

The praying woman reminds the girl a little of her own mother – the way she wears her hair in plaits so long they reach to her knees. But the girl's mother is like Maria-Luisa, and afraid of nothing. If her mother were here, she would shout at the soldiers. She would get water for them.

But then, is it not their mother's fault that they are here? If her mother had not told Maria-Luisa she was to be married, they would never have gone to the mountain. They would never have taken the gun.

Maria-Luisa opens her eyes. 'Is it better?' she says, twisting to see. 'My foot? It hurts.'

'Yes,' says the girl. 'It is getting better every day.'

She arranges her sister's shawl, so it shields her from the sun.

No, it is not, says her grandmother's voice. *The badness is spreading. If it is not stopped, then Maria-Luisa will have to lose her foot. It is the only way.*

Her grandmother would never lie to make things better – she would make them better, and if she could not, then she would tell the truth.

On the other side of the girl, a man shuffles and coughs. She turns his way. This man's face is thin and lined, he looks like the turkey vultures – the wiiru – who squat in the trees at the edge of the village, or on the tops of the tallest cacti, waiting to pick the bones of dead creatures when all the other animals are done.

He sits alone on the edge of the ship, right beneath the flag. When the others have shared their stories, he has stayed silent, beneath his blanket, watching, apart. But he is different this morning, leaning forward, eyes scanning the horizon, as though he sees something there that speaks to him, the muscles tightly drawn on his face and neck.

Now, he opens his mouth and speaks. 'Soon,' he says, 'we will see the rock.'

His voice is low and rasping. Gentle. It is a surprise how gentle it is.

The mother looks up from feeding her baby; her young boys stare. The tall father turns towards him. The praying woman falls silent. Even Maria-Luisa opens her eyes.

'Which rock?' says the father.

'The white rock. Then this boat will dock, and we will leave it.' The listeners lean in. If this is true, then it is good news – as far as any news on this ship can be good. 'How do you know this?' says the father.

'Because I have been on this voyage before.'

'Tell us then,' the praying woman says. 'Where are they taking us?'

'To the plantations,' says Turkey Vulture Man slowly, 'to Yucatán.'

The praying woman gives a small gasp. 'So it is true? They are taking us to farm henequen?'

'Yes, sister, it is true. For some of us, at least.'

'Then how are you here? They say no one comes back.' They are all speaking quietly, so as not to draw the attention of the soldiers, their little group huddled even closer now. 'Give me some tobacco,' says Turkey Vulture Man, 'and I will tell you.'

The father reaches for his leather pouch and passes it over. Turkey Vulture Man takes a pinch in his palm, rolls it, places it carefully between his cheek and his teeth. He lets it settle there, chews it a little to release the juice. He does all of this as though he has time, plenty of it. His listeners are impatient though. 'Go on,' says the praying woman. 'Tell us.'

The man coughs and spits over the side into the water below. 'When we see the white rock,' he says, 'this boat will dock, and we will leave it.'

'Will this be Yucatán?' asks the praying woman.

The man laughs. 'No, sister. Yucatán will still be many days away. If you live that long.'

'So where, then?'

'We will be in a town beside the ocean. We will be held there in pens, like cattle. Then they will make us walk, over the mountains to where the railroad begins.'

'How far do we walk?' says the father. He does not look worried. He looks as though he could walk a long way.

'Twenty days.'

A ripple of disbelief passes through the group. Twenty days' walking? The girl feels Maria-Luisa stiffen beside her, and she reaches for her sister's hand.

'The children cannot walk that far,' says the kind-faced

mother. She says this simply, as if this truth were enough to protect them.

'True,' says Turkey Vulture Man. 'They can't. But if they cannot, they will die.'

The woman puts her hands over her children's ears, but it is too late – they have heard. 'Mama?' says the bigger boy. Their mother shakes her head: no, no, this will not happen to them.

'Hey,' the tall father says. 'Enough. You are scaring them.'

Turkey Vulture Man shrugs, and falls silent, but the girl knows that the tall father does not want him to stop. No one wants him to stop.

'Go on,' says the praying woman. 'Speak. When was this?'

Turkey Vulture Man shifts the wad of tobacco in his mouth. He looks to the tall father, who nods, just slightly, for him to go on.

'It was four years ago. I worked in the mine. At La Colorada.'

They nod. They have all heard of La Colorada.

'There was an attack on the company stores. The Rurales came, they rounded us all up. We had had nothing to do with it, but they did not care. They said we were to blame. They needed their quota for the ships. So they took me, my wife and family. We had three children, like you. We had no idea of what would come.'

'Go on.'

'The voyage was hard – but it was the walk over the mountains that killed. Between my wife and I we carried our two smallest children. Our eldest walked alongside. After many days she grew weary, but they would not stop for her. She tried to walk further, but she fell. I could not carry them all.'

The listeners cross themselves, whisper a prayer.

'They would not let me bury her.'

He closes his eyes briefly: a small flicker beneath his lids, then he opens them again, and gestures to where the soldiers sit. 'They have no pity, none. If you falter, they will leave you. If you sit down, they will threaten to shoot you. If you fall, they will leave you for the vultures and the jaguars.'

Maria-Luisa's palm is burning. The girl can feel the ragged gallop of her sister's heart.

'After the walk, those that are still alive are taken by train to Mexico City, and there we are sold.'

'Sold?' says the tall father.

Turkey Vulture Man nods. 'We are slaves now, brother. All of us.'

Slaves. This word falls between them, but does not settle: it thrashes like a fish on the deck.

'And then?'

'Then, if we are bought, there is another train, another boat, and then we are in Yucatán. And then we are in hell.'

For a long time no one speaks, then – 'In Yucatán,' the tall father asks, 'in the plantations. We work there, yes?'

The girl can feel the man's strength rise with his words; he knows how to work. He has worked hard all his life. All will be well if he can work.

'We work,' the Turkey Vulture Man says, 'but not as you know it. You must cut two thousand henequen leaves a day. You must leave thirty leaves on each plant: you leave one less than thirty and they whip you, one more and they whip you. If you do not make your two thousand you are whipped. If you trim your leaves raggedly you are whipped. If you are late at roll call you are whipped.'

And then, though no one has asked him, the man lifts his shirt and shifts a little so they might see his back – riddled with raised red welts.

'They say they want us to work,' he says, as he puts his shirt back, 'but you know what they really want?'

'What?'

'They want us to die.'

'No.' The tall father leans in and shakes his head. 'You are wrong. They know we are the strongest workers in Mexico. That is why they take us.'

'Perhaps that was true – once. But look around you, brother. You think they are bringing these old people, or these mothers, or these children, because they want them to work?'

They all do as he says, and look up and out, over the packed deck. He is right. There are many older people here. Many children. Their faces raw in the morning light.

'If they wanted us to die, they would shoot us,' says the father in a low voice. 'They could do it now. They have their guns. They can shoot us and throw us over the side.'

'They cannot do that. They do not want to be seen as barbarians. How many of us do you think are on this ship?'

The father shakes his head.

'I have been counting. There are more than six hundred. You cannot just shoot six hundred people. You must find other ways for them to die. So they march us over the mountains and the old ones fall. The young ones fall. The women with children fall. But no one has killed anyone. Do you understand?'

The mother brings her children closer, but they wriggle from her grip. Turkey Vulture Man watches her.

'Can I tell you something, sister? And you, brother?'

The woman looks at him. The tall father looks at him. Slowly, they nod.

'In this town of the white rock, the Mexicans will come. They will look at the children. Perhaps they will take some of them away.'

'Take them where?'

'To different families. To become Mexican. When our children become Mexican, they breed the Yoeme out.'

'Your wife?' says the praying woman. 'Your other children? What about them? Where are they now?'

'They bought them. In Mexico City.'

'Who?'

'Hacendados. Perhaps they took them to Yucatán. Perhaps to Valle Nacional. I never saw them again.'

'But you might.'

The man laughs and shakes his head. 'They are dead, sister.'

'How do you know?'

'Everyone dies.'

'But you didn't die.' It is Maria-Luisa who has spoken.

Everyone turns to her. Her eyes are wide, dark-bright with fever, fixed on the Turkey Vulture Man. 'You went to the plantations,' says Maria-Luisa, 'and you came back.'

Turkey Vulture Man looks at her. 'Perhaps,' he says softly. 'But I am just a ghost.'

'No.' Maria-Luisa's eyes snap. 'You are here,' she says. 'You are alive. And I want to know how.'

Turkey Vulture Man looks at Maria-Luisa's foot, then back up into her eyes. The girl knows what he is thinking: that her sister will not make it over those mountains.

But you do not know my sister, she thinks back.

'I am sorry for you,' he says to Maria-Luisa in his rasping voice. 'I am sorry for you all.' And then he sits back, spits over the side, settles the tobacco on the other side of his mouth and pulls his hat over his eyes.

As the small group retreats, the girl turns to Maria-Luisa, but she, too, has closed her eyes, as if by doing so, Turkey Vulture Man and all his terrible truths will disappear.

The sun is over the mast now, she can feel it burning her scalp. She can feel the raw edge of her panic, and fear. She pulls her shawl so it tents above her, and beneath it she is in a shaded space: the ship has gone, Turkey Vulture Man has gone.

But soon they will dock. And they will walk. And Maria-Luisa cannot walk.

She must do something.

She must go back.

There may be no herbs here for Maria-Luisa's wound, but if she can follow the thread of days back to that morning, to the dawn of Carlos's death, then perhaps she can draw out the poison, drain the wound, and make her sister well.

'Pass me the huchahko,' says her grandmother.

It is morning, almost dawn, and her grandmother is tending to a man who is lying on a rush mat on the floor. This man came in the night – carried in by two others who left soon after.

The girl knows where the huchahko, the Brazil wood, is; she knows where all the herbs are that her grandmother uses to cure. She finds it on the altar and passes it over.

Her grandmother knows the properties of all the plants. She is teaching them to the girl: toloache leaf, put on a splinter, to soften it until it falls out. Coyote fat for rheumatism; hu'uapa, mesquite leaves, mashed in water, for eye drops. Beeswax and tobacco for an aching tooth.

But this man does not have a toothache. He has been shot by a gun.

'Fetch water,' says her grandmother to the girl. 'And tell Maria-Luisa to get up and grind the corn.'

The girl goes out into the morning. A thin river mist hangs from the trees, but the high sky is clear. The large mesquite tree in the yard looms. Beneath it, the dogs stir: they know something is happening, but she shushes them, and they tuck their heads beneath their paws and go back to sleep. She goes into the rama, where Maria-Luisa is sleeping, lying on her mat. She kneels and shakes her sister by the shoulder. 'Wake up. Grandmother says you must grind this morning.'

'You do it,' says her sister. 'I'm still asleep.'

'I can't.' She shakes Maria-Luisa harder. 'Grandmother is curing, and I am helping.' She tries not to make her voice sound proud, but perhaps she can't help it. 'Wake up.'

Maria-Luisa sits up in bed and rubs her eyes. One of her plaits has come loose and her hair spills over her shoulder like black water. She yawns and stretches, her mouth wide open like a cat's. 'I was dreaming.'

The girl goes to the old earthenware olla and draws water from it into a jug. The olla is cold to the touch, a green mist on the outside edge. 'About what?' she says, although she knows the answer already.

'About him.'

Maria-Luisa is in love. She goes about with a secret smile on her face, but it is not so secret really – it is like her smile is made up of great big letters that spell his name.

CARLOS

The girl knows Maria-Luisa would like to tell her all about her dream, but this morning she has more important things to do. So she leaves Maria-Luisa in bed and carries the full jug of water out of the rama and into her grandmother's hut.

She had her own dream this morning. One she has been trying to remember. But there are only fragments, like a broken pot she does not know how to mend: a jackrabbit in the dawn, the pink of the sun lighting its ears from behind. The animal running away, zigzagging down the side of a mountain. A feeling of something bad, just out of reach.

The girl puts the jug down on the ground beside her grandmother's altar. She watches as her grandmother shaves the huchahko bark in the water, then pours a cup and holds it to the man's mouth. He drinks, then her grandmother puts the rest of the water onto the altar, amongst the flowers and antlers and crosses made of palms.

The girl watches: if the water turns red the man will live. If grey, then there will be nothing to be done.

The girl knows already that the man will live.

She knows this is because of her seataka.

She has had this since she was born, since her grandmother took her and held her and saw the whorls of growth on her scalp – the way they make two cowlicks, circular patterns on her head. It means she is good with plants. With looking at the stars and finding her way. It means that sometimes, too, she can see inside people, feel inside them, and that sometimes, like this morning, she knows what will happen before it does.

It also means her hair will not lie straight, that it sticks out from her head and twists itself free of her plaits. Not like her sister's hair. Her beautiful sister with hair like water, who is likely still in bed and has probably fallen back to sleep.

Now her grandmother starts to sing, the song to bring the man's spirit back inside him. The girl sits in the shadows and listens. Once, a woman died on the mat in her grandmother's hut and her death filled the room with flowers. Her grandmother sang her out of life. The woman was young, but she was wise enough to follow the thread of the grandmother's song, into the sea ania, the flower world, and she died well, with no fear. But this man is not going that way: he is coming back. His mind, which was milky and hazy before, is getting clearer now. He is following the thread of her grandmother's song, back to his body, back to this room, where he is lying on a rush mat on the floor. Where he is still alive. Where, for now, he is safe. Where, for now, he is hungry, hungrier than he has ever been.

Quickly, her grandmother begins to ask him the things she needs to know: What happened? Where were you? How many died?

The man tells her everything she asks. He tells her because she is Augustinia Morales and she is the mother of Ernesto Morales, the leader of the forces in the Bacatete Mountains, and she is more trusted among the rebels than anyone in the eight pueblos.

He tells her that there was an attack, that they were surprised by a band of Rurales, high in the mountains, and that their camp was taken. That several men were killed, but not their captain – the grandmother's son and the girl's father. He is still alive. But the Rurales have poisoned the water holes, and the men have had to move camps. Now they are close to the pueblo, and they desperately need supplies: food and guns and bullets. That soon, if they do not get these supplies, they will have to go to Arizona, two days and two nights of running across the mountains. In Tucson they will be safe.

The girl hears all of this from where she sits in the shadows. As the man's words land in the room, it feels to her as though she must remember them, and this feeling of being here, with the earth beneath her, the mesquite smoke, the way her grandmother listens, holding this man's hand.

When the man has finished speaking, her grandmother turns to the water. The water is red.

Later, when the man has gone, smuggled from the house in a blanket, the girl goes about her morning chores. She boils water, soaks beans, rinses them. Puts them in a pot to cook.

She makes tortillas, slapping the dough between her hands, putting them on the fire.

When breakfast has been eaten and coffee has been drunk and the yard has been swept, her grandmother puts down her mat in the shade and goes to sleep. Her sister appears beside her, casting the girl into shadow, blocking out the sun. 'So,' says Maria-Luisa.

The girl looks up.

Maria-Luisa reaches down and pulls one of her plaits. 'Who was here, Little Shadow?' she says. 'Who was being cured?'

Little Shadow. This is the name that Maria-Luisa gave her, when she was small. Because she always used to follow her sister around. She hates it, but it has stuck to her the way the burr of an echo cactus sticks to the hem of your dress.

The girl looks over to where her grandmother is asleep. Sometimes she sleeps with one eye open, watching, but she is snoring now.

She tells her sister the name of the injured man. Maria-Luisa frowns.

'But he is fighting with Father in the mountains.'

'Yes.'

'And with Carlos too.'

The girl nods.

Maria-Luisa puts her hand over her mouth. She crouches down. 'What happened?' She grips the girl's arm. 'Tell me. Now.'

'He had a wound. From a gunshot.'

'How old was the wound?'

'A day.'

'An attack?'

'Yes.'

'Were men killed?'

'Yes.'

'Was Carlos killed?'

'No. I don't think so.'

'Was Father killed?'

'No. But they lost their camp. They had food there. And weapons. They say they may go to Arizona.'

Maria-Luisa stands up. She walks three times around the rama. 'No,' she says, while she walks. 'No no nonononono.'

The girl knows what Maria-Luisa is seeing in her mind – Carlos. He is with a plump girl in Arizona, and she is ripe like a fruit. He is touching the plump girl's cheek and now he is kissing it and now her cheek has a dimple in it where his tongue has been. The girl is touching his beautiful chest. The dip between the muscles of his chest.

The girl knows all about Carlos's chest because she has seen it many times, as has Maria-Luisa, when they watched the young men practise dancing deer on a Saturday night.

Carlos danced with his torso bare – his forehead covered by the deer mask. In his hands he held a gourd rattle, and around his waist were more rattles, made from deer hooves. And all the way from his ankles to his knees were rattles made from the cocoons of moths.

They took it in turns, all the young men. Carlos would fool around, looking out to Maria-Luisa, almost embarrassed, but then, just before he danced, he would go somewhere else, staring off into the night. Then, as the other men sang and drummed, he would leap into the centre of the room, his own body mimicking the movements of the deer – turning his head at the slightest sound, dipping to drink, then suddenly still, coiled with tension, understanding the hunt had begun, that he must run for his life.

This was before the attack on the railroad. Before Carlos was part of the band of men who sabotaged the tracks, so the locomotive was wrecked. Before he had to run to the Sierra to join the fighters, to escape the soldiers who came looking for him.

'No.' Maria-Luisa shakes her head. No. No. No. This will not be.

She stamps her foot.

'But they are close, for now,' says the girl.

As soon as she says it, she wishes she could bring the words back. But they are out now. She sees them flashing like knives in the sun.

'Where?' Maria-Luisa crouches down.

The girl names the place the injured man had stated: the summit of a nearby mountain. Not a very high one. A mountain that can be reached in not so many hours of walking from the place where they sit.

Maria-Luisa bends closer. 'We have to help them. To take them food and water. We have to take them the gun.'

The gun. The word is heavy and cold.

They found the gun last week when they were out collecting water at the river: a fine shiny pistol, its handle decorated with flowers, wrapped in a white cloth and tucked behind a stone, deep in the canebrake, just by the bend in the river. Hidden by someone for someone else to find.

'When?'

'Tonight.'

The girl feels a clenching in her stomach, her bowels.

'We know the way to the mountain. It is not far. We can see Father. We can take him the gun. He will be proud.'

Maria-Luisa knows the right thing to say.

'Are you scared, Little Shadow?' she taunts.

'No,' says the girl.

'Good. Then we will go tonight.'

Maria-Luisa looks just like their mother when she speaks. Her whipping eyes. Her mouth with her straight white teeth. *They are too alike*, their grandmother says. The girl knows that means that they are both too beautiful; that both have a beauty that makes men follow them with their eyes. Their mother caught their father in this way.

Their mother lives in Hermosillo and works on the Hacienda Las Playitas, two days' journey to the north. She walks with another man now, since their father has been away fighting in the mountains, and they see her only rarely.

Maria-Luisa bends over the fire. Pokes it. Tries to peer at her face in the side of the battered pot. To check she is still as beautiful as she was earlier this morning.

She is.

More, even. There is a new, high colour in her cheeks.

But despite her beauty, Maria-Luisa is angry. She has been angry for a long time. Lately, this anger has reached a new pitch. A pitch so shrill that often, when her sister is beside her, the inside of Maria-Luisa's head feels like a scream.

She is angry with their grandmother, who makes her get up before dawn and grind corn. She is angry with their father, who has been gone for years, fighting in the mountains. But she is angry, most of all, with their mother. This is because their mother has decided that Maria-Luisa is to be married to a boy in Hermosillo. She broke this news the last time she visited them at their grandmother's house.

'You are crazy, woman,' said their grandmother. 'You have lost your mind. The father of that boy is a torocoyori. He's helping Izabal kill our men.'

'She will be safe there. I am trying to protect her.'

'If you want to protect her you leave her with me.'

Then their mother said it was their grandmother who was

crazy: that they were not safe in the village. That everyone knew who she was – who her son was. That they knew all the news from the fighters in the mountains came through her house.

Her mother spoke quickly and low, as though afraid of being overheard:

'They sent out an order that all Yoemem north of Hermosillo should be rounded up. They are putting soldiers all the way along the border to Arizona. They are putting everyone on the boats now. *Everyone.*

'You think you are safe,' she said. 'You think they are leaving you alone because you burn herbs and you speak the old prayers in the old ways, but they will come for you soon, and then who will protect my girls?

'The young one can go live with her sister when she is married. Maria-Luisa can look after her. This is the only way.'

When her mother told Maria-Luisa she was to be married, Maria-Luisa laughed at her. Then, when it was clear her mother was not joking, Maria-Luisa ran away, and only came back later that night, when their mother had gone.

'We will go when Grandmother is asleep,' says Maria-Luisa now. 'She is tired. She will sleep early tonight.'

'What if Grandmother needs me? For curing? In the night?'

'She won't,' says Maria-Luisa. 'And I can't go alone. I need you. You hear better. You see better than me.'

The girl knows this is true – that Maria-Luisa is a creature of daylight, but she can see in the dark.

'I will carry the food,' says Maria-Luisa, 'and you can carry the gun.'

'Me? The gun?'

'You are still a baby. They will not shoot you if they find us. Are you scared?'

'No,' she lies.

Maria-Luisa's words stick in her like a burr. She is not a baby. She is twelve years old.

'I have a bad feeling,' she says. 'I can see –'

'What? What can you see?'

She closes her eyes – but what she sees is confusion, that same jumble of images: a jackrabbit, looking back at her. A yellow flower.

She shakes her head. She cannot see, not really. There is only this feeling, which swells in her stomach like corn in water.

They should not go.

She turns to Maria-Luisa. She knows she needs to tell her, now.

But Maria-Luisa has gone.

The girl watches as her sister walks away. The way she moves her body. The way the air around it moves back to let her pass.

Was there a time when she started to do this? Or did she always do it? Did the air always do it too?

In the afternoon, they take the dirty clothes to the river to wash them. They take their canteens with them, hidden beneath the clothes. They climb down the slippery bank and they dunk the clothes in the water. They pound them on the rocks.

Two soldiers come and stand on the bridge. Somehow, they always manage to appear just when Maria-Luisa is at the river. The girl knows they like to stand and watch her sister, the way the water flows around her, the wetness on her arms, the way her skirt grows heavy and clings to her legs. They stand with their legs apart, their rifles held in their hands. They never let go of these rifles. They cradle them like their children as they watch Maria-Luisa.

The girl hates the way they watch, but her sister seems to like it. It is a game to her. She says things about them. Smiling.

'The thing about the Rurales,' she says today, 'is that, even though they think they have the power, they are stupid. Very, very stupid. Look at them, with their stupid hats, and their ugly grey uniforms. The ridiculous shiny braid on their trousers. They think they are so fine.

'They have no idea of what we are planning. Of how we will see Father and Carlos tonight. They have no idea of the gun, just along the river.'

When Maria-Luisa speaks it is like a song, one that chimes with the river as it moves over rocks. It is as though she is saying the sweetest words in the world. Stupid stupid stupid, goes her song.

'Stupid. Stupid. Stupid,' Maria-Luisa says, with the sweetest of smiles on her face.

And all the time she says this and other things like it, the men can't hear, because of the river; they can only watch. And even if the river were silent, they would not understand – they only know Spanish, not Yoeme – they understand only the way her sister's lips part, the way her cheeks dimple, the white flash of her teeth.

After a while of watching, the soldiers move on.

As soon as they have gone, Maria-Luisa puts down the skirt she is washing and drapes it over the rocks to dry. 'Wait here and fill the canteens,' she says. 'And I will get the gun.'

She disappears through the canebrake and the girl is alone.

The girl starts to shake. If they find them here – if the soldiers come back and they see Maria-Luisa with the gun, they will take them both and kill them.

Or worse. She knows there is worse than killing for girls.

Perhaps they will cut off their hands and display them in the village square.

She saw that once. It was last year, during Lent, when the

severed hands of a man were nailed onto a board in front of the church. The soldiers who had nailed them there were laughing, pretending to shake them, but when they grew bored and walked on, the girl went towards those hands. She made herself study them: the way they curved inwards, the thin lines on the palms. The broken nails with dirt all around them, the sticky red parts where they had once been joined to the man's arms: hands that had worked and touched and lived. She was looking for the marks that would say they were her own father's hands. But they were not her father's hands – her father's hands were wide.

She longed for her father then. For her father to come home. So he could place his wide hand on the back of her head and she would understand she was safe. That he was safe too.

The girl takes the canteens and leans towards the water. Her stomach feels slippery, like the river mud.

The river is high. It has muscles, like an animal, and it is strong with the strength of the season, the recent rain, ready, almost, for its second flood, deep and quiet in the centre but loud here, moving fast over the rocks. She likes it best like this, carrying its smells of mud and secrets and the flowers and creatures that live along its banks. Soon, the snakes and the woodrats and the frogs will flee to the trees and its banks will overflow – pouring all this life into the waiting fields.

But even though it is high, the girl knows the river is lower than it should be. And that this is because it is being stolen.

Their grandmother says that from the vatnaataka, the beginning times, since the great flood receded, the Yoemem have lived with their river and it has not changed course.

But now it is being drained: they are everywhere, the Yankees, on the south side of the river, with their machines and their guns and their measuring sticks, standing in the fields, with their fair hair and their red faces twisted against the sun. They bring machines to clear the scrub and turn the earth. They dig canals. They parcel up the land in long straight lines, making huge fields where they raise crops: field upon field of wheat as yellow as their hair. They bring soldiers to guard the fields and the land and the water that they have stolen. They put up signs which are in their language and in Spanish and in Yoeme.

KEEP OUT KEEP OUT KEEP OUT.

But this is what her grandmother says – this is what the governors and the generals and the Yankees from the north do not understand: the land is not just the land you can see or the land you can measure. It is the worlds that live together, the yo ania, sea ania, huya ania – the enchanted world and the flower world and the wilderness world. All these many worlds cannot be sundered or measured with sticks.

God gave this land to all Yoemem, not one piece to each.

The girl knows this stealing of the river is a crime so huge it cannot truly be understood. And from this crime all others follow: the men fighting in the mountains to resist it, the hands nailed onto the board in front of the church. The soldiers on the bridges with their open mouths and rifles in their hands.

And now they bring the railroad and the men who build it.

It lies just north of here – cutting a path between their pueblo and the mountains. She and Maria-Luisa have sneaked up and watched it – watched the men who built it: Chinese and Russian men and Mexicans and Yankees, with their different clothes and their different hats and their different tongues and their different-coloured skin, hammering and hammering their way east, laying down the rail.

There were Yoemem too, who worked with them, but there

were others of their men who did not – who attacked at night, burning the sheds, like Carlos, blowing up the rails.

Maria-Luisa is back, hair dark and long and wild, her skirts wet. She is like a creature of river, smelling of mud and high water. She carries a small bundle wrapped in dirty cloth.

'Here.' Her sister gives her the bundle.

The girl takes it, opens it. Inside is the gun. The handle is decorated with curling vines, she traces them with her fingertip. It is almost pretty.

'It is heavy,' she says.

'Good. A gun should be heavy. Come on,' says Maria-Luisa. 'Quickly, hide it in your pack.'

When the sun begins to set, they eat. It is hard to make the food go down. Then they go and lie on their mats. They listen to their grandmother's breathing. The breathing of the dogs. The low creak of the mesquite tree. The way the fire sighs as it settles for the night.

Dry leaves skitter in a little breeze – and then, in the distance, when all other sounds have settled, just at the edge of hearing, is the river, moving west through the night.

There are no sounds of alarm, nothing to suggest there are strangers close, or soldiers moving through the night towards their grandmother's house. The dogs sleep soundly. Their grandmother snores. For a moment the girl thinks that Maria-Luisa is asleep too. But then her sister reaches over and grips her hand.

'Now,' she hisses.

They reach for their shawls and wrap them around their shoulders. They lift their packs onto their backs. They move silently across the yard, past the big mesquite tree, out through the gate. They do not need to cross the square where the soldiers sleep. They head towards the river. The sky is clear. The girl looks for Machiwa Choki, and there he is. There is also a moon, very bright and almost full. This is good and this is bad: good because they can see where they are going, bad because they can be seen.

'Stop,' says Maria-Luisa. 'Wait. Give me your pack.'

The girl takes off her pack and hands it to Maria-Luisa. Maria-Luisa reaches in and takes out the gun, opens the chamber, then bends to her own pack, where she takes out a handful of bullets. Maria-Luisa puts the bullets in the round chamber, one after the other.

'Where did you get them?'

'Grandmother. I know where she hides them.'

Now Maria-Luisa stands and lifts the gun. 'I am Lola,' she says, 'Lola Kukut.'

She points the gun. Its small black eye stares at the girl.

'There is nothing for me here,' says Maria-Luisa. 'I am not marrying the son of a torocoyori. I am going to find Carlos in the mountains and walk with him. And we will be like Jose and Lola Kukut.'

The girl knows about Lola Kukut. Everyone does. Lola is a fighter, the Señora of the Sierra. She is married to Jose and they walk together in the mountains and kill as many Mexican soldiers as they can. Jose Kukut got his power from the yo ania, at Sikili Kawi, Red Mountain. He went there at high noon and heard the music coming from the centre. He was tested there, by the Surem, and he passed, and they gave him his power. And now he can kill as many Mexican soldiers as he likes.

'Why did you ask me to come with you then? If all you want is to stay with Carlos, then you can go alone.'

'Shh.' Maria-Luisa brings down the gun. Her voice is soft,

consoling. 'I am sorry, Little Shadow. I need you. I need you to find the way.'

'Besides,' says Maria-Luisa with a smile, 'think of Father's face when he sees us. He will be so proud. Perhaps he will take us to Arizona with him.'

The girl shifts her weight from foot to foot. She does not want to go to Arizona, but she wants to see her father.

'Alright,' she says.

In the distance, in the moonlight, where they are going, the mountains rise.

The girl goes first, leading the way across the bridge and then ducking into the fields, avoiding the main path to the railroad tracks. Sometimes she hears a sound, and stops, listens harder, but it is just the scuttle of a woodrat in the thorn, or the wind in the trees, this wind that is sending the high thin clouds across the moon.

She leads through cane thicket that gives way to huge cottonwoods, bending over the places where the river will flood and turn the hard dry earth to mud.

She hears something then – a long moaning, right at the edge of hearing, borne on the wind. It is coming from the west. Behind her, Maria-Luisa comes close. 'What is it? What can you hear?'

The sound comes again – plaintive and low.

It is far away for now, a small light, coming down the valley towards them.

'The train.'

They walk quickly, and now they are running – running towards this train, as though its whistle were calling them – taking a long looping way around the fields, making sure to avoid the pueblo where the train will stop. And as it comes towards them it is growing bigger, its light spearing the darkness, throwing itself forward and forward through the night, until in a great screaming it starts to slow. They have seen the train before, but this is the closest they have been; it is like a monster from a story – a sierpa, a creature under an enchantment, turned into twisted form for doing something bad, rending the night with its lament.

The girls crouch by the side of the tracks, staring up at the lighted carriages above. Inside, people move in the brightness, people wearing heavy clothes and hats. Some look out, through the windows, but the girl knows they cannot see them, out here in the dark desert night.

Then the train begins to move again, and the girls watch as it picks up speed: faster and faster it goes. What happens, the girl thinks, to those inside? How can a soul travel so fast? Faster than a horse can run? All the souls of all these people plucked from the places they have grown – as if, if you saw underneath their clothes, you would not see legs but white roots, dangling, longing to be planted again in dark soil.

They run across the tracks as silently as they can. Their bags bump on their backs. They run till their lungs are sore and they bend over and spit on the ground, then they make their way north.

They walk and walk; they are in the desert now, and there is much to be afraid of here – creatures of this world and of the other realms: coyotes, rattlesnakes, sierpas. There is aachi and echo, so much of it that there are barbs and the burrs that spear you and catch your skirt or your shawl or your hair. Sometimes, a sauwo rears up before them – its limbs raised high. Once, they disturb an owl, and it takes to the air like a ghost. The bad feeling had gone away, but now it is back.

It is harder for the girl to find her way; she feels as though she cannot find the ground beneath her – as though the noise and chaos of that train has rent the night in two. But the moon is high. It throws their shadows on the ground in front of them, and she has been here before – many times, gathering plants with her grandmother – and so she leads and Maria-Luisa follows, and they walk on.

When they have walked for a long time, they stop, and sit, drink a little from their canteens. The girl slips off her sandals and rubs the arches of her feet.

'How far now?' asks Maria-Luisa.

The girl looks back the way they came. 'We are halfway.'

Maria-Luisa gives a small sound of impatience. 'I wish we could get there faster. I wish we had a train to get there.'

The girl turns to her sister, who looks back at her, her face clear in the moonlight, a challenge in her eyes.

'I would like to be on that train with Carlos, travelling far away from this valley.'

'That train is bad. Carlos would never get on it. He hates it. That train is why he is fighting in the mountains.'

'Perhaps.' Maria-Luisa shrugs. 'Perhaps he would.'

'Where would you go?'

'Mexico City. Or Arizona.'

'But – this is our home. Everything is here.'

'*Everything*? Don't you ever want to see anywhere else?'

The girl closes her eyes, imagines sitting like those people on that train, travelling so fast on a beast that tears the night. It would be like being blind. Looking out onto the land beyond but seeing nothing.

She opens them again and shakes her head.

'Come on.' Maria-Luisa gets to her feet and puts her hand out for the girl.

But she does not take it. She feels mutinous. Like a mule

that stops dead and refuses to move. 'That train is bad,' she says again.

'Maybe,' says Maria-Luisa. 'But the train is here, whether we ride on it or not.' She puts her hand on her hip. 'What about Yomomuli?'

The girl looks back at her.

'Remember how she said the train would come? Shall I tell you the story?' Her voice is coaxing.

The girl feels herself relent: after her grandmother, Maria-Luisa is the best storyteller she knows. So she gives Maria-Luisa her hand, lets her sister pull her to her feet, and they start to walk again.

'Once,' says Maria-Luisa, 'in the vatnaataka, there was a father, and he had two daughters. The younger of these daughters was called Yomomuli – Enchanted Bee – and they all lived together, on the edge of things, when the world was becoming new.

'This was the time of the Surem, the Little People, when all beings – men and women, insects and flowers – understood each other well.

'Over on Omteme Kawi there was a tree, and one day it started to make sounds, hmmmmm hmmmmmm, like swarms of bees.'

The girl knows Omteme Kawi – Angry Mountain. She knows that if the sun were here and she turned back to the valley, she would see its flat-topped peak below.

She is beginning to feel better, feel the dark spell of the train lifting, feel her feet find their way; the stars order themselves above her head.

'All the wisest men gathered round. There were twenty men there and not one of them could understand the tree.

'*Do you understand this tree?* they asked each other.

'No,

    no,

        no,

            no,

                no!'

Maria-Luisa makes the voices of the men sound funny, each one different, and the girl laughs at them: these wisest men who did not know.

'They scratched their heads and their chins, but they could not understand – it was the first time this had happened. No one could understand the sounds of the tree.

'So they decided to ask the question of all the animals, of all the birds who were there.

'*Can you understand the tree?*

'No,

    no,

        no,

            no,

                no.

'Until one of the birds, the littlest one of all, spoke.

'*I know a girl*, said the bird, *who lives out there at the edge of things.* She *will know.*

'So they all went there, to the edge of things, all these wise men, and they asked Yomomuli's father if he would bring his daughters to the mountain.

'And Yomomuli's father said he would, but he must do one thing first. And do you know what he did?'

Maria-Luisa stops in her tracks and turns to her sister.

'No,' says the girl, even though she does.

'He took his daughters to the ocean, and the girls dived into the water, and swam with the fish, and the fish gave them the gifts they needed to understand the tree.

'And so they went to Omteme Kawi, and Yomomuli, the youngest daughter, stepped towards the tree, sat beneath it, and listened, and listened, and listened.

'And the wise men were impatient: *What does it say?* they asked. *Tell us! Tell us! What does it say?*

'But Yomomuli was afraid.

'*Um . . . I am not sure you will like what it says,* said Yomomuli.

'*Speak!* they all cried.

'*Just tell us!*

> *Speak!*
> *Speak!*

'So Yomomuli told them what it said: it said there would be men coming in ships, from the west, that they would try to take the river and the land. It told of much suffering to come: plague and hunger and new diseases. It told of baptism. And it even told of the railroad: *A road will be made of steel*, the talking tree said, *and an iron monster will ride upon it.*

'It told of much, much more to come, then it said, *Now, you must decide what to do.*

'So the Surem held a meeting, and at this meeting some of the Surem decided to leave, while others decided to stay and to see these new things.

'And those that left went underground, into the land, into the yo ania. Some of them went into the water and the waves. And there in those places the Surem now exist as an enchanted people. They are our ancestors. And if we need them, they will come to our aid.

'So you see,' says Maria-Luisa softly, 'Yomomuli told it all.'

The two girls walk on, but things are different now, in the wake of the story. The girl can feel it: it is in the way the moon shadows fall on the ground, the whisperings that thicken the air around them; they are in the yo ania, the place of the Surem.

It is always here, but you cannot always feel it. She knows they are being watched now. She knows that if they need, there are beings here who will come to their aid.

They are high and getting higher, following a track that is lit by the moon, and Maria-Luisa is leading, and she is following – the story has given her energy and Maria-Luisa is walking fast, faster, crazy to get there; behind her, the girl must dodge the little rocks that tumble in her sister's wake. She can feel the way all of Maria-Luisa is thinking of Carlos now, like a dust storm that whirls round and round: Carlos when he dances the deer dance, the way his chest moves like the deer, his feet on the ground, the rattles keeping time. The sweat on his torso. The way he leaps into the centre of the rama. She wants all of him. She is flying towards him.

And the girl is thinking of her father: of his face when he sees them, of how proud he will be that they have come all this way, with water and bullets and the gun. Of his steady hand on the back of her head.

And now they are here: on the plateau at the top – they stand in the clearing, catching their breath. The girl's blouse is sticking to her back. Maria-Luisa whistles. Two long whistles followed by three short ones – the signal their father taught them. Then nothing. Then Maria-Luisa whistles again. The high rocks stand looking down at them, their dark shapes etched against the slowly lightening sky.

Nothing.

'Perhaps they have gone,' says the girl.

Maria-Luisa lifts her hand to shush her. Just then a small rock scuttles down the pass above. Then the answering whistle comes, and the girl's heart skips.

'Who are you?' comes the call from above. A man's voice. But it is not the voice of their father.

'We are the daughters of Ernesto Morales,' calls Maria-Luisa. 'We are the granddaughters of Augustinia Morales. We bring you food. And weapons.'

There is a long silence, then – 'Stay where you are, sisters,' says the voice.

Slowly the men come down from above: five dark, tattered forms. The first man steps forward. He has his gun raised towards them, bullets criss-crossing his chest.

'Lios em chaniavu,' says Maria-Luisa.

'Lios em chania,' says the man. 'You have water?' he says, and his voice is low and hoarse.

'Yes.'

'Throw the water on the ground.'

The girls reach into their packs and take out their canteens. They place them on the ground. 'Now step away.'

The girls do as he says.

'Who sent you?' The man's rifle is still raised.

'Our grandmother, Augustinia Morales, cured one of your men. He told her where you were. That you needed help. And so we came.'

'Two girls alone?'

'Yes.' Maria-Luisa thrusts her chin in the air.

Slowly the other men step forward. In this dawn light they look like birds picked to rags. 'Where is Father?' the girl whispers to her sister. But Maria-Luisa does not respond, she has seen Carlos – the last of the line. He looks thinner, and older, and he stares at Maria-Luisa, standing here on the top of the mountain, as though she has come from a dream.

'Where is my father?' says the girl. Her voice sounds strange, up here on the ledge. It bounces off the high rocks. It echoes.

'Gone,' says the first man.

'Where?'

'Tucson. He left with ten men.'

The man is not lying. The girl can feel his truth: her father is long gone. She feels her disappointment rinse through her, pool and puddle on the ground at her feet. And behind that, something else. Exhaustion. Fear. The bad feeling from her dream: they should never have come.

Slowly, slowly, the first man approaches the water. He picks it up. He unscrews the lid. He drinks. The girl sees that he is thirsty – terribly thirsty, that he could drink the whole canteen and then more, but he stops himself, passes it down the line. 'Only a little,' he says to the other men, and one by one they drink. Carlos is last. He tips the canteen and pours the last into his throat.

'You said you had weapons?' says the first man.

'We do.' Maria-Luisa gestures to the girl and the girl takes out the gun from her backpack. Hands it to her. Feels again the flowers on its handle. The weight of it in her hands. She passes it to her sister and Maria-Luisa holds it out. 'The pistol is yours. We have bullets too. But . . . I have a condition.'

'You? Have a condition?'

'Yes.'

The first man stares. The girl knows what he is thinking – he cannot believe this crazy girl.

'I wish to have an hour with Carlos first.'

'Carlos?'

'Yes.'

'This Carlos?'

The man gestures behind him to where Carlos stands.

'Yes.'

The commander whistles once, long and low, and Carlos steps forward. He stares at Maria-Luisa. Maria-Luisa stares back. There is wild air between them.

The commander laughs. 'Alright,' he says. 'He's yours.' He turns to Carlos. Jerks his head.

The girl is proud of her sister then. There is nothing more powerful in the whole of the eight pueblos than her sister here, high on this mountain, taking what she wants.

'One hour,' says the commander. 'No more. We will be back for him.'

The other men melt away.

Maria-Luisa turns towards the girl. 'Be good,' she says quickly. 'And go and wait behind that rock.' She gestures towards a large rock that stands nearby – more than the height of a man. 'Don't look,' she says. 'And we will come and fetch you when the time has gone.'

The girl does not move.

'Go,' says Carlos, and his voice is warning now.

'Go, Little Shadow,' says Maria-Luisa. 'I promise I will come for you when the time is done.'

The girl wants to stamp her foot. To shout at her sister. To tell her that she is selfish and crazy, and she is not proud of her any more. That this is what Maria-Luisa planned all along. And she is just the stupid Little Shadow who helped her. That she has had a bad feeling since this morning, since her dream. But she does none of these things, she does as she is told and goes over to the other side of the big rock. She leans her back against it. It is cold, and her body is cooling now the climb is done.

She kicks off her sandals and brings her foot into her palm, presses her thumbs into the pad beneath the toes. But when she looks up she forgets to be angry, for she has never been so high before. From up here you can see the whole valley. And all around her now, the world is flushing with light: turning the river to gleaming thread.

She can just see the flat top of Omteme Kawi below, the place where Yomomuli listened to the Singing Tree; the place she gave her prophecy. And she can feel but not see the vastness of the ocean to the west, where Yomomuli went to learn from the fishes. It was here. All here.

And was it here, too, that the story-bearers were left, after the great flood? In the vatnaataka, the beginning times? That terrible flood that destroyed almost everything that was living on the earth?

Was the water as high as this peak, covering the valley, moving against the sides of these rocks? Did those few people who were left alive sit here, as she is doing now, high on these mountains – islands then – watching the water rise and rise, waiting for the dawn?

And when the water retreated, did they come down, carrying nothing but their stories inside them, to make the world anew?

Maria-Luisa and Carlos are silent now. Perhaps they are asleep.

Small birds are singing somewhere behind the rocks, and the newborn sunlight hits the yellow flowers of a kovanao bush beside her.

See how it grows? says her grandmother. *How it holds its water, when everything around it thirsts?*

The girl is starting to learn the ways of this bush: how they are the oldest plants in the desert; that they were living in the vatnaataka and are still here today; how the limbs grow leaves and then flowers, then seeds, and how those limbs will die, but from the same root more limbs will sprout and grow.

And she thinks the stories are like that, the etehoim: the way they flower and blossom on the tongue of the teller, who only lives a short time, but whose tongue tastes the root, which has lived on, all the way back to the time of the flood.

We will take the leaves and flowers: for fever, for salves, for wounds, for easing pain.

Four of each, from the east side of the plant. Do you see – where the sun lights them?

The girl reaches for one of those yellow flowers, but her grandmother stops her: *Wait – you must ask first.*

And so she asks permission of the plant, and promises to offer its leaves back to the roots of another shrub when she is done.

Then she picks four of its flowers and four of its greenest leaves, rubs them between finger and thumb to release their scent, and holds them to her face: their smell is intoxicating – like the desert after rain.

Just then, a movement on the other side of the bush catches her eye – a jackrabbit, feeding on its leaves, its pink ears lit by the rising sun. As she watches, it stands on its hind legs, ears pinned back: listening, listening.

Then it turns its head towards a skittering sound – a falling rock.

It looks back, holds its amber eyes to hers, then turns and runs, as fast as it can, in zigzag paths back down the mountainside.

She can hear words, clear in the mountain air. Spanish. There are animals – horses, their large dark shapes coming up the pass. Riders on their backs.

She puts her hand across her mouth to stop the scream from coming.

And she understands, the jackrabbit is telling her to run. The little birds are calling in alarm now too. Telling her to run. The whole bright dawn world is telling her to run.

She comes out from behind her rock, calling to her sister where she lies with Carlos on the ground. 'Maria-Luisa,' she hisses. 'There are men coming. Up the pass. Soldiers. They are nearly here.'

Maria-Luisa and Carlos become two people again, coming quickly towards her, pulling on their clothes. 'What? Where?' They whip their heads – which way? The fear is loose and moving between them all: dark purple and red and blue, it sparks off them, like the beginnings of fire.

But it is too late – or too soon – the soldiers are already here. On their horses. On the plateau. They have rifles, and the sharp blades on the ends of the rifles are pointed at them. The sun lights the blades. The girl is shaking, shaking, and there is hot wet on her legs.

But then the girl feels something, behind her back. Heavy and cold: the gun.

Maria-Luisa is holding it, pointing it towards the soldiers.

'Turn around,' she says. 'Turn around and go back down the mountain. And you will live.'

The girl can feel the tremble in Maria-Luisa's body. But her sister's voice is clear and strong.

The first soldier lifts his rifle.

The girl closes her eyes.

You are Lola, she thinks to Maria-Luisa.

You are Lola Kukut.

You are Lola Kukut and you have killed so many Mexicans it's easy. So easy.

You are afraid of nothing at all.

Maria-Luisa shoots. The gun jumps back like a live thing. There are more shots: snapping and cracking off the rocks, scattering birds across the sky.

The girl turns, sees Carlos is on the ground. His head is half off and blood is pouring onto the earth.

And he is twitching like the deer in the dance – the deer as it knows it is slain, and his breath rattles and bubbles as it drags in and out of his chest. Maria-Luisa kneels beside him, she is lying on him, pulling his arm over her body, drenching herself in his blood, calling to him – calling from a long way away, but he is already travelling, already leaving Maria-Luisa, leaving the men hiding above. He is with the mountains, he is in the folding of the flowers, in the place beneath the dawn.

Machiwa Choki is there, steady, waiting. The morning star. The last left in the sky. *Come*, he says, as he greets the dying boy. *Come*.

Someone is screaming. The sound of her sister screaming brings her back. And she is shaking, and the men are shouting, and the horses are bucking and there is the smell of horse piss and Carlos is dead. His breath has stopped, and his eyes have turned to the sky. And now she is pulling at her sister, telling her to run, *run!*

And she is strong, somehow, strong enough to wrench her sister to her feet, to push her ahead, to make her run, the way the jackrabbit did, to follow in its tracks. But Maria-Luisa is not in her body – she is still with Carlos, still lying on him, still lifting his arm – and she slips and falls, tumbles, the girl hears the snap of bone, her sister's howl of pain.

The girl reaches her sister, bends to her, and she knows it will not be long now – that the soldiers will be on them soon. She reaches for her sister's hand and waits for the flowers to come. But the flowers do not come. Instead, the soldiers come – the rough cloth of their uniforms. The cooked-meat smell of their bodies – their hot breath. They take them both and truss them in ropes. They haul them onto the backs of their horses and strap them down, and they leave Carlos where he fell.

They bring them down the mountain, but they do not take

them back to the village; instead they deliver them to the pueblo by the railroad where they put them in a cell. The girls sit
in the cell and bring their arms across their knees. They do not
speak. Sometimes Maria-Luisa weeps in grief and pain. She
calls his name. Her skirt is stained scarlet with his blood.

'Little Shadow! Little Shadow!'

Her sister is calling her. The girl opens her eyes, and the
harsh light of morning floods her gaze. Maria-Luisa's eyes are
open wide, her breath is coming fast – and the girl's heart
skips, because her sister is back, and perhaps the poison is
retreating, perhaps this is the cure she has been seeking all
along.

She looks for her sister's wound, but it is still there, as bad as
before. It did not work, she thinks. Whatever she wished for,
whatever cure she wished to find, it has not worked.

'No,' says Maria-Luisa, '*look* – over there.'

The girl follows where Maria-Luisa is pointing and sees a
rock, rearing high on their side of the boat. It looks like a face,
a face with hollows for eyes, and at the bottom, a jagged row
of teeth.

'Little Shadow.' Maria-Luisa is gripping her, pulling her
close. 'Listen to me,' she says. 'We have to jump.'

Every part of her sister is burning, inside and out: her eyes,
her skin, her palms, her heart. Her sister's fever is higher even
than before.

The girl looks out at the rock. She can smell it, salty and
deep, can see the slap and suck of the dark green water where
the crabs move across its belly, hear the call of the birds on its
crown. But the rock is jagged and there is nowhere to land.

'No,' she says, and pulls back. 'We will die.'

'There is only one sure way to die, Little Shadow, and that

is to stay on this boat. You heard what that man said. As soon as we leave this boat, they will make us walk across the mountains. I cannot walk. You know I cannot.'

'We will find another way.'

'What way?' Maria-Luisa says, gripping her. 'Tell me. What way?'

'You have a fever,' she says. 'You are not well.'

'Tell me another way and I will stay.'

'We will find one . . .' the girl says, but as she speaks she knows her words are weak – that she herself does not believe them.

'Help me,' says Maria-Luisa.

The boat is arcing, now, turning towards the shore. No one is looking their way, everyone is occupied, gathering their belongings, their children, intent upon themselves. If they were to jump now, if they were to slip off the side, no one would notice – no one would see.

It will not take much, it is only a few handspans between where they sit and the edge of the ship. Slowly, Maria-Luisa turns towards the railing. Slowly, she brings her legs around. The girl does the same. They are sitting now, both with their calves dangling – their skirts billowing. From here, like this, the girl cannot see her sister's wound. She could imagine she was well. That the poison has gone.

'Help us,' says Maria-Luisa, to the sky, the water, the rock.

The girl can feel the heat of the side of the ship, as though it carries a fever too: the hot spray of the water below, the way it is churned into foam. She knows that, beneath the surface, the boat must be churning the water this way, and that when they jump they must try to jump clear. But she knows there are creatures in the water, dolphins and whales, and that there are Surem there too – their ancestors – the enchanted people, and perhaps they can hear Maria-Luisa calling. Perhaps they will come to their aid.

Then, just as though she has heard her thoughts, Maria-Luisa grabs her hand. 'Look,' her sister squeezes her hand. 'An eagle – can you see?'

The face of the rock has changed again, and the girl's stomach swoops, because Maria-Luisa is right, she sees it: the face of an eagle, its proud beak facing north.

'That eagle will protect us,' says Maria-Luisa. And her words are certain: so certain that perhaps they themselves are strong enough to will a place to land. 'Look at me,' says Maria-Luisa. 'Look at my face. There were two sisters, remember?'

The girl nods.

'They went to the ocean, remember?'

'Yes.'

'The ocean taught them how to understand the tree, how to understand the future, how to know what was coming next – remember?'

Her stomach pitches, but she feels light – so light.

She wonders if these are the last moments of her life: the thrum of this ship, this green-blue water, this sunlight, this rock.

'Keep looking at me.'

The girl looks at her sister. Her beautiful sister is all she sees.

'Now –' says Maria-Luisa.

The girl feels the air rush up – she waits for the water to hit them – but she does not fall. She is pulled – yanked back towards the ship by a great force.

'No,' says the force. 'No.'

The tall father is behind them.

He has them both, one in either arm.

They struggle and kick, but he holds them tight.

'Stay, little sisters,' he says. 'Stay.'

The Lieutenant
1775

'Sir!'

It is the Galician, calling from the foredeck.

'Yes?' The lieutenant is standing at the stern, hands lifted, palms flat, checking the breeze.

'I think you should come and look at this.'

'Not now.' The lieutenant turns – the very slightest of movements to the east, then back again, the very slightest of movements to the north. Always a moment where you doubt yourself, where you believe you might be conjuring the wind you have longed for, but no – here it is. He bends, makes the note in his journal:

Six pm, wind NNE. Horizon fair.

'Sir!'

He puts down his pencil. It takes him all of thirty paces to travel the deck of the *Sonora* to where the young Galician stands, eyeglass pressed hard against his eye.

The lieutenant takes up his own glass, finds the island, which is not truly an island, just a long spur of land hugging the mouth of the tributary of the Grande de Santiago. Behind it, just visible, rising two hundred feet from the flat plain around, is the hill of the Contaduría. The low flicker of the flag high on the flagpole confirming the direction of the breeze. The cannons catching the evening sun.

'What am I looking at?'

'Lieutenant Manrique, sir.'

'Manrique? Where?'

'In the water, sir. Near the rock.'

He brings the rock into view: this odd, white excrescence around which their ships have been anchored these last three days. From most sides it presents an unpromising picture, but from where he stands, facing north-north-west, it appears uncannily like the face of the Lord, the white cowl, the eyes cast down in tender contemplation, the beard, pointed in the Spanish manner, darker where it meets the waves.

His glass catches Miguel, head just visible, arms rising and falling as he swims. Objects litter the water around him. He squints – the tide bears all manner of flotsam to this rock, vegetable and animal and human refuse from the ships, but the glass shows these to be small gourd coracles and candles. There must have been more Indians, in the night, coming to the edge of the shore, casting their offerings on the waves.

As the two men watch, Miguel reaches the rock's northern face, where a small spit extrudes into the sea. He hauls himself onto this spit and kneels, half-dressed, his long brown torso slick with wet. He wrings out his hair, reties it, then leans forward, scooping something from the water. From the distance and the position of his body, it is hard to see just what.

But now he is standing, arms outstretched as though in supplication. He appears to be speaking to, to be beseeching even, the rock.

He looks like an actor. In a playhouse. But this is no performance. Miguel seems oblivious to the fact that anyone might be watching.

'What in God's name is he doing?' says the Galician.

The lieutenant says nothing, not at first. This is how power works, he has learned, or a version of it at least. You simply stay silent for longer than the other man.

Whatever it is that Miguel is doing, it is better that he is not observed.

He swings his glass over towards the other boats: the *San Carlos*, Miguel's ship, anchored closest, is all but empty, only Cañizares, the young pilot, is on deck. Cañizares would not be able to see Miguel from where he is, as the *Santiago*, the frigate and lead ship of the expedition, is in the way. It is just possible that those men gathered on the *Santiago*'s deck, all one hundred and sixty of them, might turn and see him, but their view too would be partially obscured, this time by the rock, and besides, they are occupied, standing in line, shuffling forward one by one to receive their pay.

He can see the Basque, commander of the expedition, seated at the head of the line in full dress uniform, overseeing the payments as he does everything, with that superior expression which never seems to leave his face, a mixture of hauteur and disgust, as though Mexico and all the horrors it holds were a dream from which he might wake and find himself on the clean-swept streets of Bilbao. Beside the Basque sits his second, the old Majorcan pilot Pérez, face still ravaged by the scurvy he suffered last year.

The lieutenant finds his own small crew huddled together towards the end of the line, the Peruvian with them. Ten of them, all present. (He is in the habit of counting them, since they have been at anchor, always somewhere at the back of his mind the fear that they might make a bolt for land.) The men look dumbfounded, as well they might; only four of them have ever been to sea before.

'Sir –'

'Yes?'

'Lieutenant Manrique, sir. Look.'

He brings Miguel back into sight – bent now, pressing his forehead against the pocked and pitted surface of the rock. He appears to place something into one of its many crevices, then turns, shakes himself like an animal and dives.

A few moments later he surfaces again, swimming in easy strokes back towards his ship.

The lieutenant brings down his glass. Wipes the sweat from his skin with his handkerchief.

'Do you think,' says the Galician, into the silence between them, 'that Lieutenant Manrique is quite well?'

The lieutenant can feel something stir inside him. A small, blind creature worming its way through his guts. 'What do you mean?'

'Well . . . the men talk . . .' says the Galician.

'Do they?' He turns to his pilot. 'And what do they say?'

'That Lieutenant Manrique has been . . . disturbed. They believe it is something to do with his ship. The *San Carlos*. They say that it is cursed, sir.'

The lieutenant holds up his hand. 'Spare me. Please.'

He knows the stories – has no desire to hear them again:

She has been cursed since her maiden voyage to Guaymas. The Indians there brought the wind that wrecked her. When she last sailed to California, they could not drop anchor. Almost all the crew died.

'Yesterday,' says the Galician, 'one of the crew of the *San Carlos* came here to deliver some sugar for the stores. He said Lieutenant Manrique had locked himself in his cabin.'

'What of it?'

'I don't suppose *you* have an idea, sir, what might be troubling him?'

The lieutenant turns to his pilot.

'It's just – I know he accompanied you, that day. When you went to seek the pine, for the mast. I wondered – if he was troubled then – whether he took the chance to confide in you . . . ?'

The blind creature moves its head, seeking the light.

He stares at the pilot: his youth, his slab of a skull. His sharp little eyes. He knows they miss nothing, those eyes.

Just as well he has nothing to hide.

'I am surprised, quite frankly,' says the lieutenant slowly, 'that you seem to have nothing better to do than stand here and hazard opinions on the relative health of your senior officer.'

'Yes sir. No.' The pilot's face changes. His eyes flinch. He looks suddenly, terribly, young.

'Judging by the breeze, I'd say we will set sail around ten o'clock.' He snaps his glass shut. 'The Peruvian will be back on board soon with the crew. Speak to the storekeeper. Get him to tap a barrel of brandy. Give them double rations. Settle their nerves. We will gather for the Oration at sunset. Till then I'd rather not be disturbed.'

The Galician salutes, walks back down the deck – almost forty paces on his stumpy little legs – then swings himself through the hatch.

The lieutenant lifts his glass again, quickly finds Miguel, who has reached the *San Carlos* and is climbing its dangling ladder onto the deck. Cañizares, his second, is there. All, thank God, appears to be well.

Miguel has taken a swim. Nothing more. He has done the same since he was a boy.

Hopefully it has steadied his nerves – they have all been stretched to breaking these last weeks, tested by the Sisyphean effort of provisioning a year's expedition from this God-forsaken place: everything must be brought along a supply line to the capital – a single mule track across torturous mountains, taking weeks to traverse.

There are curses here, that is certain, but one needs no recourse to the metaphysical to attest to them – the whole damn place is cursed: cursed with a harbour that is little more than a tidewater channel, in constant danger of silting up, by the lack of prevailing sea breezes, by unhealthful vapours, by fever-carrying mosquitoes and other, smaller, even more maddening insects which emerge every afternoon and torment your skin. With spiders as big as the palm of your hand. With ticks that set up their home on your ballsack and bloat obscenely with your blood. With birds that screech you awake as though calling calamity forth with the breaking day.

There have been many times, in the last four months, when the lieutenant has, under his breath, cursed Gálvez, the visitador whose decision it was to make this swamp the outpost of the Spanish in the west of New Spain.

But as for the supernatural – no. Look – there lies Miguel's ship: the *San Carlos*, the *Golden Fleece*, rigged and ready in the sun. And whatever strange mood has overtaken his friend these last few weeks will be dispelled by this fair north-easterly: the wind and the water are Miguel's elements; for all his many eccentricities, he is the finest natural sailor the lieutenant knows.

Over on the *Santiago*, the line of men is dispersing. He can see the Peruvian loading the first launch full of seamen, ready to row back to the *Sonora*. He feels a familiar sensation: that old, strange admixture of elation and disquiet that always prefigures departure. Soon his crew will climb back onto this tiny ship, and they will understand there is nowhere else to go. No space to walk, hardly any below deck to shelter from the waves or the cold or both. When his small crew are back on board with their pay in their pockets, the men who have never been to sea before will look at each other, or back at the land they have left – the mountains they have known all their lives, the river which has emptied itself here from the beginning of time, the trees which drop ripe mangoes and avocados into your lap – and they will understand that there is no going back. They will start to apprehend, in these last few hours at anchor, that they may not see their homes again, their hearth fires, the faces of their children, the bodies of their wives.

The lieutenant is a man excessively fond of mathematics, but he would not like to calculate the odds on their safe return. It is a good idea, in his experience, to have brandy ready for such times.

The lieutenant lifts his palms up again – the wind holds good. He paces towards the stern and climbs down, glad for the darkness below, even though it is no cooler and hardly possible to stand – just a little over five feet of height in some parts. A sort of hunched walk, head bent over, is necessary to move about.

He runs his hand along the wall, feeling for any bumps and splinters in the wood. He has spent the last eight weeks overseeing the careening of this tiny ship – twenty-seven feet from stern to bow – to make her seaworthy for the far north. The horror of laying eyes on the *Sonora* for the first time – built six years ago at the local shipyard, by local men (amateurs compared to those in La Coruña or Havana) for short voyages, nothing more than crossings between Guaymas and La Paz, a packet boat to deliver mail and transport men.

She will suffice, he had said, that first day, with a calmness he did not feel. *Our job is to chart. Her shallow draught will aid us.*

Her draught was revealed, all ten feet of it, as she lay on her side for careening, two months stripped back to her ribs at the tiny, rustic astillero like an animal mid-butchery, as they replaced planks and strengthened the keel and generally harried ship-builders who had no sense of urgency or time.

And then there was the excruciating wait for their crew: ranch hands, mango farmers, whose hacendados agreed, only reluctantly, to let them go, on the condition that they brought in the harvest first. Insanity. But there have been insanities upon insanities, here at the end of the world.

They turned up eventually, machetes in hand, the red dust of the fields still on the cuffs of their white trousers, men who hardly spoke Spanish, let alone understood practical naviga-tion, rounded up at the point of a gun.

They hate us, the Galician said to the lieutenant, as the men were apportioned to their ships.

They don't hate us, the lieutenant replied. *They are like chil-dren. Children do not hate.*

Seriously? The young Galician shook his head. *You must not know many children. I hated everyone when I was a child.*

He and the Galician and the Peruvian have had to rig the *Sonora* alongside the crew in the small time left – nerves stretched to catgut, knowing each fumble has meant lost time, that each day spent in this latitude means a day later in the far north, a day closer to winter storms. A day more likely to be wrecked on frozen coasts far from home.

How well they have rigged, how thoroughly they have stop-pered the leaks and patched the hull, will only be proved once they hit weather. He himself has never sailed above 20 degrees, but he has sailed south round the Horn and knows what it is to be cold – how timber shrinks and the sides spring leaks while the fingers that might fix them swell and blacken and fumble and fail.

On the shelves and in the sacks lies a year's supply of food: dried beef, dried fish, hardtack, a half-ton of lard, quantities of beans, rice, wheat, lentils, onions, cheese, chilli peppers, salt, vinegar, sugar, pork, cinnamon, cloves, saffron, pepper, chocolate, brandy, wine, fruits and vegetables. Fresh water enough for four months. The decision was taken not to bring live animals on the voyage, and so the livestock was slaughtered last week before being dried in the sun – a huge matanza on the shore, the sand drenched scarlet. The Indian crew, newly arrived, watched it silently, but sometimes, as the animals were still twitching with the last of their life, they stepped forwards and knelt beside them, dipping their fingers into the blood of the cattle, daubing it onto their own brows and the small coins they carried. The Spanish officers stood back and let them: they were in the business of compromise, not coercion – the viceroy had said it himself. Only God knew what lay ahead.

Past the men's quarters, where after only three days at anchor there is already the heavy musk of men living in close confinement. There is no room for possessions, although in their small chests, beneath their bunks, the men have all been provisioned with woollen garments. It is hoped that there will be trade possible with the Indians in higher latitudes for furs: they are said by the Majorcan to dress themselves in the pelts of sea otters and wolves.

The lieutenant can hear the Galician speaking with the storekeeper at the other end of the ship, rattling out his orders in his rapid-fire Castilian. The quiet of the other man's voice. The smell of frying onions.

The Galician is a good pilot – only twenty: plucked from the ranks in the colegio in Seville for his accuracy and skill.

Whether he is a good man or not remains to be seen.

In truth, it is not only the Galician's character that concerns the lieutenant. It is years now since his last command. Years since his illness in Guayaquil. He knows he appears awkward; not like the Peruvian, with his easy demeanour – the way he has of crouching beside the crew, speaking gently, moving his hands through the air, managing to find ingress. Not like Miguel, who can compel a lifetime's loyalty with a look. He knows the men think him aloof – not so bad as the Basque perhaps, but still.

He reaches his cabin and shuts the door.

No matter.

Here, he must attend only to reason, to the science of exactitude. Here are his instruments: the quadrant, the sextant, the azimuth compass, all of them guarded with excruciating care during the torturous three-month journey from Cádiz. Paper for charting – the finest paper he has been able to find, brought one hundred and fifty miles from Guadalajara.

The sun slants in through his tiny window, landing in a fierce band of light on the map on the wall: the only map of the northern coast in existence.

Carte réduite de l'océan septenrional, comprise entre l'Asie et l'Amerique. Suivant les découvertes qui ont été faites par les Russes.

A chart drawn by Bellin, the famous French cartographer (although, as far as the lieutenant is aware, despite his stellar reputation amongst the Encyclopédistes, Monsieur Bellin has never left France).

The map, in truth, is little more than a revised, prettied-up version of one he has known since his days as a cadet at the

Academy in Cádiz, over fifteen years ago: the Russian discoveries of 1741, when Bering and Chirikov first sailed over the Kamchatka Sea. At best, Bellin's map is speculation and errors; at worst, a tissue of Russian misinformation and lies, thrown out to keep them off the scent.

He finds his position on the chart: latitude 21 degrees, thirty minutes north and 110 degrees west of Paris. In a few hours, as soon as the Basque gives the command, all three ships – the *Santiago*, the *San Carlos* and the *Sonora* – will swing due west, sailing through the night, following approximately 19 degrees north until they clear the Cabo San Lucas and then, once they have gained a northing, follow it up the coast of California to Monterey, where the three ships will part: Miguel and the *San Carlos* to provision Father Serra and the mission there, then to enter and chart the bay of San Francisco; he and his crew to follow the *Santiago* north, to where the map is all but blank.

Their mission, closely guarded, is to reach 65 degrees north and make landfall, there to carry out the Ritual of Possession, to find wood, fashion a cross and erect it, then walk up and down the shoreline, speaking a text the lieutenant knows by heart:

In the name of His Majesty the King, Don Carlos III Our Sovereign . . . I, as captain of this ship, am taking and take possession, am seizing and seize possession, of this land where I have at present disembarked, which I have discovered forever and ever in the said name of the Royal Crown of Castile and Léon . . . as its own property, which it is . . . by reason of the Donation and Bull of the Very Holy Father Alexander VI, Supreme Pontiff of Rome . . . given at Rome on May 4th of the year 1493.

The Doctrine of Discovery: which must then be signed and placed into a glass bottle, stoppered with pitch, hidden within a cairn of stones, beneath the cross, where it might be found by any marauding Russian or British sailor who dare encroach on Spanish land, then – and this is where the *Sonora* will come into her own – to travel back home, surveying every bay and inlet and mapping each with as much pinpoint accuracy as he can.

Only one man in the Spanish Navy, Pérez, the Majorcan pilot, has sailed a version of this voyage before.

They were there on the dock to greet him: it was November, only four months ago, and they had just arrived in this God-forsaken outpost. The Majorcan and his remaining crew limped into port with the strange, spasmodic movement of men who had been too long at sea, faces sunken with hunger, teeth loose or lost from their swollen gums. It soon became apparent that they had failed, that the Majorcan had turned back for home on account of the cold and the scurvy at 42 degrees. And as if that caution (cowardice?) were not enough – when the Basque asked him for the charts of his voyage, Pérez could not produce any but the most rudimentary of maps. The old pilot had plenty of excuses:

We hardly saw clear skies.

We could not see the sun.

We could not see the stars.

We could not take measurements.

It rained ceaselessly.

It was fog-bound.

The rolling of the ship.

But despite the failure of his mission, the Majorcan kept a journal: under the orders of the viceroy, each captain has been tasked with copying it out by hand. The lieutenant knows therefore that the land they are sailing towards is mountainous, chilly, foggy, gloomy, that the Indians there seem peaceful, with a great appetite for the beauty of the nacre of the shells of Monterey. That they greeted the Spanish ships by singing, and casting feathers on the water. That they hunt the sea otter for its pelt. That they weave the most extraordinary cloaks: cloaks which depict mythical, monstrous creatures, heavy, fringed, woven all over with eyes; cloaks that in their workmanship evince a culture far in advance of that the Spanish have found in the Indians around Monterey; cloaks that have been duly sent to the viceroy – and thence to the king.

But higher? At 65 degrees?

No Spaniard has ever sailed so high.

And the map says nothing, or rather, it calls, a high thin singing as of ice and snow, but behind that another sound – just at the edge of hearing – the hiss and whisper of ambition, the push and press of the Great Powers, converging on that northwest coast.

Here are the navy-coated British, owners, these last twelve years, after victory in the French and Indian War, of the colony of Canada, probing ever westwards, searching – as they have since the days of Drake and Cavendish, for the greatest prize of all: the Northwest Passage – the strait that will link the Atlantic with the Pacific and unite the two sides of the map.

Here are the Russians, making their way east over the steppes of Siberia at the behest of their ambitious tsarina, first hunters, searching for pelts, then ships fitted with scientists and astronomers, crossing the cold Kamchatka Sea and finding a continent there, unspoiled, unsettled bar by natives. It is news of these Russians that has been whispered into the ear of the Spanish ambassador in Saint Petersburg, tales relayed in turn to the king in Madrid, which have forced the Crown to rouse itself, to understand that in all the years it has been dealing with the Indians in Sonora and the Apaches and their raiding parties, there have been other, more imperial threats to its sovereignty in the west. Which in turn has led the king to pick four of the finest, most talented officers of the Spanish line, and send them to Cádiz for further training with the greatest cartographers and hydrographers in the Empire and supply them with the finest instruments money can buy. *The Four*: the Basque, the Peruvian, Miguel, himself.

The lieutenant goes over to the square mahogany box, opens it, takes out the sextant. It really is a thing of beauty, made (whisper it) by Jesse Ramsden of Fleet Street, bought by an agent of the Spanish Crown in London and shipped incognito to Cádiz, where it was handed to the lieutenant on departure by Tofiño himself. Each of the four captains was gifted one: the finest, most accurate marine technology there is – capable of measuring an angle with precision to the nearest ten seconds.

Its solid brass frame makes one-sixth of a circle, 65 degrees (a degree divides into sixty minutes, a minute into sixty seconds: the rendering of the priest's first teaching, of time into distance and distance into time). Small enough to fit into the palm of his right hand, and yet able to map the heavens; able to take a line from any horizon, triangulate with any celestial body, and, with the right longitudinal calculation, show you where on the vast trackless ocean you are.

If you can ask the right question, if you can solve the right equation, then you can always find your way out of the dark.

He has understood this ever since the priest took him out onto the terrace in Osuna and showed him the bright heavens above his head.

Osuna, Andalucía, a small town in the middle of a large plain thirty miles from the sea.

His father was a nobleman who lived off his estates. He never knew his mother, she died at his birth – a blank space where a woman might have been.

He spent his childhood alone, a lonely boy in large rooms. He could not understand if his distant, silent father was cruel or unhappy, or both. Sometimes – not often, but for no reason he could understand – his father beat him. But even in his beatings he was silent. The boy learned to cry silently, then not to cry at all.

The only real sound in that house was that of the clocks: there was one in each room, wound every day by servants whose job it was to make themselves invisible. Sometimes though, the boy woke at night – thought he could hear the sound of a woman crying. That it came from the room his mother died in. The room in which he had been born. But the door remained locked.

There were people paid to feed him, clothe him, teach him. From the age of eight he had a tutor, a local Jesuit who came to the house. His father showed little interest in the proceedings, and so the young priest was free to teach him what he cared to: first, the priest taught him French, *for when you learn French you learn of the world*, and once the boy's French was good enough, he taught him in that language only – Greek and Latin, Botany, Mathematics. Geometry from Euclid's *Elements*. It was the last he looked forward to most. There was a particular feeling he had in his body when the solution to an equation emerged, of rightness, belonging; a key turning smoothly in a lock.

The priest was also an amateur astronomer. One night, when the boy was eleven, he took his charge outside onto the terrace, where he had set up a telescope trained upon the Milky Way.

'Oh,' said the boy, when he looked through it – for the sight was more beautiful than anything he had ever seen. He saw the stars as pinpricks, small rents in the fabric of the night, which showed a brighter world beyond. 'Is that where my mother is? In the light behind the darkness?'

'Your mother?' The priest sounded surprised. 'No. Your mother is in heaven.'

'Is that not heaven then? The brightness behind the dark?'

'There is no brightness behind the dark. Only more darkness. Each point of light, each star you see, is a sun. Some far greater in size than our own. Sometimes,' said the priest, 'I think of knowledge like that. Bringing light to the darkness around it. We are all stars – only our knowledge determines how brightly we shine.'

The priest spoke to him of Galileo, of Newton, of a universe that moved like clockwork. He showed him how, in one hour, the earth rotates through 15 degrees. The young priest spoke with certainty, and in his words there was no strain, no tussle with his faith, and the boy understood: here in these very calculations was the face of the divine watchmaker who presided over his infinitely complex design. For the first time in his life the boy saw, and was comforted: there was nothing random, nothing left to chance; everything, every part, operated according to its natural law. Now the boy no longer felt alone, and the sound of the clocks in the house was not the scoring of his loneliness but was truly the heartbeat of God.

After that, the boy mustered his courage to ask his father for a telescope, and his father, to his surprise, agreed. Perhaps he was relieved his son had something to occupy him. The priest showed him how to train his glass upon the face of Jupiter, so its moons appeared: four bright shining discs. He taught him to watch for them: to wait, and wait, and wait, and then, on their appearance, showed him how he, standing on his father's terrace, in Andalucía, could record the times of their emersions and occultations, tabulate, and with patience and skill, fix a position on the map.

The boy spent hours outside, short summer nights scented with almond and orange and thyme, long winter nights when his breath froze in crystals in the air. Sometimes the priest would accompany him, but most often he was alone. The young boy recorded everything meticulously in journals – would spend hours, watching, waiting for the arrival of those moons, always that feeling when they appeared, just as expected, just as they were supposed to: they were predictable, to be depended upon – the faces of those shining discs became his friends.

As he grew out of boyhood, he imagined he would, like his tutor, enter the priesthood. The seminary was close. It would simply be a matter of leaving that unhappy house, packing a bag, and walking the two miles or so across the valley. Taking his telescope along with him. There he would spend his life with books and with instruments, and an arrangement with faith that understood that science and God were not mutually exclusive; that one might, indeed, illuminate the other.

But his father had other ideas, and at the age of thirteen the boy was enrolled at the Naval Academy in Cádiz.

The priest gave him a book to say goodbye: his own copy of Euclid, translated into French, beautifully bound in kidskin, a gift of such generosity that the boy could say nothing in return.

He had hoped that his father would take him to Cádiz, but

he was detained in Granada on business, and a servant of the house accompanied him instead, leaving him with his case on the steps of the Academy before turning for home.

The boy hated the city on sight: the incessant wind from the ocean that still did not shift the faecal stink of the close-packed streets, the rats which swarmed in their droves, the sense of all those lives lived so close together. He hated the Academy too, where he was made to share a dorm with twenty other boys. He could not understand the delight they appeared to take in their terrible proximity. He watched the way they were with each other, these boys, and understood that he did not know how to be, did not know the codes these young men had, their games, their high strong smell, their way of talking, of touching each other as though they might at any point be about to break out into violence, the play fighting and the real fighting that ensued. The unpredictable mutations of their bodies, and his own, which seemed on the verge of fulfilling some dark promise made at birth.

They were all there already, *The Four*, classmates even then.

The Basque: scion of an ancient northern family. Handsome. Arrogant. Offensive in his humour. A bully by nature. Fourteen and already affecting a beard, imagining himself another Cortés.

The Peruvian: quiet, gentle, determined. Ambitious. The Basque taunted him for having been born in Lima, for being a Creole.

And then Miguel: dark and slight, an Andalusian like the boy – equally as noble as the Basque, but he wore it more easily, a lighter cloak. Something in Miguel, some self-possession, irritated the Basque, who called him the Moor, for the colour of his skin.

'Who makes the best sailors?' the Basque would say. 'Basques or Galicians? Andalusians or Balearics?'

The answers did not vary much, although were subject to endless embellishment, and the Basques always came out on top: Andalusians were filthy and no better than Moors, Galicians liked to fuck the sheep that roamed the rainy hills.

The Basque had a Galician joke he liked to tell:

A Galician was told his wife was fooling him with his best friend.

The Galician shot the dog.

The boy kept his distance. He knew enough to know that. He missed the space he had known, the emptiness of the valley, the nights spent alone with the stars. He had not been permitted to bring his telescope with him, and he yearned for it. He missed those moons, those dependable, shining discs.

But, inevitably, one day, the Basque's attention turned to him. 'You. What are you reading? You're always reading.' He plucked his Euclid from his hands, held it high. He was a good half-head taller than the boy. '*French?* You fucking traitor. We'll have to call you Frenchy then.'

'Give it back.'

But the Basque chucked it up in the air, where its pages fluttered like frightened birds before falling to the ground.

'No!' He lurched for the book, as the Basque laughed, kicking it from his grip.

'Leave him be,' said Miguel.

'What's it to you?'

'Just – give him back his book and leave him be.'

The Basque shrugged, turned. Miguel walked over to it, picked it up, handed it to the boy. When he had done so, he turned back to the Basque.

'By the way,' he said lightly, 'France is our ally now. Haven't you heard?'

After that, when he looked up from his reading, it was Miguel who drew his gaze. He moved differently to the other boys, trod lightly, seemed not to need to push and jostle and shout. His voice was low and quiet. He often carried a sketch-book with him, and the boy watched him sometimes, from a distance, frowning over his paper, the heavy brow, the steep slope of the cheek, the fierce indent in his chin, as though someone had come along and pressed their thumb there while he was still being formed.

On Saturday afternoons, when they were free to do as they liked, most of the cadets would clump together, wander around the streets, or go down to the Lameda and gawk at women in the carriages pulled by mules. The boy tagged along – he found their company as oppressive as the city but did not know how to escape or to refuse. Only Miguel did not join these outings. He would disappear and come back hours later, in time for food, his skin a shade darker, hair matted and smelling of salt water. 'Where have you been?' the Basque would ask with a curl of the lip.

'Swimming.'

'The water's filthy. It's full of shit.'

'Not when you dive from the rocks.'

'We're training to be sailors, not swimmers, you fool.'

But Miguel would just shrug, as though the Basque's words were the dirty water, and it was pouring off his back.

The Academy housed an excellent library, and the boy spent as much time as he could there, with the collection of maps, many of which dated from many years before: Juan de la Cosa's map of the world, from 1500, covered with drawings; here were the three kings riding to Jerusalem, here was the Queen of Sheba, here was the coast of the New World, a large green mass. With each new map, coastlines became more distinct, the naive figures disappeared; with ever-finer instruments of measurement, the world was translated, expunged of story, made rational.

But it was not the Conquistadors who compelled him, not Cortés, not Pizarro, nor Columbus, it was the sailors of his own century, those Enlightened men, scientists, rationalists: Antonio de Ulloa, who had been trained at the Academy, and at the age of nineteen joined the French Geodesic Mission, sailed around the world for eight years, and Jorge Juan, who accompanied him, and whose findings, showing the earth was not a sphere, was, in fact, flattened at the poles, vindicating Newton's *Principia* – and who were both elected Fellows of the Royal Society as a result.

The cadets took their courses in Mathematics, Cosmography, Trigonometry, Cartography. Forced to do the most elementary of calculations, he would finish in minutes. But then, in their final year, they studied with Tofiño, the great hydrographer, classes that took place in the Observatory, newly finished, built to rival those in Greenwich and Paris, set high above the city in a medieval lookout tower. The windows commanded the compass of the horizon, and when you stepped out onto the gallery there was a full view of the sky. The boy liked it best up there: held between sky and water, high above the streets below, the filth of the city resolved into white towers, gold domes, the hard bright glitter of sun on sea.

Tofiño was only twenty-seven, though he was already a lieutenant – had been since he was twenty-three. His reputation as the finest charter in the Empire already sealed, it was Tofiño whose gaze they all courted. *To be able to take measurements at sea*, he taught them, *one must first learn to take one from land*.

In the Observatory the cadets were taught to use the quadrant – an eight-foot brass instrument secured to the stone wall. Tofiño taught them the lunar method: how to measure the angle between a given star and the moon, the exact position of which was shown on the star charts, or ephemerides, calculated for a given meridian, and then how, by measuring the discrepancy between the tables, longitude could be found.

While the other cadets struggled to grasp the basic concepts, the boy understood innately that what mattered above all things was precision, finding ever-smaller angles. The longitudinal calculations could occupy his mind for hours: at first the numbers would elude him, race ahead, a chaos, a storm, and then, suddenly, they would be within his grasp, tamed, unsheathed of mystery; the path was clear, and he had found the way home.

Alongside the priest, astronomy had been amateur, but there, with Tofiño, in Cádiz, on the edge of the Atlantic, the boy understood it was about power. Each year two fleets left Cádiz with European goods for New Spain: wine, oil and vinegar; pepper, olives, raisins, almonds, needles, scissors, steel, paper, tin, linens from Brittany and Belgium and France. The cadets would watch from the Observatory as the fleet sailed, thirty, forty, fifty ships with their military escort, their sails patterning the horizon. And then, twice a year they would arrive back, and the city would erupt: the tumult of the bells, the flags unfurled from the watchtowers, merchants swarming the dockside, desperately accounting for their wares, women everywhere – as though the city had bred them suddenly, in their bright skirts and jewellery – and everywhere in the life of the streets the sense that this was what the city was built for.

The cadets would race down to the ships when their lessons

were done and watch them unload, crate after crate: silver and gold, indigo, cochineal, cocoa, tobacco, sugar, copper, porcelain and silk from China. The treasure of half the world arriving back in Cádiz, and all of it due to the mathematical abilities of the mariners who had brought these riches home.

But the boy never spent long down at the dockside. Something about these objects seemed too dense, too *material*, too smeared with trade. It was not for these he wished to sail.

He would peel away from his companions, walk back alone to the Academy, know it would be deserted and he would be able to find a rare, quiet corner in which to study undisturbed.

Once, one searing afternoon in summer, when the fleet was in harbour, walking back from the dockside the boy turned a corner and saw Miguel. He was sitting amongst a small group, along the shaded wall of a warehouse, and they were passing a flask of wine between them and laughing, playing cards with a ragged deck. The boy stared. There were four of them: Miguel, two other boys, one of whom was, astonishingly, a barefoot negro, and a girl. Miguel was dressed simply, in shirt and britches; he wore nothing to denote his rank. He, too, was barefoot.

The boy pulled back into the doorway, to save Miguel as much as himself, for no one would wish to be caught like this – they had had it drilled into them that wherever they went in the city, they represented the Academy and therefore the king. He watched, heart hammering. Was the girl his lover? She sat beside him, a pair of sandals kicked off, one slim brown calf visible beneath her skirt. Her long hair was loose, only a scarf lightly wound around it. All those bodies tumbled so close together that it was hard to see whose limb was whose – there was something infinitely troubling in the way those legs were touching, black skin and brown skin and fair skin, with no thought of propriety or degree.

Then – just as though his name had been called, Miguel looked up.

The boy's heart stalled as Miguel stood, advancing towards him across the clamorous street. 'It's you,' he said.

'Yes. I'm sorry.'

'Why are you sorry?'

'I –'

'No one is with you?'

He shook his head.

'Thank God.' Miguel smiled, and his teeth were stained with wine. Then – 'Come and join us,' he said.

Four simple words. And then that touch again, a hand, light and easy on his arm.

Come and join us.

As though it were that simple – for the boy to leave his doorway and walk through the racket and heat to sit in the shade and sup and play.

'You are not wearing uniform,' said the boy. His voice was tight.

Miguel looked down at himself, as though surprised: his shirt, his trousers that stopped above the ankle, his blackened feet. 'No,' he said, with half a grin. 'It's easier like this.'

A call came from his companions, Miguel turned back, and in that moment the boy jerked himself free of the doorway, walked quickly, head high, as though Miguel were just some unshod boy of the streets, far beneath his gaze. But as he walked the boy felt the severity of his own clothes in the heat – the tightness of the buttons on his gaiters, the heaviness of his long dress coat, the sweat in the band of his hat, the handkerchief knotted at his neck – and in their constriction, he understood his unthinking compliance: it had never occurred to him that he might break the rules.

When he reached the corner he stopped, turned, but Miguel was not watching, he was back, already, sitting with his friends, caught in the next thing. And the next. And the boy thought that life for Miguel would be like that – a series of next things, all of them lit and glowing, beckoning him on. Whereas he himself would move forward only slowly. For how could one advance without fixing one's position first?

His first posting upon graduation was as alférez de fragata, a midshipman, on a vessel escorting the commercial fleets to the Caribbean, then on ships that ferried prisoners to gaols on the other side of the world. He sailed with captains who were brutes; the first time he sailed over the equator he was blind-folded, along with the other novatos, his face smeared with excrement, then ducked three times into the ocean by the other sailors and thought he might die.

He sailed, too, with captains who were men of understanding; he found he liked the naval day: the bells, the watches, the simplicity of an ordered life. The way, once the lights of the land disappeared, you were left to find your way on the vast trackless water, as though God had designed the ocean as a great puzzle for men to solve.

He saw battle, saw surgeons hacking off limbs and staunching wounds with tar. Sometimes the ships he served on had slaves, shackled in the hold, bound for the sugar fields of Havana and the cotton fields of Louisiana. When the slaves died, they threw the bodies over the side. There were always sharks that followed these ships, waiting for the bodies, scenting blood.

Throughout it all he taught himself to look away – whatever the stink and press and horror of human life, he could look up: the stars were always there, unchanging, ordered. He learned to contend with the variation of the needle, learned to correct for the parallax. He learned that, as Tofiño had taught him, any calculation taken on land was many times harder on the water, where, even on the finest of days, all was pitch and roll.

He rose through the ranks, developed a reputation for efficiency, for skill. The men seemed not to mind him, which was not the same as them liking him, but it would suffice.

He kept, as always, his journal. His meticulous calculations. He was rising, steadily rising.

And then, when he was twenty-five, an aberration, a moment of weakness: a visit to a local whorehouse in Guayaquil at the behest of a boorish captain. The third man to take his turn in a room that stank of semen and sweat. A silent Indian girl with a face like the moon, who closed her eyes and twisted her head away. A coupling that lasted all of three minutes. Then – pain when passing water, a burning, followed by a swelling, and a fever that gripped him for weeks. His ship and his captain sailed back to Spain without him.

He was tended to by silent priests who smelled of garlic and hemp. Sometimes his mother was beside him: he knew it was her because across her chest was cast the night sky and the stars and the Milky Way. Sometimes she held his head and calmed him as he cried. Sometimes she was covered in blood and viscera, holding out her hands to be saved. Sometimes his father was there, looking down at him, shaking his head.

Once, he was in his father's house and all the clocks had stopped. He wandered the rooms and the silence was more white and more frightening than anything he had ever known. He opened the door to his mother's bedroom. There was a figure lying on the bed. He approached, touched its shoulder, it turned – but it was not his mother, it was the young priest. He was dead, yet he spoke in rasping French to tell him there was no God. *Il n'y a rien après* – there was nothing beyond this but nothing. No brightness, nothing at all.

Mostly, when he was lucid, he understood that he would die alone, thousands of miles from a home that was never truly his own. That he had no one in the world who loved him. No one who ever had.

Slowly, the poison in his blood retreated and he came back to Spain on a merchant ship. Still weak, he went to Osuna, where he slept in his childhood room. He went to see the priest, only to find he had died, taken by plague the summer before. Perhaps, he thought, it was true; perhaps the priest had come to tell him there was nothing afterwards – nothing but nothing. Sometimes, when he woke in the night, he could not breathe, his hands clawing at his chest. Once, he walked into the room he had been born in, the room his mother had died in. Her portrait was there on the wall. He searched her eyes for something, some clue as to his loneliness. Had she touched him, did she speak to him, before she died?

One morning, with the fierce sun outside the shutters, his father came into the room.

'How old are you?'

'Twenty-six.'

'I had a child and a dead wife at twenty-six. What have you got?'

He had no answer to that.

He wrote to the navy. Told them he was quite well and ready to serve again.

His next commission arrived – an armaments officer at the fort in El Ferrol. Galicia was cold and damp, but he was glad to

155

be on land. Land was so much easier to take measurements from, land did not slip from your grip. He sent, as always, his calculations to Tofiño, and one grey morning in late autumn, he received a letter back, summoning him to Cádiz to undertake further training at the behest of the king.

It was there they all met again: the Basque, the Peruvian, Miguel, himself. *The Four.* It had been fourteen years since they had seen each other, and they were men now, nearing thirty, no longer young.

The Basque was a senior lieutenant, paunchy and choleric, still a bully and a brute. The Peruvian as steady and determined as before. And then Miguel – also a senior lieutenant, said to be the most talented young sailor in the Armada. The familiar contours of his face, the heavy brow, the steep slope of the cheek, the fierce indent in his chin. The same self-possession. The same sketchbook never far from his side.

'It's you,' said Miguel, that first day.

'Yes,' he answered.

It's you.

Come and join us.

'You look different.'

'Do I?'

How?

That evening he stared at himself in his glass. *You look different.*

He saw that it was true, that the world had marked him. He looked thinner. His eyes grown more wary, his mouth downturned. His shoulders had a different cast. He looked, if anything, astonishingly like his father.

The Basque lost no time in getting reacquainted.

'So, the Pope divided up the world in Tordesillas in 1493 and we got all the women west of forty-seven degrees. And in the last fourteen years we have seen more of them than most. So, come on then – where are the best rides in the Empire? I'll go first shall I?' He clapped his hands together. 'The Chinese whores in Manila who can grip your cock like a vice. Who's next?'

'The girl I love in Lima,' said the Peruvian. 'I will marry her when I return home.'

'Ahhhhh,' said the Basque. 'How tedious. What about you,' he said, turning to the lieutenant. 'Still a eunuch then?'

He thought of the moon-faced girl. The poison inside her, ready to detonate in his blood.

He looked down at the title of the book he was holding. It was Abbot Chappe's *Voyage en Californie*, his account of the Venus transit of '69.

'The French,' he said. 'I had a woman in Paris who taught me more than any other.'

'France doesn't count, you damned idiot,' said the Basque. 'France is France. Last time I checked it wasn't part of New Spain.

'And you?' he said, finally, turning to Miguel.

Miguel just shrugged. 'I hate paying. I prefer the chase.'

'Go on then. Who was the last one you had?'

'A countess. Last night. I licked her while she bled.'

The lieutenant watched the flicker on the Basque's face. His arrogance dimmed. He was outplayed. 'For God's sake, Manrique. You're an animal. Man, woman, beast, you don't care.'

In the first class with Tofiño, now the director of the Academy, the great man looked out at the four of them, unsmiling. 'You have all done well. You would not be here if you had not. But what you have achieved so far means nothing. I do not care. The viceroy does not care. The king does not care.

We care only of what you might do.' He told them how the discipline of navigation was changing, of the advances the British had made with the marine chronometer, the determination of compass readings by azimuth variation, but above all, it was in the use of the sextant they were to train.

They were told nothing of their posting, not yet, and so it became a game with them. *Where are they sending us, then?*

The lieutenant joined in the game, but he knew – surely they all did – there was only one possible posting. He went back to the library, pored over the old maps again, and in them he heard the call of destiny: there was only one mission deserving of such care – it could only be the Far North they were training for, only be the ice calling, for where else was left so blank on the map?

He and Miguel were given a room to share. Miguel had the habits of a cat; he would disappear at night, coming back much later, while the lieutenant was asleep. Sometimes he would take his sketchbook, sometimes not. One evening, when Miguel had gone, the lieutenant saw he had left the book behind. He lifted it, began leafing through its pages: it was recent, that much was clear; neatly divided, the first section was devoted to natural history – sketches of the large umbrella pines that lined the coast, the salt marshes at low tide, saltwort and cordgrass and sea lavender, each plant rendered with minute attention. The middle of the book was taken up with portraits: an old woman in Andalusian black, sitting in her doorway, her chin on her hand, her skin marked, but something in her gaze that arrested you. A young fisherman wearing no shirt, bent over his skiff, his britches rolled over his knees.

Looking at these portraits in the light of his candle, these faces rendered in loose, swift strokes, he saw these people were alive. More alive than he had ever felt. Close to something he had never touched. In the back were different sketches: women in their nakedness – many different women, many of the same woman, here seen from behind, the long flat planes of her back, her hair tumbled over her shoulder. Here lying on her back – the heavy fall of her breasts.

A countess, last night. I licked her while she bled.

It was clear that intimacy had occurred, or was about to. But there was a tenderness to the portrait. He stared at it, transfixed: felt that if he were ever looked at the way this woman was gazing out at the watcher, then some splinter might be drawn out of him. Something essential. Something hungry for the light.

He could not sleep, and so sat awake, working until, many hours later, Miguel came back.

'What are you working at so late?' he said, as he took off his hat and cloak. He smelled of the city, of the night, a strange complex mix of scents, rousing and disturbing in equal measure.

'It's early,' said the lieutenant. The dawn was grey beyond the window.

'So it is.'

Miguel leaned over him, peering at the heavily inked paper on the desk. 'What is the calculation?'

The lieutenant looked at the long chain of numbers before him. Minutes before he had been within them, but now they seemed senseless. He could not find his way back in.

'I am attempting to calculate our longitude, by the distance to the moon from Venus.'

'Surely you know our longitude.' Miguel moved away from him, seated himself on the edge of his bed and began unlacing his boots. 'We are in Cádiz.'

'Of course.' He felt the low flicker of irritation. 'But this is practice.'

'And what is the answer?'

'I don't know . . . I haven't corrected for parallax or refraction yet.'

'All this measuring. All these calculations,' said Miguel softly.

'What about them?' He turned to where Miguel sat, easy in his shirtsleeves and britches.

'Well, Columbus didn't need them, did he?'

'Columbus lived three hundred years ago.'

'I know, but sometimes I think –'

'What?' said the lieutenant.

'That you could measure the body of a woman but it would still not tell you how she feels when you are inside her.'

The lieutenant felt his face grow hot.

'The analogy is a weak one,' he said.

'Why?'

'Because, as you well know, we are being trained to navigate. Not to feel.'

In June they set sail. Just before their departure they were joined by a fifth sailor – a young Galician pilot, plucked from the ranks for his talent and his youth.

They were told their mission: to travel to Vera Cruz as passengers on a frigate, then overland to Mexico City. There were more details, but they would be provided by the viceroy on arrival in the city. Each of the captains was given a bonus of five hundred pesos prior to embarking, ostensibly for travel expenses.

'Dear God,' said the Basque. 'That's an awful lot of whores.'

From Vera Cruz, there followed an arduous two months' travel over appalling tracks to Mexico City, where they were guests of the viceroy, and where, on their last afternoon they were called to his private rooms. They stood, a small semi-circle, while the viceroy addressed them. Told them they would leave for the west coast in the morning, where three ships – the *Santiago*, the *San Carlos* and the *Sonora* – were waiting. From there they would sail north-west.

He pressed upon them the urgency with which they must prepare for the voyage – a departure no later than February, March at the very latest.

And then the commissions were given out. The Basque: commander, captain of the frigate *Santiago*. Miguel: captain of the *San Carlos*. And captaincy of the schooner *Sonora* that would accompany the *Santiago*, to himself.

That evening the viceroy hosted a lavish dinner: Iberian ham, wine from the vineyards of Málaga, candles which brought moths the size of small birds to their flames. The lieutenant was seated to the left of a wealthy mine-owner and his wife, Miguel to their right. The couple were dressed as though they had decided to wear all their most valuable garments at once, the husband in a cochineal waistcoat, laced with gold and silver gauze, the wife's hair studded with gemstones, her wrists cir-cled with ropes of pearls, diamonds on the front of her dress. Two silk beauty spots in the shape of a small sun and moon were fixed to her temple.

'Itching to get going, are you?' said the mine-owner over the entrées.

The man smiled, spoke low. 'I'm sure you're sworn to secrecy, yes? Don't worry about any of that with me. I know full well what you're all here for. I lent the viceroy the money for the ships.'

He gestured towards the viceroy, who was deep in conversa-tion with the Basque.

'He won't tell you but he's in debt to me to the tune of a million pesos. I came here,' said the mine-owner, 'a third son from Asturias, and now,' he nodded to the head of the table, 'he's going to make me a count.' The man's breath was heavy with meat and with wine. 'Bring me something back, eh?'

'What sort of thing would you like, sir?' said the lieutenant. The man sliced his beef, loaded his fork, and licked his lips.

'Something for my wife.' He put his thick hand on her wrist. 'I've heard the Russians are hunting the sea otter. That they wear their pelts in Saint Petersburg. That they fetch fortunes in China. I'd like one of those.'

Miguel leaned forward. 'Is it not a little hot here, sir, in Mexico, for fur?'

The man frowned; he was clearly unused to being contradicted.

'We go to the mountains in the winter, to escape the city. She can wear it then.'

On the other side of the man, Miguel raised his eyes, and the lieutenant met them. He could feel the thin, tensile thread of his friend's disapproval.

Then – 'Of course,' said Miguel smoothly, and smiled, and raised his glass.

They left the next morning: two weeks to travel another hundred leagues by horse and mule, and then the terrible, unforgettable bathos of their arrival here – a half-built town of wood and thatch, huddled in the lee of a lava escarpment, sweltering in fetid heat, surrounded by a choking tangle of mangroves and crocodiles and God-knew-what-else for a hundred miles north. Three hastily built ships, all in various states of disrepair.

'My God,' said the Basque that first day, when they all rode down to the docks. 'It's the arsehole of the fucking Empire.'

And he was right.

But whatever horrors this place has spawned, soon there will be only the ocean ahead.

The lieutenant weighs the sextant in his hand, sets the index arm to zero, lifts the telescope to his eye, shades it, brings the sun into the centre of the sight, releases the clamping screw on the index bar and then slowly, slowly brings the burning orb down until the lower limb of the sun just kisses the rock.

Here is time (the movement of the sun) laid across timelessness (insensate rock).

There.

It is an illusion – the sun at the horizon captured in coloured glass – but it is an illusion of the best sort: no myth, no camp-fire lantern show, no offerings cast onto the water. An illusion that fosters progress, that furthers truth.

See, Miguel?

We must navigate by calculation, not by instinct.

This is my ritual. Here is my daubing of blood.

It is these instruments of measurement, of exactitude, that will keep us from being smashed on rocks or caught by hidden shoals, that will bring us to glory, then beat the odds and help us home.

He lowers the sextant and places it carefully back in its case. It is time.

He can hear the low laughter of the men above. Good. They have been given a decent amount of brandy. Footsteps, then a soft knock, and the Peruvian's face around the door.

'Captain?'

'Yes?'

'The men are gathered on deck. They are ready for the Angelus.'

'Give me a moment.'

He fetches his Bible and makes his way out, up onto the deck, where the men are gathered. The Peruvian, the Galician, the cook, ten men: four seamen and six ranch hands. Now, he knows, is when this ragged bunch of men becomes a crew.

He opens the Bible, fingering the damp edges of the pages, and finds the passage he marked earlier in the day. The breeze is quickening now, as the sun begins to set, and he feels the answering quickening in himself.

He is good at leaving – for there has never been anything truly for him to leave. He cannot wait to be gone.

He clears his throat. 'Let us pray together.'

The men bow their heads.

'Then they said to him, "Please inquire of God to learn whether our journey will be successful." The priest answered them, "Go in peace. Your journey has the Lord's approval."'

His voice grows stronger as he reads, as he feels the word settle with the men, their skin touched by the setting sun. The white rock behind them, the face of Our Lord flushed wine-red.

Then the silence is pierced – a great tearing. Cannon fire.

The men drop to the deck: cries, confusion, smoke.

It is the Galician who moves first, crawling fast over to the side of the ship, hauling himself up by the railings to see. 'It is no enemy fire,' he shouts. 'It is the *San Carlos*, sir. She has raised her red flag.'

The lieutenant hurries to the side of the ship, brings out his glass, sees men swarming the deck of the *San Carlos*. Sees Cañizares, Miguel's second, climbing into the launch, rowing himself over the small stretch of sea between the two ships.

He calls to him as soon as the launch is in earshot. 'Good God – what is it, man? What has occurred?'

'It is Manrique, sir,' he shouts. 'He has gone quite mad. He is raving.'

'*What?*'

'He has locked himself in his cabin. He is armed, sir.'

'With what?'

'With four pistols. He says he will kill us all.'

The White Rock

This is the west.

For a long time there was only water here, water that boiled and thrashed and spoke only to itself:

Sometimes the water was an eagle, with the horns of a deer.

Sometimes a great two-headed serpent.

Sometimes a large ear, listening to the ancient briny dark.

Then, one day, a rock appeared, a white peak above the waves: the first solid object in the world.

The water moved against it: slap, sting, suck, pull.

And this motion, this friction, made vapour, became clouds, fell as rain, gave life.

Here was the place that formlessness first fell in love with form.

And so, and so, and thus and then, was how the world was born.

The Lieutenant
1775

The lieutenant climbs down the rope and hauls himself into the small boat below, where Cañizares waits. He seats himself, and the young pilot lifts his oars and starts to row.

There are shouts from the *Sonora* behind him – further noises from the *Santiago*, anchored close. Wrapped around them all a strange quiet – the way that sound behaves in the wake of cannon fire, the warp of it, ears pummelled by a noise so loud that everything is small and far away, laced by a high thin ringing, inside or out, he cannot tell.

The night is falling. The breeze is strengthening from the north-east: the breeze that is to carry them away. If he blinks, this might disappear – he might be back on deck, finishing the prayer, giving the order to weigh anchor. Sailing west.

'Tell me then,' he says to the pilot, and his voice also sounds strange to him, 'quickly – what has occurred?'

'Lieutenant Manrique has been . . . distracted. These three nights at anchor. He has spent most of his time in his cabin. His door closed. The men have heard him, speaking in there.'

'To whom?'

'To no one, sir.'

'I see. And today?' says the lieutenant. 'I saw him earlier, through my glass. He swam to the rock. He seemed well enough.'

'Yes. We took our walk together after that. Everything was in order, everything readied for our departure. He said he had to retire, went into his cabin. Not long after, there was shouting. I went in, and – he had a gun pointed at my head.'

'Did he speak?'

'Yes.'

'What did he say?'

'He said – *There is one here for each of you*. And then he fired.'

'Dear God. Were you hurt?'

'No. He fired just wide. There were men behind me. They stormed the cabin, overcame him after a struggle. Secured him.'

'Was anyone injured?'

'Lieutenant Manrique, perhaps.'

'Badly?'

'I don't know. Then, when he was tied, he began speaking, raving.'

'What did he say?'

'That I had to find you.'

'Me?'

'Yes sir. That he had to speak to you. To only you.'

The lieutenant shifts and the boat rocks. 'What happened then?'

'I stationed five men on the door. Gave the order to fire the cannon and I came.' The pilot looks at him. 'I know you are his friend, sir. I thought perhaps you could bring him to himself.'

He puts his hand to his pistol, aware of the dull fast thud of his heart. His left hand grips the wood of the boat. They are rowing close to the *Santiago* now. The lieutenant can hear commotion from her deck: men shouting, the Basque's voice issuing orders. The pilot rows them to within calling distance and the Basque appears above them. He climbs down and into the launch. 'Tell me,' he says.

'Lieutenant Manrique is raving,' says Cañizares. 'He had four loaded pistols. He shot at me.'

'Who is guarding him?'

'A watch of five.'

'All armed?'

'Yes sir.'

'And you?' The Basque jabs his finger towards the lieutenant. 'Why are you not with your men?'

'Manrique asked to speak with him,' says Cañizares. 'I thought –'

'You thought what? You'd grant the request of a madman?'

'Give me some time with him, sir,' says the lieutenant. 'I believe I have the best chance of bringing him to reason.'

'To *reason*?' the Basque barks. 'Dear God – he deserves to be shot in the head.'

'Not until we can establish the cause of the disturbance –'

'*The cause of the disturbance*? He tried to shoot his pilot – clearly he's lost his mind.'

'Just give me a little time with him. I have no more desire for delay than you.'

The Basque looks between the two men, his face strained in the torchlight.

'Alright,' he relents. 'I want soldiers at the door. And then you bring him here. *Under armed guard*. We will prepare for the junta in the meantime.'

'Yes, sir.'

The Basque climbs out of the launch and the pilot begins to row them towards the *San Carlos*. As they approach, the sour tang of gunpowder loads the air. The pilot starts to shake – a shaking that begins in his hands and moves all over his body, until the oars are shaking too. 'What is it, man?'

'There are already the stories. About the ship. The men were already nervous. It will be hard,' says the pilot, 'to bring them back round.'

'It is nothing that a gun cannot resolve.'

'No sir.'

'And pull yourself together. Show some strength. The men will take their lead from you now.'

They climb the ladder onto a deck thronged with men. All silent, watching. Their eyes follow them as they cross the deck towards the hold.

Below decks the air is close; it reeks of shit and sulphur.

The cabin door is shut fast. Guarded by five men. The lieutenant holds his pistol high as the pilot opens the door.

At first it is hard to see – there is only one candle, low in its burning, throwing long snaking shadows across the room. Then there is Miguel, bound at the chest and ankles to a chair. There appears to be a wound on his forehead. His shirt is torn, and his face is bruised – one eye swollen and purple – and there is the dark stain of blood on the white cloth of his shirt. On the table before him are four guns.

The lieutenant inhales the smell of burning paper, the greasy tallow of the candles in the close confines of the room. And then, emerging from the darkness, he sees something extraordinary, something unexpected: drawings, many of them, covering the walls. At first they convey only disorder, dissolution, then he stares at them, astonished, as he sees; they all have only one subject: the white rock. Here is the rock from the *San Carlos* – Miguel has managed to make it look like a monster, but a monster in pain, its eyes dark gouges in its collapsing face. Next the angle which shows the face of the Lord, but the face is far from serene, it is crosshatched, troubled, dark. Here another angle, and another and another: twenty, thirty drawings of the rock.

And he understands, with a sense of inevitability that makes no sense at all, that here, in this room, is something he has been trying to outrun.

He arranges his face, turns to Cañizares. 'Leave us,' he says to him. 'And pull your men from the door.'

'But sir, the Basque said –'

He waits. He counts. He speaks as calmly as he can.

'I heard what the Basque said, but Lieutenant Manrique is secured. Thirty minutes, and then we take him to the *Santiago* for the junta. As agreed.'

'Yes sir,' Cañizares salutes.

He hears the murmured command. The men's footsteps moving away. And then they are alone.

The lieutenant goes over to a small cabinet where a jug of water stands alongside several pewter cups. He pours a cupful, drinks the warm liquid quickly himself, then pours one for Miguel.

He brings Miguel's cup over to the table, holds it to his mouth.

Miguel looks up at him. 'If you untie my hands,' he says, 'I will be able to drink the water myself.'

He hesitates, and Miguel speaks into the silence.

'I am bound at the chest and at the feet. I am going nowhere until they take me. And once they take me, it is unlikely I will be untied again for a very long time. Please, untie my hands so I may lift the glass.'

The lieutenant moves slowly around the back of the chair. Miguel's hands are secured so tightly the rope has cut the skin. He loosens the knot and for a long moment the other man's arms hang, as though dislocated. The lieutenant moves back several paces and waits. Even if Miguel were to swing, he would not reach him from here.

He watches as Miguel brings his arms around – slowly, slowly. Reaches for the water, brings it close. Lifts it. Drinks.

The lieutenant looks at the guns. Counts again, to make sure.

'Which one was for me?'

'I did not choose.'

'Choose now.'

Miguel puts the cup back on the table.

A look – and then Miguel's eyes skim the weapons on the table. 'That one,' he says, jerking his head towards a small gun, closest to where the lieutenant stands. The lieutenant reaches out and brings it into his palm. A handle made from mother of pearl. He checks the barrel – all chambers are loaded. He points it at the other man. There is five foot of table between them.

'Who was the fourth for?'

'What do you mean?'

'The Basque, the Peruvian, myself. Who was the fourth for – yourself, or the young Galician?'

'The Galician.'

'You intended to survive this?'

'I did.'

'And what did you plan to do? Once you had murdered us all?'

'Rouse the crews.' Miguel's voice is steady. 'It would not take much. They are here by coercion. Everyone knows their allegiance is paper-thin. Set light to the ships and everything in them. Row to the shore. Burn the astillero. The timber yard. Burn it all.'

'And then?'

'Tell the world of the madness of this endeavour. Of our collective sin.'

'The *madness of this endeavour*? You didn't think that they might think it is you yourself who is mad?'

'Perhaps,' says Miguel. 'It matters only to me now that I speak my truth.'

The lieutenant lowers the gun, puts it on the table between them. 'Listen to me.' He speaks quickly. 'They are preparing the junta now.'

'Yes.'

'You will be disgraced.'

'Yes.'

'Stripped of your post.'

'Undoubtedly.'

'Executed.'

'Perhaps.'

'There is still time. If we were to walk out of this room together – if you were to tell them it was a spasm, no more: the heat, the insects, the toll of these last weeks. Then perhaps . . . you would be free to sail. They need you. *We need you.*'

'What part of me do you need?'

'My God. We need you to captain this ship. To sail to the bay of San Francisco. To map it. To chart it. To claim it for the Crown. To *do your duty.*'

'My duty to whom?'

'To your king. To your country.'

'My duty is to my conscience.'

'And what does your conscience tell you?'

'It tells me we are sinners.' Miguel opens his hands as he speaks, and the lieutenant remembers him, on the white rock, earlier today – the way he stood, arms outstretched as though in supplication. 'There are voices here. They speak to me. They have been speaking to me since we have been at anchor. Perhaps before. Perhaps for a long time. Only I could not hear them clearly then.'

'And what do they say, these *voices*?'

'They tell me that we are the curse.'

The lieutenant shakes his head. 'You are raving. You are not yourself. You will be better once we are sailing. Better once the breeze is moving through here.'

'No,' says Miguel, softly. 'I will not sail. I will never sail again.'

'This is madness.'

'It is the only sense I know. Will you do something for me?'

'What?'

'Bring me my sketchbook.' Miguel gestures to where it lies, open on his bunk. 'Please.'

The lieutenant hesitates, then goes to it, brings it over to the table.

'Bring it to the light, so you may see.'

The lieutenant opens it in the light of the candle: there are few pages remaining, most of them have already been torn away, but the book falls open on a heathen *Pietà*, an Indian mother cradling her son.

'Do you recognize them?'

The lieutenant stares: remembers the way she cradled him – like this, so tenderly. The way it had made him furious, somehow.

He looks up at his friend.

'Please,' says Miguel. 'Do not lie.'

'What do you want from me?'

'I want to hear you tell me about that day. *They* want to hear you tell me about that day.'

The lieutenant pushes the sketchbook away. 'Listen to me,' he hisses. 'Soon they will come for you – you will be taken from this cabin to a junta on the *Santiago* which is being prepared as we speak –'

'So, then, let us spend the little time that remains to us well. Please,' Miguel gestures with his hands to the seat before him, 'won't you sit?'

The lieutenant curses under his breath, pulls at the handkerchief around his neck, loosens it, then brings out the chair and sits upon it.

'Thank you,' says Miguel, and his eyes are steady. 'Now, please, tell me, from the beginning, from the timber yard.'

'You are serious?' he laughs.

'I am.'

The lieutenant places his hands on the wood of the table before him, breathes in, breathes out. He has the strange, discomfiting sense it is he who is about to stand trial, not Miguel. 'I had found the mast of the *Sonora* was rotten,' he says. 'Worm-eaten. So I went to the timber yard. They did not have the pine to repair it. They had cedar – acres of cedar, planks and planks of cedar, but no pine. I was . . . frustrated. Time was running out.'

'Time was running out,' Miguel says softly. 'Yes, go on.'

'The chief of the astillero said he was waiting for the pine. There was a place upriver, at the spur of the mountain, where the pine forest could be found. A group of Indians had been sent there to log. They had not appeared for a week. He said he would send a party of men after them.'

'And then?'

'I said I did not trust any party of men and I would go there and fetch the wood for myself. You were there.' He looks up at Miguel. 'Speaking about another matter. You said you would come with me. You said it would be good to escape. A day's excursion. You said you had worked for forty days straight. You said your crew would manage without you for a day.'

'I did. Then?'

'We went alone, the next day. We rode to the end of the bay, and then into the interior.'

'You are rushing.'

'What?'

'Do not rush. Tell me. How it was.'

The lieutenant closes his eyes briefly. 'I remember how thick the jungle was. How slow our progress. We tethered our horses, and took a boat together, up the inlet.'

'Do you remember the birds? You must remember the birds.'

'I do. There were hundreds of them, thousands.'

'And how did it feel?'

'I don't understand.'

'How did it *feel*? To travel up that river?'

'I –' He sees again the mangroves' twisted, contorted shapes. The presence of Miguel, close beside him in the boat – the way they were alone, but watched everywhere: by the birds, and from the slimy banks, down which slithered crocodiles and other, unnameable creatures.

'It felt – obscene.'

Miguel nods. 'Go on.'

'We rowed for a long time, then we arrived at the headwater. There was a lagoon there. A spring. The Indians were there. There was a pool, and they were swimming.'

'How many? Do you remember how many there were?'

'There were . . . two men, two boys, and several women and children.'

'Do you remember the sound of the children laughing? The way it echoed around the pool?'

He nods.

'What happened then?'

'You said we should join them and I refused.'

'I dived and swam, and I heard you shouting. Do you remember?'

'Of course.'

'*Why*? Why did you shout like that?'

'Because they were not working! We had caught them in the act.'

Miguel nods. 'And then?'

'Then, they got out of the water. You got out of the water.'

He remembers their bodies: all of them, on the bank. And Miguel's too: all of them in their near-nakedness.

'I told them to cover themselves. I told them they would all be flogged. That they were being paid by the Crown. That they were the subjects of the king.'

'Then?'

'Then . . . a boy stepped forward. He was eleven, or twelve. He said he should be the one whipped. He said it was his idea to swim.'

'And then?''

'Then I whipped him.'

'Yes,' says Miguel. 'Yes, you did. I remember his blood. Do you? The sight of it. The way it sprayed in arcs. The way it touched the leaves of the trees. The scarlet against the green.'

'There is usually blood, is there not, when a man is flogged? Surely you have seen a man be flogged before? Surely you have had to perform the deed yourself?'

Miguel gives a small smile. 'Indeed. But I remember thinking how precise you were. How you took your time. How suddenly you seemed to possess the time you had craved so badly. How slow, in fact, the whipping seemed to be.

'I remember how ugly you became. Uglier and uglier as you hurt him more and more. But how you did not stop.

'And I remember thinking that, a moment before, that boy's body was being used differently. That boy's body had been swimming. A moment before it had been free.'

'They needed to understand the urgency of the matter. An example needed to be made.'

'I remember the cry of a woman. His mother. The way she went to him. The way she cradled him. The hopelessness of it all.'

The two men are silent, then – 'Do you think you killed him?' says Miguel.

'I know that we had to finish the ships. That we had to find the pine. That they were the servants of the Crown. They were wasting time.'

Miguel regards him, then – 'Shall I tell you what I thought,' he says softly, 'when I watched them? When I swam with them?'

'Go on.'

'I thought this was the first place I had ever truly been where time held no sway. And do you know what I saw? When you whipped that boy?'

'What?'

'I saw that here was the garden. Here were God's children. And here we were, casting them out. Bringing sin. *We* are the fallen. Not they.'

'You have lost your mind.'

'If I have, then I have found myself. Tell me. Answer me this. If you killed that boy – what did he die for?'

'He *needed*,' he says again, 'to understand *the urgency of the matter.*'

'I will tell you what he died for. He died for Time. Now you must take his time. You must not squander it. This is what I am told to tell you. This is what they say to me. These voices.' He casts his hands about him. 'They say we must learn to live.'

'And how do you propose we do that?'

'I see you. Inside the cage you have been given. The cage you have made. The cages we have all made. You can still escape. You can be free.'

He is like a conjuror, here in his cabin, his eyes in the candle-light. His voice – that low clear stream, so certain, somehow, of its course.

'How?'

'The junta will convict me. They will have no other choice. They will send me back to land to face my fate.'

184

'Yes.'

'After the junta has reached its verdict, if they do not shoot me there and then, offer to be the one who takes me to shore.'

'And then?'

'Ask for forgiveness.'

'Ask who?'

'The rock. The white rock. That is what I have been doing, these last few days.'

'You speak as though it were alive.'

'I believe it is. As alive as you or I.'

He laughs, shakes his head. 'And then?'

'Ask to be forgiven. Live.'

'Live *how*? And live on what?'

'Live as we were intended to. Slip our cages and become something else. Without uniform. Free upon the earth.'

'We will be hanged for desertion.'

'Only if they find us.'

His voice is soft, consoling, cool.

Footsteps approaching – a knock at the door. The lieutenant holds up his hand to silence Miguel as the pilot enters, salutes. 'They have raised the flag on the *Santiago*. The junta is prepared. They expect us on deck.'

'Very good. We have finished our business here. I will wait on deck for the launch.' The lieutenant walks through the door without looking back, moving through the thick fetid air, then up onto deck. The wind has gathered in the time he was below, warm, from the land, *north-north-east*.

He feels, suddenly, an immense fatigue. He would like to rest – to lie down and sleep – but he can hear them bringing Miguel up from below. When he emerges, he is trussed, the rope wound around his body, a black hood on his head. The lieutenant climbs down into the launch, alongside the pilot, and both men lift their arms to receive the prone body in the boat. Miguel is hot, his shirt soaked with sweat, silent beneath his hood.

The pilot takes the oars and begins to row. The lieutenant feels his eyes on his face. He makes his own face blank, wonders if the man was listening at the door. Were they overheard?

'Will he be shot?' says the pilot, as though Miguel, wearing the hood, can no longer hear.

'I do not know.'

'Who will shoot him if so?'

'I do not know.'

Let it not be the Basque.

They approach the *Santiago*, where torches have been lit all along the deck and the water seems to burn with orange light.

There are calls, negotiations, a rope is sent down, pulled through the ropes that bind Miguel, and the men on board begin to winch his body high. When his body is level with the gun deck they stop, there is a commotion on deck, someone struggling with the winch, and Miguel is left to hang, swinging twenty feet out over the sea. Then someone loses control of the winch and it sheers wide – Miguel's body dangles above their heads, then he is smashed against the side of the ship. The men grab hold again of the winch and gain control, as hands reach out for him and haul him onto the deck.

When Miguel's body is clear, the lieutenant climbs the ladder. He looks at the other men's faces as though in a dream. The Basque – his face shining with sweat in the torchlight. 'The Majorcan stays here with the men. We will go below, to the surgeon's quarters.'

They follow Miguel's body down to the orlop deck, where he is placed in a chair and the hood is taken from his head. His face is a bloodied pulp. And the lieutenant feels it again – that same sensation he had when seeing those pictures of the rock: the edges of a terrible disorder. A dissolution. A chaos in which anything is suddenly possible.

He blinks. Clears his throat. 'He has sustained more injuries, I believe,' he says to the surgeon. 'As he was being lifted onto the ship.'

'Examine him,' says the Basque.

The surgeon feels Miguel's ribs. 'They are broken. At least five of them.'

The Basque nods. 'Lieutenant Manrique. From every report it appears that you have taken leave of your senses. Before we begin the junta let us first see if we can bring those senses back.' He turns to the surgeon. 'Bleed him.'

The surgeon selects a small, two-bladed knife from his cabinet. He moves to Miguel's upper arm where he makes several small incisions. Holds a bowl for the blood. He draws a pint, then places it on the table. For a long moment no one speaks. It has a strange power to it, the blood. Unhoused, it seems to pulse, still, with life. Then the surgeon binds the site and steps back. The chaplain is murmuring a low prayer.

'Who will act as scribe?' says the Basque.

'I will,' the surgeon says. He sits. He writes the names of those present. He asks for the time and writes it: forty-five minutes past eight o'clock.

The Basque turns to Cañizares. 'Will you relate the events of this night for the record?'

'Yes, sir. Lieutenant Manrique's condition became apparent as soon as we lay at anchor. That is to say, three days ago.'

'In what way?'

'He locked himself inside his cabin. He appeared to be speaking, but there was no one with him.'

'And what did you do? Why was I not informed?'

'Whenever Lieutenant Manrique exited his cabin he seemed sane. He was able to give his orders, command the ship. Then this afternoon, while the crew were on the *Santiago* receiving their pay, he told me he did not wish to be disturbed.'

'And then?'

'I was alerted to the fact that something was awry when one of our crew came to find me. The door was barred. Manrique was shouting.'

'What was he shouting?'

'That it was time. That the time was now. I went immediately to the cabin. I opened the door and he shot at me.'

'Do you think he intended to kill you?'

'I do, sir. There were three more loaded pistols in there. He clearly stated there was one for each of us.'

'I see.'

'We overcame him, disarmed him, and tied him to the chair. We launched the distress signal. That was when he asked to see the lieutenant.'

The Basque turns to him. 'You were with him for half an hour.'

'Yes.'

'Who was with you?'

'We were alone.'

'And what did you speak of?'

The lieutenant opens his hands. 'I tried to persuade him to see reason.'

'And was he willing?'

'No, sir.'

The Basque turns to the scribe. 'Wait,' he says. 'Stop writing.' The Basque steps forward. 'Lieutenant Manrique – we know you to be a man of sense. A man of reason. We know you to be one of the finest sailors of the line. We know that this locale is notorious for its insects and its unhealthful maladies. All of us have fallen victim to its depredations at one time or another. We are perfectly willing to imagine that you have suffered a temporary insanity. We are giving you the *benefit of the doubt*. What do you say to this?'

The lieutenant closes his eyes. He sees this ship, anchored off this white rock, enfolded in night, the ocean around it, the miles and miles of jungle and shore, all the dark world waiting, watching, to see what occurs.

'I say . . .' says Miguel. It is hard to hear him – his words are mangled by his shattered jaw.

'Speak up, man. The scribe must hear.'

'We are the agents of the Fall. We must repent. Give offerings. Turn back.'

'My God,' says the Basque, in a low voice. He goes over to the scribe and takes the paper. 'Enough. We have wasted enough time on this nonsense.' He holds it to the flame, the paper burns brightly. 'Lieutenant Manrique, I hereby strip you of your command. Command of the *San Carlos* will pass to you.' He turns to the lieutenant. 'Command of the *Sonora* passes to the Peruvian. The Galician will serve as second on that ship.'

The flames gutter, the paper is almost gone. The Basque signals for water, tosses the charred remains in a cup. 'We do not talk of this. We do not write of this. No one will ever hear of it. Lieutenant Manrique is mad. That is all.'

The men look at each other. *Yes*, they nod. *This is the only way*. 'Someone must take Manrique ashore,' says the Basque.

'I will,' says the lieutenant.

'You?'

The men watch him. He feels their eyes. The closeness in the room. The noisome air. His heart is racing, but the lieutenant makes his face expressionless – his eyes blank, without need. 'My instruments and my belongings will need to be moved to the *San Carlos*,' he says. 'I cannot sail without them, and I will not use another man's.'

The Basque nods. 'Deliver him to the gaol. Tell them to keep him there. Tell them to write to the viceroy. He will decide whether he lives or dies. While you are gone the Peruvian will see your belongings are transferred to the *San Carlos*.

'We are finished here,' says the Basque to the surgeon. 'Put the hood back on him. Make sure he is secured, then get the men to take him into the launch.' He moves to leave the room then turns back, goes over to where Miguel sits, takes his pistol, and slams it into the other man's side, and Miguel lets out an animal howl of pain. 'You always were a fucking Moor.'

The Basque leaves, the Peruvian behind him. The lieutenant follows them up onto the deck. He gives the Peruvian his instructions for his instruments, then, when the Peruvian has gone back to the *Sonora*, he finds himself a spot of darkness, leans and retches over the side. He stays there for a long time. He can hear them, bringing Miguel up from below. Lowering him into the launch again. Inside him he feels the wild useless spin of the needle. The sky above him is an anarchy of stars.

The Basque calls his name, and the lieutenant straightens himself, wipes his mouth with his handkerchief, and makes his way out of the darkness to where the other man stands.

'You are quite well, Lieutenant?'

'Quite.'

'Up to this?'

'Of course.'

'No need for anyone else to accompany you?'

'No.'

'Good. You always were such . . . allies. I know.'

The flag at the stern is rippling in the breeze.

'Be quick about it,' says the Basque. 'There is still time for us to catch the wind.'

The lieutenant clambers down the rope into the launch. Miguel is there already, slumped in the bottom of the boat, the hood tied over his head, his hands secured behind his back.

The lieutenant takes the oars in his hands and begins to row.

It is a long time since he has rowed for himself. Strange to have the roughness of the oars in his palms, to feel his arms pulling them through the water, feel the small skiff respond.

Blades in, blades out, blades flat; blades in, blades out, blades flat.

The sweat rises on him.

Silence. Faster now: only his grunts of effort, only the sound of the oars in their locks.

Miguel lies slumped in the keel, his head on the riser. The lieutenant tries to keep the small craft steady. He must be suffering greatly, the lieutenant knows, with the extent of his injuries, but he does not speak, there is only sometimes, when the skiff hits a swell, a stifled moan of pain.

The lieutenant rows until the white rock rears beside him, dark grey in the moonlight.

When they are on its north side, invisible to the ships, the lieutenant stops rowing. He pulls the oars into the boat.

He leans forward and lifts the hood from Miguel's head – sees the bloodied mess of his face, his jaw. 'We are here,' he says. 'This is your rock.'

The boat bobs in the water. The moon is just past full, hanging low over the mountains. The air very still. The lieutenant can smell the land of the island: the heat and the scrub, and, closer, the salt-piss smell of the rock. Something female and ancient and infinitely disturbing. There are animals, moving along the waterline: crabs, he imagines, the whole lower part of the rock is alive with their clicking movements. Closer still, Miguel's sweat. His blood.

'I have done as you asked. Now – what would you have me do?'

The other man does not move, his broken body curled over itself. 'Ask forgiveness.' Miguel speaks with difficulty. 'Then choose.'

'Choose how? Choose what?'

'Choose differently. Row to the island. Head into the interior. There are no settlements for miles.'

The lieutenant looks at his friend where he lies, sees the expressions which flicker over his countenance: pain, hope – and then, the apprehension of defeat.

'You are injured. You cannot walk. Let alone run.' As he speaks, he is flooded with a feeling, one he never expected to feel for Miguel: pity. 'It is happening anyway,' he says. 'If not us, it will be the Russians. If not the Russians the British. We are in a race, don't you see? Every day. Every hour. Every minute. We cannot let them get there first.'

'I know where this race ends. It ends in ruin.'

The lieutenant shakes his head. 'You are mistaken. It ends in glory.'

Even as he speaks it, he understands the truth of it. 'There is no choice,' he says, as he moves to put the hood back on the other man's head. 'There never was.'

He ties the hood back into place, and when he has done so, he lifts the oars, pulls the boat, feels the strength return to his arms, his hands.

He rounds the point and now he can see the dock. There are lights there, torches. Soldiers, waiting on the shore with lanterns and with guns. He had not thought there would be so many. They call out as he nears. They are armed, all of them, with muskets and pikes. It is as though they expected a marauding army. Not one slight, injured man.

They are silent, he and Miguel, as he rows the last yards – oars cutting through the torchlight, which reflects on the water like orange blood.

Miguel does not struggle. He does not fight as he is pulled from the boat. As he takes his leave, Miguel speaks, but it is hard to hear what he says, through his shattered jaw, from beneath the hood. Something about forgiveness. That he is forgiven.

The lieutenant gives the commander the Basque's orders, then, when he has delivered them, he climbs back down into the launch.

For a moment, as he rows, he feels unmoored, and then, as he reaches and rounds the point, he sees the ships, waiting. And his heart leaps at the scene laid before him: the white rock, dwarfed by the magnificence of these ships and all they hold, these ships which are ready, their sails unfurled, and he feels the leap – *yes* – they will sail tonight, west through the night.

He stares up at the great clock of the heavens. There is time yet.

It is a long time yet until the dawn.

The Girl
1907

The ship has turned, completed its arc, and they are steaming slowly along a narrow strip of water. They are close to land, now, very close – the prisoners cluster at the rails, staring out at the buildings that dot the shoreline, the wooden boats tethered to little posts. There are tall trees, and groups of children dart in and out of them like small shoals of fishes, calling, pointing, laughing, watching the ship steam past.

The tall father is busy, occupied with his own family now, gathering their things; every so often he glances their way, checking, nodding – glad they are here, happy he has helped them. The girl knows he was kind, but she knows that his kindness may have killed them: she can no longer see the white rock, or the mountains, or the open ocean. She knows that their chance has gone.

She looks to her sister, but Maria-Luisa has her eyes tight shut. Her hands in fists.

And now they are slowing, and there are soldiers, visible on the dockside, more Rurales, waiting to meet the ship, and at the sight of them, in the same grey uniforms as the men in the village and the men on the mountain, the girl's stomach pitches. One of the soldiers jumps onto the dock and passes a thick oily rope to another, who loops it over a big metal round. The boat strains and heaves, lowing like an animal, sending out smoke through its funnel, but the rope pulls taut, and more ropes are thrown as the ship is caught, captured and tethered, and, as though it has understood this captivity, it gives one last anguished groan, then shudders and is still. The flag above the girl's head flutters and droops, heavy against its pole.

A plank is lowered, and the soldiers run down it onto the dock, shouting and gesturing at the men on land. Soon the soldiers are holding up their guns, shouting at the people at the front of the boat to descend.

The prisoners start to walk, moving with jerky, awkward steps as they use their legs for the first time in days. The girl watches – the women with their heavy bundles on their heads, the children holding their mothers' hands.

But a strange thing happens when they reach the top of the plank – they hesitate, as though filled with a sudden reluctance. And the girl knows what they are thinking: however bad the ship was, however terrible the smell and heat and fear, it still had something of home in it; it was where they ate their last tamales, where they drank the last of the water they brought from their springs and wells, and when they descend, they will move onto an unknown land. They will not know where they are. But the soldiers prod them with the blades on the ends of their rifles and make them walk, which they do, slowly, their legs stiff, and when they finally reach the shore, they stand and look about them, still dazed, unsure what to do or where to go, until the soldiers herd them into a penned-off area, a place with no shade from the sun. More and more people leave the ship in this way, until, finally, it is the turn of those who sit here, at the back.

'Come,' the tall father bends to Maria-Luisa, 'I will carry you. Come onto my back.'

Maria-Luisa does not respond, and so, as though she weighs hardly anything, he lifts her onto his back, then his younger son onto his front. His wife carries their baby in a sling across her chest. The older boy walks alongside.

The girl follows. She and Maria-Luisa have no belongings, so she helps to carry one of the family's bundles – while the mother balances another, larger bundle on her head. Each step the tall father takes hurts her sister, she knows that – the redness has spread now, it is moving towards her knee.

When they reach the pen, the father bends, puts Maria-Luisa on the ground; she sinks down with a long, low hiss of pain.

The pen is thick, heavy rope, the sort that is used for cattle in the markets in Hermosillo. The prisoners are made to sit in straight rows. The girl sits between Turkey Vulture Man and Maria-Luisa, both of whom have their eyes closed. The ground feels strange, as though it is moving beneath them still, as though her stomach is still there on the waves.

When the last of the passengers is off the ship, the soldiers start to count them.

There is one who looks to be in charge: his uniform is smarter than those of the others, the gold braiding on the sides of his trousers shinier in the sun. He walks up and down, up and down in his polished boots, numbers rattling from his mouth. When he passes, the girl sees his eyes are grey, grey like his cloth, grey like a rattlesnake's. The girl looks straight ahead and makes her face blank.

They sit facing west. She knows this because the sun is at their backs and their shadows clump on the ground in front of them, as though whispering with each other, conferring as to what to do.

In front of them is the great metal hulk of the ship, behind it is the narrow strip of water, and then, on the other side, a small stony hill where buzzards circle, climbing high and wide. She knows that beyond that hill is the white rock.

Would they have lived? If they had jumped?

The water close to where they sit is held in a narrow channel and is greenish and foul. Wooden boats lie, upside down, their planks missing, like the carcasses of creatures which have been picked clean and bleached in the sun. Nearby, a fisherman sits, mending his net. He pays no attention to the people who are so close, prisoners in the sun.

Then, a call from inside the pen. 'Water,' the speaker says, in Spanish. Agua. Agua. 'We need water. The children need water. Are you trying to kill us all?'

And then more voices join in – *agua agua agua*.

But no water comes.

The only water is in small brown puddles on the ground.

A strange stillness falls over everything – it feels as though they might stay here forever. Sweat gathers and pools at the base of the girl's back.

She is aware of her thirst as something huge and terrible, something that if she turned towards it, might devour her. It squats there, just at the edge of sight, with her hunger, with her fear.

She looks to Maria-Luisa but her sister has retreated. She is in a place deep inside where there is no pain. There is nothing at all.

Sounds – the barking of a dog nearby. The soldiers laughing as they speak to each other. The woman from Hermosillo, chanting the litany of her children's names. Maria-Luisa's breath. Fast now.

The two boys are whispering together. She watches as the older one leans towards the younger – drawing a picture in the dirt with his finger.

'Chuu'u,' says the younger boy with the jolly face, laughing and pointing. Dog.

The older boy smiles, nods, rubs it out, draws another with his fingertip.

Kuchu – fish

Maaso – deer.

She is glad to be close to this family. It still feels like luck. These boys who even here can find a way to play. But she knows that it will not feel so lucky on the walk. The father might carry Maria-Luisa for a while, but not for twenty miles. He will have his own children to think of, and when his own two boys tire of walking, he will have to choose to carry them. There will be no room on the father's back.

She looks over to where Turkey Vulture Man sits, impassive, still chewing his tobacco.

She remembers what he said on the boat:

In this town of the white rock, the Mexicans will come. They will look at the children. Perhaps they will take some of them away.

To different families. To become Mexican. When our children become Mexican, they breed the Yoeme out.

She can feel her heart start to race, if this is tree, she understands: this is the only way. They are good workers, can cook and clean and grind corn and take care of the smaller children; they will do all this and do it well, and then, when Maria-Luisa's foot is better and all these Rurales have disappeared – over the mountains with their prisoners, all the way to Yucatán – then they will escape. Then they will find their way home to their grandmother's house.

She looks across to Maria-Luisa, who sits, eyes closed, her shawl over her head, and she sees her sister is filthy, her skirt still stained with Carlos's blood, crusted brown. And the terrible wound on her foot. No one will take them if they see those things first.

The girl bends down, dips the end of her shawl into the brown water of the closest hole, and wipes the edge of her shawl on her face, over her dirt- and salt-encrusted arms.

Then the girl dips again, and cleans the white flecks from her sister's mouth; gently wipes the blood from her burning cheeks. Maria-Luisa flinches, but allows it.

Just then, for no reason that it is easy to see, the soldiers point their guns and shout at them that they are going to move. People start standing, putting their bundles back on their heads. The tall father leans in and lifts Maria-Luisa.

'Alright, little sister?' he says, to the girl. 'Not long now.' And although it is not clear what he means, it is clear he says it to give her comfort.

They walk for a short distance and then they turn into a wide street, and they are in a town; there are houses made from bricks, and stores, and there are people, going in and out of the stores.

What had she expected? She does not know. But not this – not this everyday town.

A group of children on their way to school stand and watch them. They point and laugh. Some of them shout; a rock lands in the dirt close to her feet.

The line halts before a building with big stone arches out-side. The soldiers shout at the prisoners to stay still. Up ahead, people are being taken into the building; here at the back they are standing in the hot sun.

After a while of standing like this, people start to sit down again, to huddle together and create what shade they can. The tall father bends, puts Maria-Luisa onto the ground. She opens her eyes, but they are glassy. 'I'm cold,' she says, and starts to shake. The rash is angry-looking now.

The mother reaches out, puts her hand on Maria-Luisa's arm. She frowns.

'I'm cold,' says Maria-Luisa again.

The mother unties her bundle, reaches into it, brings out

a warm shawl and wraps it around Maria-Luisa's arms. The girl stares: it is beautiful, this shawl – the colours sing in the sunlight; it speaks of a time, far away from this one, when there was time to embroider, to choose these threads, to sit in the shade and stitch.

On the other side of the road is a low red building, a fine house – there are large gates to the side, and gardens visible behind. There is green grass, people move across the grass, tending to its greenness, and it is calm in there, and cool-looking. A man stands staring out – and there is something in his expression, something searching, that holds the girl's gaze. Perhaps, she thinks, he is looking for someone to help him in his home. Perhaps he has children, and perhaps his wife needs someone to help those children get to sleep, to walk them and sing to them in those blessedly cool gardens. She sits up straighter. After a while of standing, looking like this, the man moves away.

The line inches slowly forward and now they are beneath the arches where it is cool. The soldiers usher more people inside. The line inches forward again and as they near the front, the family rouse themselves: Maria-Luisa is lifted again by the father, the woman balances her bundle, the boys hold hands and the girl follows behind.

As they pass into the building the girl's heart starts to pound: inside is a large room with tables on either side, there are people and soldiers everywhere, many of the prisoners have their belongings spread out on the tables. The praying woman is already inside, she has been brought to a table and her bundle has been opened. A soldier is rifling through her things as though looking for something he has lost, while she stands, weeping, to the side.

'Children,' one of the soldiers calls. 'Those with children over here.'

The soldier is speaking in Yoeme. His face is Yoeme too. He is young, no older than Carlos, but he is wearing the uniform of the Rurales. A torocoyori – traitor. 'Those with children over here.'

The girl follows the family, a few paces behind: like this, it is easy to believe that they are all together, all in the protection of this same tall father, who will stand between them and the soldiers. This kind mother, who will help them in whatever way she can. These boys, who will continue to play, however bad things seem.

Perhaps, she thinks, this family's strength is enough to protect them. Perhaps all will be well after all.

They follow to a part of the building away from the windows. It is darker and cooler here. There is a desk, and a woman sits behind it. 'Put your children down on the ground,' says the woman to the tall father.

'Why?' says the father.

'Just put them on the ground. Let us see them. Let them stand.'

The torocoyori soldier points his rifle at the father, who bends and places Maria-Luisa beside the girl, then he stands again, and holds his younger son close to his chest, speaking something into his ear.

'Hey,' says the woman behind the desk sharply. 'Both of them. On the ground.'

'They are all yours?' says the torocoyori soldier.

The tall father looks to Maria-Luisa and the girl, his eyes questioning, but the girl shakes her head. She grips Maria-Luisa's clammy hand, her heart pounding.

'No,' says the girl, in Spanish. 'We do not belong to him. We are not his daughters.'

The father's eyes flinch – but the girl nods to him. 'Please,' she says, in Yoeme. 'It is better this way.'

He turns back to the woman. 'Just these boys,' he says.

The woman makes a note in her big black book. Then she puts down her pen. 'Now,' she says. 'Come forward, boys.'

The soldier still has his rifle pointed at the father. The woman smiles at the boys. It is a strange smile, but the smallest one, the one with the jolly face, smiles back. The woman nods, points at him, says something to the soldier.

There is a moment when everything is slow, then the toro-coyori soldier is lifting the boy, and the boy is screaming, and the father is moving towards the soldier with his big bare hands. Another soldier has appeared, and has his rifle pressed to the father's head.

'Take me,' the older boy is shouting at the woman. 'Take me instead.'

But the little boy has gone. Bundled away. Where have they taken him?

The mother begins to howl. A terrible, animal sound. She grasps her baby to her. The father pulls his remaining son towards him. The soldier keeps his rifle to the father's head. 'Outside,' he says. 'All of you.' He gestures to the girls. 'You too.'

The family begin to walk – pushed by the point of the gun – but the girl hangs back.

'Wait.' She touches the torocoyori soldier on the arm.

He turns his eyes to her and his eyes are wary, and will not hold her own, but she speaks quickly, in Yoeme, before he can resist.

'My sister is ill. She cannot make the walk. Please – we can work. I will work for two. And I will make her better. And then she will work too. We are strong. We can cook and clean. We can look after the little ones. Please.'

The soldier looks at the girl, he looks at Maria-Luisa. She feels him hesitate. She can see he is more of a boy than a man.

She knows his story is not an easy one, she can feel it inside him – despite his uniform he is not yet numb. He can still feel shame. His eyes are despairing – they ask her not to ask him, but she stands firm.

'Please.'

'You are too old,' he says.

'For what?'

'They only want the children.'

'*But we can work*,' she says again.

The soldier hesitates. 'Wait here,' he says. Maria-Luisa's hand is slippery. She is away somewhere else. She knows that none of this is touching her, not really – that she feels it all as something far away, but the girl is here, and everything is etched sharply: the torocoyori soldier's boots clipping on the tiled floor, the way the sunlight falls in a long slice on his face as he speaks to the woman, something in Spanish, the way the woman looks towards them, half in shadow and half in sun. A brief flicker, then she shakes her head.

The torocoyori soldier walks back over to them. 'I am sorry,' he says. 'You must go outside. Now.'

She puts her arm around her sister's waist and her sister leans into her. They move slowly, slowly, Maria-Luisa's weight on her shoulder, blinking into the sun, and they take their place amongst the other prisoners in another pen, in a scrubby square on the other side of the building, leaning against the trunk of a small tree.

A terrible silence hangs over that yard.

The tall father is sitting, staring at the building they have just come from, as though his young son may yet emerge. The mother is weeping, bent over her baby, and the older son sits, curled over himself, staring at the vacancy his brother has made.

'Console yourself, brother,' Turkey Vulture Man says, into the silence. 'Your little son is spared the walk.'

They look up at him: the father, the mother, the older boy.

'Your son will live,' he says.

'Do not speak,' says the tall father. 'We do not want to hear you speak.'

Despair presses like a heavy stone on the girl's chest, pushing out her breath. She wants to hurt something.

On the other side of the rope, people come and go. People who barely glance their way: fishermen, coming back from the sea – carrying their catches in buckets, trousers rolled to their knees. Women carrying shopping bags on their arms. Children running, laughing. Leaping. Every so often one will glance their way, and the girl feels the quick flicker of pity and fear, before they look away again, then hurry on. The sun reaches its height. Clouds come. They thicken. They cover the sun.

What would she be doing at home? Soaking the beans. Tending the fire. Sweeping the yard. Following the ordinary rhythms of the day.

Often, in the afternoons, when the chores were done, they would comb each other's hair.

In her mind, the girl fetches the comb – a burr from the organ cactus, the spines on two sides burned off so it is easy to hold – and loosens her sister's plaits. Maria-Luisa's hair falls to her waist like dark water. The girl brushes it evenly, slowly, bringing the world back into rightness.

Just then there is a trundling sound, and a man walks down the street rolling a cart, a large cooking pot on it. He goes past the red-walled building opposite, crosses the street towards where they sit, then trundles on to the far corner, where he stops.

The girl watches as the man lights his fire with charcoal. In a short while the smell of cooking oil, then onions, drifts over the square, and the people gathered lift their heads. Then comes the smell of meat. Beside the man with the stall sits a woman, perhaps his wife, and she is patting out dough, pressing it into shape, then piling the tortillas to the side. She places them onto the grill pan, six at a time. The girl watches her – how she tends to them, how she turns them. How many times has she done the same herself? The cool, lime-soaked dough moulded between her palms, the way the tortillas curl a little at the edges on the heat of the stove, just enough to reach in and flip them over, to show you they are almost done.

The girl imagines the feel of the warm tortilla, heavy with food. Potatoes fried in the fat from the bacon. Nopales. Coffee. Her mouth fills with saliva and her stomach starts to cramp and groan.

People come to the stall. They stand around and talk with each other. They smile and laugh. No one looks over towards the square where the prisoners are held. The sky is growing darker, the clouds thicker above.

A handsome young man walks along the street to the stall. He is smartly dressed, in a dark suit, with a hat and a cane. He has a large moustache. The girl recognizes him, the searching look he carries. It was he who was standing in the hacienda garden earlier, staring out. He speaks with the stallholder, then steps back and waits for his food, looking towards the square where the prisoners sit.

The girl sits up a little straighter, but something else has caught the handsome man's eye.

The tall father has rolled up his trouser leg. He peels off a note from the roll then hands the rest to his wife, who puts it in her dress. Then he stands and goes over to the torocoyori soldier.

'My family are hungry,' he says. He speaks slowly and carefully. 'There is food here.' He gestures towards the taco stand. 'I have money. I would like to buy them some food.'

'No.' The soldier shakes his head. 'Go and sit down.'

The man does not sit down. He is a head taller than the soldier, who is not a short man. 'My family are hungry,' he says again. 'My wife is feeding our baby. There is food here. I have money.' He gestures to the food stall, where the handsome young man in the fine dark suit is paying for his food.

Everyone is watching now. Everyone in the square has their eyes on the tall father. And something is happening in the father's body. He appears to be getting taller. To be growing. Perhaps he is growing with all the need of all the people who are also hungry, and who are willing him on.

'Go and sit back down,' says the soldier to the tall father. But this time, his voice sounds less sure. And she sees again that this young soldier is not a bad man. He is a prisoner too. 'Get back in the pen where you belong.'

'No,' says the father, calmly. 'I will not. I do not belong in that pen. Just as you do not belong in that uniform. Is it worth it?' he says to the soldier. 'Worth it for these shiny buttons? For this gun?'

The soldier says nothing.

'My family are hungry,' he says again. 'And I will buy them food.'

Now he turns away from the soldier and he starts to walk. It is only a little way to the taco stand – perhaps ten paces to the corner. At the corner the man turns left, then continues along the top side of the square.

The tall man's boots hit the ground. He walks like he

speaks – slow but steady. One two, one two, one two. Everyone is watching. It is as though no one is breathing. The girl feels her own breath, caught in her chest. The handsome man at the taco stall is watching too, a small smile on his face.

There is a gunshot. Another.

The girl closes her eyes. She sees Carlos, his insides glistening. The red mess of his death. Another shot. Another. Somewhere close by, someone is gasping for air.

The tall man is still standing. He is not hurt, but the soldier in charge – Rattlesnake Eyes – has his gun pointed at his head. He speaks in Spanish, and yells at the torocoyori soldier to translate.

'Next time,' says the torocoyori soldier, in Yoeme, 'I will not shoot in the air.'

The man's wife calls to him, 'Please,' and she says his name. She is weeping as she says his name. 'Please come back.'

The tall father hangs his head.

'I am sorry, brother,' says the torocoyori soldier, in a low voice. 'If you know what is good for you, you must get inside the pen.'

The tall father walks back along the side of the rope, and when he reaches his family, he climbs back into the pen. He goes and sits beside his wife, his two children. Rattlesnake Eyes comes over to the little family.

'Your money,' he says.

'It is my money,' says the man. But his tone is different. It is full of shame – the shame that he could not feed his wife or his children. The shame of his child being taken from him. The shame of this and the terrible shame of what he knows now is to come.

'Your money,' says Rattlesnake Eyes calmly.

The wife gives the man the money, and he hands it to Rattlesnake Eyes, who puts it in his jacket.

All of his money.

How long did it take him to save that money? How many days of work?

Everyone casts their eyes away from the family as though they cannot bear to see.

Only the handsome man at the taco stall has not taken his eyes away.

He finishes his food. He hands the wrapper to the woman, wipes his hands on a cloth and walks back along the square. He walks close, very close by the girl and Maria-Luisa and the tall father and his family, and all the time he is looking, looking, then he turns and crosses the road, and stands before the low red house, his eyes casting about as though he is waiting for something. He looks up and down the street. Then she sees him smile – someone is coming towards him. A little girl – she is five perhaps, or six, walking hand in hand with a woman and the woman is dressed more finely than anyone the girl has ever seen: she looks as though she has robbed several forests of their birds – the feathers she wears stick right up from her hat. Both the girl and the woman are wearing dresses that sweep the floor and come right up to their necks. They look like strange stiff creatures – in these dresses and feathers – neither humans nor birds but something in between. The little girl's hair is curled like her mother's in tight ringlets, which bounce when she walks. When the girl reaches the handsome man, she calls out in delight, and the handsome man lifts her high in the air. He lifts her so high her legs kick and the girl laughs: a tinkling, high-pitched sound.

The girl knows the way her body must feel, so free up there, her stomach swooping, and held, too, by her father's arms. She watches as the girl puts her hands on her father's face. The smoothness of his cheek. His thick, bristling moustache.

The father puts her back down and her mother fusses around her, making her dress straight again, tidying her hair. Her shoes are so shiny they look as though they have never been worn. Now the girl puts her hand in her father's and they cross the road. As they get close to where the prisoners sit, the man stops abruptly. He seems to consider, then he beckons over the torocoyori soldier, says something to him in Spanish. The man's wife pulls at his arm, but he brushes her off. Her eyes dart between the prisoners on the ground, the darkening clouds above. The girl can feel the mother's heart, flutter, flutter. She is frightened of them all. But the father is not afraid.

The handsome man starts to speak to his daughter, but he uses his hands, as though to encompass the girl, and Maria-Luisa, and the tall father and his family and all the people around – and the ringlet girl, listening, stares back at them with her big brown eyes. When he has finished, he gestures to the torocoyori soldier to translate his words.

'These Indians,' says the torocoyori soldier, 'are being deported.' He draws the word out – de-por-ted. 'They are going to work in the plantations. They are going to become useful.'

The handsome young man speaks again; he lifts his voice higher.

The soldier translates. 'The Indian,' he says, 'sits in the way of progress. He is lazy. He is feckless. He understands nothing of the modern world. He prefers to suffer hunger than to fatigue himself with agriculture. Therefore, he must be forced to do this by his superiors.'

Then the man smiles. He puts his hand on the top of his daughter's head. His voice changes, become lower, almost sweet.

'But,' the soldier translates, 'they help us in the end. These Indians. Once they have been put to use.

'Our world is built on their world.' He goes on. 'They work hard in the plantations, the henequen is sold and our republic grows strong. Our president grows strong. We eat because of them. We have our clothes because of them. We have our homes because of them. We should thank them. For giving their lives for the advancement of our nation. Order and progress. This is the motto of our president.'

The man says something to the soldier. The soldier speaks back, telling him the word for thank you in Yoeme. *Liohbwana*. As he speaks it, the girl sees his reluctance. He does not want to give this man this word. Does not want to hear this word in his mouth. But it is too late –

'Liohbwana,' says the father.

'Liohbwana,' says his daughter, then gives a smile which shows her white teeth. Her mother makes a sound like a tortured chicken. But the father just nods, as though at a job well done. 'Liohbwana,' he says again, and lifts his hat.

Then he takes his daughter's little hand gently in his big one. And they walk away, down the road. The little girl skipping, her ringlets bouncing.

The girl watches them. She can feel how safe that little girl feels. How protected she is with her father's big hand closed around her own small one.

Our world is built on their world.

She can see how they are to him, to his daughter. Only Indians. Only the brown dirt on which their world is built. She knows who she wants to hurt – she wants to hurt that girl. And her mother. And the handsome man. All of them. She wants to curse them. She wants a witch's olla to explode on the road before them, filling them full of nails and frogs and pins.

She feels fury travel through her, lighting up her bones.

How is it that some fathers can protect their daughters and some cannot?

How is it another father has his hands nailed to a board in a village square, and this girl has her father's hands upon her head?

How is it this girl is skipping down the street, and she and her sister are here, held behind this rope?

How is it some daughters can feel safe?

But then a thought comes to her – a thought that is huge and terrifying and satisfying all at once – how safe is that little girl's world, if it is built on something so fallen? All the fallen people and all the fallen things? The fallen world of the tall father? The boy they took away? Turkey Vulture Man and his family? Carlos, dying in the dawn?

How long will it be until their world falls too? The mother with all her feathers? The little girl with her tight curls?

What if there is a greater falling coming?

For how can worlds continue after this?

'Little Shadow,' says Maria-Luisa.

She turns to her sister.

'Oh,' she says, because her sister is back – back behind her eyes, and her eyes are crying.

'I am sorry,' says Maria-Luisa. 'I am so sorry. This is all my fault.'

'No.'

'Let me speak. You did not want to go. That night. If I had not made you come with me, you would be in the village still. You would be safe.'

They put their foreheads together. They find each other's hands.

'Not for long,' says the girl. And as she says it, she knows it is true. 'They would have come soon enough. They are coming for us all now.'

'Listen,' says Maria-Luisa, gripping her arms. 'You must run. As soon as you can. As soon as the soldiers are not looking, you run, you hear me? You run and you do not look back.'

'No –'

'You must.'

The girl looks down to where Maria-Luisa's nails are digging into her skin, so hard they are drawing blood. 'I cannot walk,' says Maria-Luisa, and her tears flow more now. 'But you can run.'

The girl looks up into Maria-Luisa's face, and she sees her sister's death there. Hovering beside her. She knows it has been there all along, this death of her sister's, getting closer and closer. She knows that somewhere she has understood this, but has not wanted to look.

'No.' She shakes her head to make it go away.

But she can see Maria-Luisa clearly now. She is dead, her sister is dead, fallen by the side of the road. Her death is coming soon. It is almost here.

'No,' she says to her sister's death. 'It will not be.'

But her sister's death, which has kept them company, quietly keeping pace beside them, is now just ahead, waiting. Her beautiful sister's death. Waiting to greet her, sitting, calmly, waiting to pull her into its lap.

'I am afraid,' says Maria-Luisa. And the girl feels her sister's fear, stealing across her, chilling her heart.

'No.' She smooths her sister's hair from her face. 'You are Maria-Luisa,' she says, 'and you are not afraid of anything. You are braver even than Lola Kukut.'

A drop of rain lands on the ground beside them.

The girl looks up and sees the sky is opening itself. The prisoners tip their faces to the sky and open their mouths.

They put their swollen tongues out to catch the rain. She puts her own tongue out. She can feel the dry cracked surface soften. Beside her, Maria-Luisa does the same.

And now the rain is hammering, bouncing on the ground, off the leaves of the trees in the square.

Water the colour of coffee is filling the holes in the middle of the street. People are running for shelter. Over in the corner of the square the man and wife with the taco stall are running around, pulling out the awnings so everything does not get wet.

The girl looks over to the soldiers who are guarding them, they have turned towards each other – huddled together, gathering beneath the furthest of the trees.

'You must go,' says Maria-Luisa. 'You must run.'

The girl looks at her.

'Go,' says Maria-Luisa.

The girl leans in, pressing her cheek against her sister's.

'Run,' says Maria-Luisa into her ear. 'Run. *Now*. Run away.'

And Maria-Luisa pushes her, gently. And the girl stands. And turns.

No one looks at her as she slips behind the tree. She is invisible. She is Little Shadow. She has been a little shadow all her life.

She pulls her shawl over her head and runs across the street. And she is just a girl, a young girl running through the streets of a little town, her heart slamming against her ribs, her feet hardly touching the ground. She does not look back, although she longs to – does not look back at the square and the soldiers and the prisoners and Maria-Luisa and the family and the praying woman and Turkey Vulture Man.

She is waiting for the shout. For the gunshots. But the gunshots do not come.

She runs faster. She runs past stalls: meat stalls and fruit stalls,

stalls with glittering fish, their eyes only half-dead. There are dogs. There are chickens scratching around in the water. There are other children, running and laughing in the wet. There is a stall stacked with fruit, its owner nowhere to be seen. As she passes the stall the girl reaches out and takes two ripe mangoes and slips them into her shawl. She darts down a side street, comes out on the corner of a street, ducks into a smaller alley-way, and stands, looking out. She fingers one of the mangoes beneath her shawl. She peels the skin off one side of the fruit and lifts it to her nose. Warmth and sunlight. Her mouth floods with saliva. She sinks her teeth into it. Feels the flesh give way. Bites right down to the stone, lets the juice flow onto her cheeks and her chin. She closes her eyes. And then she eats that fruit – sucks the stone so clean there is nothing of the fibrous flesh left.

The rain drums on the ground, the water scooshes and whooshes down the middle and the edges of the street; it takes small stones with it, faster and faster it goes.

She thinks of the girl with the ringlets. The way her hair will grow damp. Her curls will droop. The way her mother will fuss in her high thin voice, and her father will protect her. Will gather her up so she doesn't get wet. How safe the girl will feel, where the rain does not touch her, but how her safety is a thin, brittle thing.

She wonders if it is raining at home, and if it is, how the river is swelling, swelling and flooding the fields, the fields on the north side and the fields of the men from America on the south side. Flooding into the arroyos and ditches – the ditches dug by hand and the ditches dug by the machines. How the rain will be filling the waterholes in the mountains where the men wait, crouched and hungry for the time when they can come down again. She thinks of the river, of the fire, of the smell in her grandmother's hut.

And she knows something, there in the rain – she will return. She will return home. For a moment, the knowledge of this – of her survival – courses through her like the river in flood, and makes her giddy.

She knows that even if she returns to that terrible pen, if she walks over those mountains and travels to those plantations, she will survive. She will see the desert again. She will see the mountains again; see her grandmother's face. The mesquite tree in the yard. Touch her father's hands. She does not know how she knows this, but she does. She can see a long way, a long, long way now – the rain is washing her eyes clean.

She knows that she will carry this story in her, to a high safe place. It is light. It weighs nothing at all. And when the waters have receded she will bring it out – stretch it like hide before the fire, dry its bones in warmth and heat. And when it is ready to be told, it will find its way onto her tongue.

And through this story – the future will listen, will find its way.

And she feels her choice, but it is not a choice, not really – not at all.

She turns. Away from the food stalls and the chickens and the other children and the dogs, away from all the complicated, tangled things that life is made of, here on this side of the rope.

She runs back the way she came, her feet splashing through the water. The soldiers are still looking the other way.

Little Shadow. She is glad of her name. She knows it suits her. She slips back under the rope, heavier now from the heavy rain, and slides back against the tree. She has been gone for hardly any time at all, for the time it takes the world to fall and to rise again. She puts her shawl above their heads so it hides them from the sight of the soldiers.

'No,' she says to Maria-Luisa. 'I cannot run.'

She leans in and places her cheek to her sister's.

Her sister does not speak. She is breathing fast, so fast, as though she cannot get enough of this bright life of hers, as though it were she who was running just now, she who was free.

The mango is there between them, heavy in the well of her skirts.

'For you,' she says to her sister.

After a moment, Maria-Luisa reaches for the fruit.

She lifts it. And she smells it. And she smiles.

The Singer
1969

The kid is setting the pace, with that off-centre lope, the singer is a step or two behind. The path they are on bends to the left and then turns right, following the beach.

He tries to keep up, figure out the stakes. Hard to say if the kid is dangerous or not. Most likely not, but you can never tell. He looks like kids he knew ten years ago, down in Florida – little skinny hips, DA tapering into the collar of his clean white T-shirt. His jeans are tight, and from the look of his back pockets there does not seem to be a weapon anywhere on him. But the kid has collateral. He knows who he is, knows he is hiding. Even the sweetest kid might wonder if he could turn this situation to his advantage. And the kid is jumpy. He can feel it coming off him in waves. The pace he is setting, for a start.

Hey – he calls to the kid. What's the hurry?

The kid half turns.

The jejenes, he says. Soon they will start biting. They are bad. He turns back, carries on.

They are walking on a sandy track, the ocean ahead. Behind them, beside them, the massy jungle. He can feel its closeness – a low green roaring at the edge of thought. A weakness in his fingertips. Down his arm. Five minutes ago he had a plan, and now here he is, following in this kid's wake. Towards – what?

He has the sudden vision of a car, barrelling towards them, two men in the front, ready to pistol-whip him into unconsciousness, tie him up, bundle him into the trunk. For a moment he cannot breathe.

He stops dead, bends double. A dull liver-ache under his ribs. He spits between his bare feet onto the sand, then straightens up. He can just see the roof of the hotel. It's not far. Five minutes away, down the track. He needs to turn around and go back to the hotel. If he goes back there he can order a cab. Get to the airport. Get on a plane. Get the fuck out before it's too late. He touches his back pocket. Feels the contours of the little blade.

The kid looks around, impatient. Sharp.

Why have you stopped?

He wiggles his toes on the sand. Makes a clown face. I need my boots, man, if we're going into town.

The kid looks down then back up at him. Moves from foot to foot.

The singer gestures back the way they came with a hooked thumb.

I'm gonna go to my room and get my boots.

No!

He makes a face. Whaddya mean – *no*?

I mean no. You can't go back there.

Why not?

They will find out who you are.

How?

I will tell them.

You serious?

Hard to gauge how serious he is. He looks desperate, his face on the verge of something – but what?

He counts – one thousand, two thousand, three thousand.

You threatening me? He gives a slow grin.

Listen, says the kid. You want to see the white rock, yes? I can take you there. I can take you everywhere. You can write a song about me. You make me famous too, right?

He laughs. Sure, he says. Keeping it light. But his heart is thudding, the blood making him dizzy. He needs to think, think. Sure I will.

He takes out a cigarette from his packet, offers one to the kid, who shakes his head as the singer lights up.

How old are you?

Twenty.

Where you from?

Mexico.

Sure, but where?

Sinaloa, he says. His voice is dull.

Where's that?

The kid points up the beach. Next state, he says. But a long way.

How come you're here?

A flicker in the kid's eyes. No work at home.

Family?

The kid shrugs. He looks very young. The singer imagines a mother, a little house somewhere. A shithole town.

He smokes. The kid does that foot-to-foot dance. A plan starts to rise – befriend the kid. Go with him into town. Get him wasted. Blackout drunk. Then come back here – pack his things. Leave. Move on. Be a thousand miles away before the kid comes to. It's crude, but he knows he can do it. Blackout drunk he can do.

He takes a slug from the mescal then hands it to the kid.

Here, he says. Drink up.

The kid looks at it, back up at him, shakes his head.

C'monnnn, he says. We're heading into town, right?

The kid nods.

We going to have a good time tonight or what?

There's a good three inches still in the bottom of the bottle.

He waggles it in front of the face of the kid, who reaches in, takes it, lifts, drinks. Coughs. Grimaces, hands it back.

He laughs, grasps him at the top of his arm. Good stuff, huh?

The kid's eyes keep sliding away, up the track. Is he waiting for something? Someone? But there is nothing there. Just empty track. Just the ocean and the beach and the jungle and a few thatched huts in the far distance. The blue roar of the ocean. The heat of the afternoon.

Hey, he says. We going to have a good time, right?

The kid nods. He seems to come back to himself. Right, he says.

That's right! And you know the best places, right?

The kid grins. Yeah, he says.

Bars! Music! Girls!

Yeah, the kid says. I do.

Well there we go, buddy. He reaches out and slaps him on the arm. Oh, hey. Here, I got these for you. He fingers the mescaline necklace. I took mine already.

The kid stares.

You eat them, he says, waggling the beads. They're good. He lifts the necklace off. You bite them. Like this. He bites another ball between his back teeth, then another, crunches them: sand and cactus and spit.

He holds it out to the kid who takes it, holds it at arm's length.

C'mon.

The kid places one ball between his back teeth. Bites, makes a face. They are not good, he says.

They are fucking great, I'm telling you. It's not about the taste. You'll see. C'mon. And another. Take a big one. Big guy like you.

The kid takes two more.

Now wash them down. He hands him back the mescal.

The kid lifts the bottle. Puta madre, he says, wiping his mouth.

Yeah. He laughs, swigging the rest down. Puta fucking *madre* is right.

The kid looks as though he's going to be sick. This might be easier than he thought.

He lights another cigarette, offers one to the kid, which he takes. C'mon then – he claps him on the back – let's do it. Let's go!

And just like that, it has shifted – the balance of power. He feels it settle with him.

They start to walk again. A little less quickly now. He is the pacesetter. There is nothing in either direction: no houses, no people, just scrub, sand and ocean.

They really did build it at the end of the world, huh?

What?

The hotel. Someone told me they built it at the end of the world.

You like it? The hotel? says the kid.

Sure I do. You?

The kid shrugs. Not really. There is a story about the hotel. You want to hear it?

Sure.

They say it is cursed. That it is built on cursed land.

He can see that this might be so. Something desolate here in these low dunes. No houses, no people, no witnesses. It could still happen easily – the car that comes from nowhere. The gun to the head.

He keeps his pace steady, feels the heat of the sand beneath his feet.

The President came to open it, the kid is saying – and the mosquitoes and the jejenes chased him away. The kid slaps his arm. And there are sounds, he says. At night.

What sort of sounds?

He shrugs.

One morning I came in to work and the night porter looked scared. He said he heard noises. Scratching. Crying. And when he went to check he couldn't find them. Then they came again. This happened all night. He was very scared in the morning. The next day he left the job. He said it was haunted.

Cool.

The kid looks at him. You believe in ghosts?

Sure I do.

You ever seen one?

Sure I have.

What ghosts have you seen?

How long you got?

They are walking easily now. A pace he likes. If the kid is a jaguar he is a bear. A big fucking grizzly bear.

The kid looks at him sideways.

Once, the singer says, walking down the street in Venice Beach, I saw a satyr.

A satyr?

You ever seen one of those?

What is a satyr?

A goat man. The singer grins. A little fucking goat man. Just weaving in and out of the parked cars. Waving. Following me for five blocks or so.

The kid wrinkles his nose. That is not a ghost.

No. Sure. Well. A spirit then. A little devil. Running behind and a little to the right.

Were you scared?

No. I was happy. I was fucking thrilled.

You like the devil?

Sure I do. You?

The kid shakes his head. He crosses himself, his eyes wide. He looks younger and younger all the time. Sixteen? Seventeen?

Ah, I love him. I love that little goaty fuck.

To the right, the jungle – the cicadas' sawtooth orchestra – ahead, the ocean, the sun.

They walk for a hundred yards or so, until low thatched buildings appear on the edge of the beach. Signs for beer. He stops outside the first cabana.

I'm going to get a drink, you want one?

The kid is jumpy again, doing his need-to-pee dance.

You got somewhere you need to be, kid? Go ahead, I'll catch you up.

No! The kid looks panicked. No. No, we go together.

Sure thing.

He has this thing he does, with his voice – he can make it low and it calms animals. He does it now. Sure thing, kid, he says.

The interior of the thatch is dank and dark; it smells of old fish and damp wood. A skinny teenage girl sits on a stool staring into space. She is wearing a T-shirt that says *Mexico '68*. The Olympic rings. The lettering jumps and shimmers in the light of the bare bulb. An older woman sits in a chair beside her with a baby on her knee. Behind them, a TV blares. Images of astronauts on the flickering screen. A voiceover chattering excitedly in Spanish.

Dos cervezas? says the kid, taking the lead, throwing a few coins onto the wooden counter. Para llevar. He slaps his neck.

The skinny girl slides off the stool and goes over to the

229

fridge to fetch two bottles of beer. The mosquitoes huddle, stack themselves in formation in the centre of the hut. The singer looks down at his arm. Sees two of them feasting. Slaps them. Watches the blood smear across his skin.

Now he is here, in this hut, he understands he is really high, really very fucking high indeed. He looks up, at the screen, they are showing the astronauts training; turning and turning on those gravity things – those Leonardo things. He watches them, mesmerized, these bland, blond heroes in their shiny suits, turning and turning in the widening gyre. How far out in space until you can no longer hear the falconer?

And then there is a shot of the rocket. Apollo 11.

Apollo – Sun God. Messenger.

Apollo was never his man. Too clean-cut. Too squeaky. Too repressed.

The rocket looks rickety, improbable, standing there, high above the Florida coast. He knows that coast – was born there, in Melbourne, just over twenty miles across the bay from Cape Kennedy.

It's all a fucking swamp.

Bad Moon Rising.

It was playing in all the bars in LA when he left – all the bars in Mexico City.

Trouble on the way.

¿Puedes abrirlas?

The skinny girl opens them, hands them one each.

The singer smiles at the girl as he grasps the cool small miracle of his beer, then steps through to the other side of the cabana, out onto the beach, where the sun is beginning to set, high feathered clouds lit from below, vermilion bleeding into blue. Little perfect breakers frilling on the shore.

He looks down the beach, finds the white rock, closer now.

Two fishermen are sitting nearby, repairing their nets, their wooden boats pulled out of the water beside them. He sits on the warm sand, lights a cigarette, watching. One is cleaning the catch, scales flicking silver from his knife. The mescal is doing its work now, and here comes the beer, steadying the peyote and everything is alive, breathing together in a great show of animus, and he can feel it, the way that the jungle stretches, all the knowing that it holds. Everything just writhing and fucking and licking and sucking itself into existence, but held here – held in place by the purity of this golden sand, this ocean, this sky. Apollo and Dionysus. Balance.

And these men – stitching their nets, their nets strung out like this, the smoke from the charcoal cooking the fish they caught, as they stitch the universe together here on this perfect stretch of sand. The men are gentle, methodical, and every so often they laugh.

He breathes out.

He could be a fisherman. Get himself a boat. Fish and write and live off the sea.

Hey!

He turns to see the kid standing just behind him. Jumpy. Nervous.

For a second he had forgotten he existed.

We have to go.

Sit down, wouldya? Take a minute.

No, says the kid, moving from foot to foot. No. You cannot sit here.

Why not?

Jejenes. They will bite you.

Ah fuck. The jejenes. Always the fucking jejenes with you. He stretches his legs out on the sand. Wriggles his bare feet. I got my jeans on.

The kid squats down on his haunches beside him.

We have to go, says the kid.

No, he says.

And it's there again – the fear. The kid has a plan, that's for sure. To deliver him up to – what? To whom?

Hey, he says. Just look at that. He gestures with his arms: the ocean the sky the jungle the fishermen. This is the best place in the whole fucking world. You gotta let it in, man. Breathe it in.

He sees the kid reach to touch his back pocket. Checking the piece of paper is still there. He does not have to touch his own pocket to feel the outline of the knife.

He pats the sand beside him. The kid sits gingerly down. He feels his blood quicken. The kid has no weapon. It would be easy enough now, to grab him, twist him into the sand. Hold the obsidian blade to his neck. Take the piece of paper. Eat it. Or throw it into the sea.

But it is too peaceful here. Too beautiful. Everything is going to be okay. The kid is just a kid after all.

You got any pot? he says.

Pot?

Marijuana?

Oh, says the kid. Mota. No.

Can you get some? In town?

I can get everything in town. The kid jumps up again. Let's go. Now.

You're in a hurry, he says. Why are you in such a hurry? Be cool, man. You feel anything yet?

The kid shakes his head.

Check out that sunset. You see that? You see those colours?

The kid squints.

You ever tripped before?

The kid shakes his head.

232

You scared?

No.

But he is, he can tell.

He stares out to sea.

Just be careful – he says, low and sweet. Those ghosts. The devil. All the things you're scared of. They might come and find you . . . when you get really high. He turns back – Boo! he says and the kid jumps.

Only kidding, he says.

Then he gets to his feet and puts out his hand for the kid.

We go back this way – the kid points to the track.

No. He shakes his head. We walk on the beach.

No unmarked car or truck can come and get him here. The sand is thick and wet and hard to walk on.

The kids frowns then shrugs. Okay.

They pass the fishermen, their upturned skiffs, their nets, and he raises a hand. They smile, show broken teeth, salute him right back.

They walk down to the place where the sand is wetter, hard-packed. He leans down and rolls up his jeans, lets the waves run over his toes. The kid stays a little higher, keeping his clothes dry.

You should try this, he says. It's beautiful.

The pelicans are back, skimming over the waves. Every so often, out in the water, a fish jumps.

To their right, the jungle is edged by shacks along the shore, the odd table on the sand, more fishermen. The white rock coming closer all the time, until they reach a small estuary where they cannot walk further on the beach, and so they turn, heading up a wide street. And they are heading away from the shore now, and there are stores, a few little grocery stores with mangoes and papaya out front. They pass a tortilleria, the smell of the warm dough on the evening air; they turn again, and there are houses now: goats and chickens and dogs in the yards. More fishermen walking home, carrying their catches in filthy plastic buckets, the smell of cooking in the air, kids playing ball in the street. Flickering streetlamps slung up with the wiring all hanging in clumps above. A beautiful woman stands leaning on a dark porch, staring out into the coming night.

The kid is jumpier than ever, swinging his head from left to right. He must be feeling it now.

Here. He passes the mescal back. We gotta finish this, kid.

The kid drinks some more, hands it back, and the singer drains it, puts the bottle on a nearby wall.

The houses are gone now and there is water again to their left – a small placid inlet and what looks like an island on the other side. A lighthouse at the top of a hill. The evening star above it. By a small wooden dock, several boats bump gently together.

The singer stops. What's that? He points to the island.

The Isla del Rey.

The Island of the King?

Yes.

Which king?

The kid shrugs.

They stand there, staring out, feeling the cool air rising from the water.

He feels the kid tense beside him.

Wait – hisses the kid, putting his arm out.

The kid pulls them back to the shadows as a small group appears on the dock: several men, two women, one with a baby in her arms. Behind them, another two men. They look like no one the singer has ever seen. Their trousers are short, stopping just short of the ankles, heavily embroidered. There are animals there, and in the dusk-light the animals seem to move: deer, leaping across the hems. The women wear scarves covering their heads, skirts to the ground. Last is an old man. He wears an elaborate hat, the kind a Chinese peasant might wear, but adorned with small feathers and with pom-poms. It should be ridiculous, but it is far from ridiculous. The people stand in a line, waiting. And the old man takes something from his bag, a stick with feathers. He moves along the line, brushing the men, the women, the child, sucking along the feathers, singing again.

That song. It's doing something to him too – he can't stop twitching, his body moving like a puppet on a string.

The kid turns – Stay still, he hisses.

The singer shakes his head. I can't.

The singer moves from the shadows, starts to move towards the old man, he wants to bathe in his song, but the kid grips his arm. *No*, he hisses. His eyes are only pupil. Do not go to them.

The old man in the hat stops singing, he looks up, stares straight at where they stand. The old man holds his eyes. The singer stares straight back.

Fuck, he breathes. Holy fuck.

Just then, a man emerges from one of the boats tethered on the water, beckons the people towards him, and they move quietly over the wooden planks of the dock. One of the young men goes first, jumping down into the boat and then helping the others down, one by one, until they are all in. And then the boat sets off, the oars hardly making a sound as the group disappears from sight, into the gathering dusk.

His body stops twitching.

Fuck, he says. *What the fuck was that?*

Indians. Brujos. Paganos. Witches. Bad.

Where are they going?

To give offerings. Sacrifices. On the island. By the rock.

The white rock?

Yes.

Let's go, he says, moving towards the dock.

No! The kid flails for his arm. *No.* Do not go there. They kill animals.

He laughs. We all kill fucking animals, kid.

They make dark magic. Curses. Spells.

Huh.

The rock is haunted. A bad place.

Aw, really? Everywhere is haunted, according to you.

No. No. The kid looks like he is about to cry. I will shout. I will shout who you are. Right now. People will come. They will see it is you. You will not escape.

Okay, he says softly. Okay. Jesus. Calm the fuck down.

He'll go find the Indians later. From the look of him, the kid'll be a wreck soon enough.

Come, says the kid. We go into town. We find a bar. Yes?

Sure, he says. Softly. Sure thing, kid. You lead.

They walk on, down a small street, to where it opens up, cobblestones, colonial buildings. On one side, a building with arches in front of it, on the other a red, hacienda-like hotel, a chapel, a swimming pool.

Hey, says the singer, you think that guy put a spell on us? The Indian? With the hat?

The kid turns to him.

He looked at us pretty strange, didn't he?

They walk a little further.

Hey, he says. You feeling okay, kid? You look a little weird.

I look weird?

Yeah.

They pass a store with a mirror in front, racks of clothes

236

inside. Clothes. Good. Clothes are good. This shirt. He needs to change this shirt.

Here, he stops before the mirror. Looks at himself. His pupils are huge. Better check yourself out, kid. You sure do look a little strange.

The kid moves slowly towards the mirror, faces his reflection – he stares at himself, touches his cheeks, his nose. His eyes have the wide panic of a cornered animal.

The singer leaves him with his own image, heads into the dark interior of the store. Behind the counter a large woman in a housedress sits, smoking, watching. A fan stirs the heavy air.

Buenos noches, señora.

The woman nods in response.

He riffles through the shirts on the racks and picks out a heavy white cotton one, one of those Mexican ones with the pockets in front, a small ribbon of embroidery on each, a small G for Grande written on the label in the collar. He takes it up to the counter.

Hey, he says to the woman. You got anything for spells? I think the kid is ill. Muy malo.

He jerks his head over to where the kid stands, still caught in his reflection, still with the rictus face of fear.

Un brujo. Es muy malo.

The woman frowns. No, she says.

Shame.

Diez dólares, says the woman. Para la camisa.

Diez dollars? Jeez.

He fishes his money out of his pocket. Three hundred-dollar bills. All he has left of the five hundred they gave him in Mexico City. He slaps one on the table. The woman looks at the bill, back up to his face, shakes her head.

No tengo cambio.

The kid looks up then, the trance broken, moves a little unsteadily over to the counter.

I will pay, he says, peeling a ten-dollar bill from the roll in his pocket.

The kid takes the hundred-dollar bill, hands it back to the singer. You should be careful, he says. With this.

The singer unbuttons his shirt, which could probably walk back to LA on its own by now, and the smell of overcooked meat rises from the fabric. Un regalo, he says. A present for you. He gives it to the woman, who takes it as though she has been passed a hand grenade, then turns and throws it into a trash can at her feet.

You see that? he says to the kid, buttoning the new shirt up. Straight in the trash. They go crazy for my shirts at home, he says to the woman. Loco. Fucking lo-*co*. He winds his finger around his temple.

Beside him the kid starts to laugh – small at first, then a little louder.

The stinkier the better, he says. They rub their little noses in them.

Now the kid is laughing harder, he he he he he. The cactus has finally got to him.

Fucking loco! the singer says again. And now he is laughing too – his whole body shaking, and the two of them are bent double, convulsing, almost retching with the force of it.

Callate, hisses the woman. Leave my store.

They straighten up, make it out onto the street before another wave engulfs them, and they are howling, holding each other up. When the tide of laughter has subsided, he feels rinsed. Empty.

A present! the kid splutters. You gave her a present! Your stinking shirt.

Yeah!

That pinche shirt really fucking stank.

Yeah, he says, that pinche fucking shirt huh?

He moves a little away from the kid, lights up a cigarette, eyes him.

If it weren't for that pinche fucking shirt I wouldn't be stuck here with you.

The kid's face contracts. What?

If. It. Weren't. For. That. Pinche. Fucking. Shirt. He moves in, jabs the kid in the chest with his finger. I. Wouldn't. Be. Stuck. Here. With. *You*.

The kid is a head shorter than him.

He remembers this, taunting his little brother – he would pin him down, hoick up a spitball, let it teeter in his face, almost fall, suck it back just at the right moment. One more jab. Harder this time. The kid topples, almost falls. *Cabrón*, he says, steadying himself.

Sure. He shrugs. Whatever. Just kidding around.

I think I am drunk, says the kid.

No. No. You're not drunk. You're not nearly fucking drunk enough. C'mon. Let's get another bottle.

Night has fallen – the way it does in towns like this, suddenly, absolutely. The little town is getting its groove on – there are young women in pretty off-the-shoulder tops and too much perfume and too much lipstick. Young men standing on street corners watching them, hungrily. A hustly end-of-the-line glamour to it all. Restaurants, their tables open to the street.

Hey – he puts his arm around the kid's shoulders. I like this place. This is a cool little town. You know what? he says. I'm glad I met you, kid. I think we're going to have a good night. He squeezes him. Up close he can smell the kid's scent – hair wax and cheap cologne and poverty. Then he lets him go. Just a little too much force. Just to show him who's on top. The kid stumbles, looks up at him. The ground beneath his feet is a little less sure. He can feel it. He doesn't trust him any more. Good.

Motorbikes, scooters, taxis, bikes. Tail lights and traces. Murals advertising beer, painted onto walls. Like someone turned up the volume on the colour and the sex and the sound. The trip is strong, getting stronger. Just about rideable, but there are things that could help.

Hey – you got any speed? Benzedrine? Dexedrine?

Speed would straighten this whole situation out.

Speed? The kid nods. The idea seems to have an invigorating effect. He stands straighter. On the plaza, he says. We can get some. We are nearly there.

The kid leads the way to a pharmacy on the corner, its white light beaming out into the night. A small bench before it. The singer sinks down onto the bench. You go, he says, waving his hand. Reds. Blues. Whatever.

Okay. You stay here. Don't move.

The kid goes inside. He keeps throwing looks over his shoulder, making sure the singer is still in place. He knows he could run, but the kid would likely catch him. And besides. This will be easy. The kid is cracking already. He might as well have some fun with him before the night is done. And when was the last time he was out incognito in a town like this? Not for years.

Opposite him is a liquor store, its window stacked high.

He hauls himself up, goes inside, takes a couple of beers from the fridge. Asks for a bottle of mescal. Another pack of cigarettes. Takes out a hundred-dollar bill. He slaps the note on the counter. The guy serving looks up at him in disbelief.

Gimme a bottle of Johnnie Walker too, he says. And let's call it quits.

Outside, the kid is standing on the sidewalk, head whipping right to left, panic on his face. The singer strolls over to him. You get 'em?

The kid shows him the bottle. Twenty pesos, he says.

Duuuude. You shoulda got two.

They walk up a little ramp into the plaza. It's a pretty square – trees and benches and lights strung up in the trees and the harsh chatter of evening birds and families doing what families do. He sits on a wrought-iron bench, lights a cigarette, opens the mescal, leans his head back and pours it down his throat. He passes the bottle to the kid, who drinks.

Come on then, he says. Open it up.

The kid screws open the jar, shakes a few pills onto his hand. How many? he says to the singer.

You want a straightener, or a rocket ship?

A straightener.

Seriously? You don't want to go to the moon?

I see the bad moon a-rising.

I see trouble on the way.

Take five, he says.

The kid shakes three out, chases them with the mescal.

Aw, c'mon, you're no fun. Take a couple more. Here. He takes the bottle of pills, shakes five onto his palm, throws them back and washes them down with his beer.

In the middle of the plaza is a bandstand with a band playing, popcorn hawkers and sweetcorn hawkers and ice-cream hawkers and jewellery hawkers. The whole Mexican street party carny roadshow.

I fucking love this country, he says. You got it all.

He leans over, pours a glug of mescal onto the hard-packed soil beneath the trees behind them. Here's to your land. La tierra. La libertad.

He takes his fingers now and rakes them through the dirt beside him, wipes a strip of it across his nose.

What is that? says the kid. Why have you done that?

I'm Tezcatlipoca, he says, low and sweet. You know him?

The kid shakes his head. Rub it off, he says.

Why?

You look strange.

He laughs. I am strange, kid.

Then he puts his head back and lets out a howl to the evening sky.

He opens his eyes again. Rainbow traces. Fuck, he says.

What? says the kid.

I'm really fucking high.

Opposite is a small family group – two women weaving, their looms tied to the trunk of a tree. Children play around their feet. A patch of cloth laid on the ground with crafts on it. He goes over, kneels before the women. A little boy looks up – eyes round. Hey. He pulls a face. The boy is one, or two. He has a cloth tied around his middle. The women look shyly to the singer and then away. Alongside the blouses and the earrings they are selling are small woven crosses. Bright colours.

What is this? he asks, reaching for a cross made from four diamonds, woven from blue and green thread.

Ojo de Dios, the woman says.

The eye of God?

The woman nods. Azul. Para el mar. Haramara.

For the ocean?

Sí. One dollar, says the woman.

He lifts it up to his face. In the centre of the diamonds the thread is black. He stares into the blackness.

He will buy it for her. For Eva. To prove he was here. To prove that he met God.

242

I'll give you a hundred, he says, and reaches into his pocket for the note.

The woman looks down at it, up at him. Her companion says something high and clattering, like a frightened bird. Quickly she reaches out her hand, takes the note. Pockets it. Starts to pack up her stall, her loom. In a few seconds it has all gone. The women, the children, their things. Disappeared into the busy square.

He turns, sees the kid is still sitting on the bench. He looks as though he has retreated somewhere very small and very dark inside himself.

Hey, he says. See this?

The kid looks up.

I got the eye of fucking God.

He holds it up to the kid. Look at that, he says. Look at that eye. It's watching you. Hey, you high? He elbows the kid. You high yet?

The kid looks disturbed. You should wipe that off your face, he says, pointing to the dirt.

No way! Hey, I need a drink. You going to take me to this bar or what? Hey? Kid? You okay?

The kid shakes his head.

They'll make you feel better – the blues. I promise. All that weird shit you're thinking right now, all that scary stuff in your head, will just – he clicks his fingers – disappear. C'mon kid, we're just getting started.

He lifts up the Ojo de Dios. See, he says. God is watching us. Better give him a good time. He turns the little woven cross round and round, round and round. The kid watches, hypnotized, seasick.

Then he stops, pockets the cross in his shirt.

Come on then, he says, leaning in and hauling the kid to his feet. Lead the way, dude.

The kid finds his feet, leads them off the plaza to an ill-lit side street: skinny dogs and pools of standing water. The bar is little more than a long, thin room, spilling blue light onto the street. In the front there are battered plastic tables, cantina-style; over to one side a small stage for the band. It's busy, for early evening, most of the tables populated.

They head over to the wooden bar – it is shaped like a dug-out canoe.

A young woman stands behind it, wearing jeans and an embroidered shirt of the kind you can pick up in the thrift stores along Sunset, except on her it looks different. Better. Real. The flowers are sending off chain reactions in his brain – he stares at the stitches, sees the needle that moved in and out of the cloth to make those flowers, the colour of the thread, the love that is in it – what texture of love would make such a beautiful thing? It is perfect. This girl is perfect. He has never seen anything more beautiful in his life.

You speak English?

Yes.

Oh, wow. Great, that's great.

What can I get you?

I got mescal, he says goofily, holding the bottle up.

Good for you. You want something to go with that? I can make it into a cocktail if you like.

Wow. Sure. Wow.

Her English is fluent. He passes the bottle over, watches as she squeezes oranges into a little ceramic bowl. Her thin fingers, the way she works so gently, so carefully. And the bowl too – the brown glaze – all of it conjuring something so perfect that there are no words for it, not really, only love – the world made up from these tiny acts of love: Cointreau, tequila, oranges, mescal.

We're tripping, he says, grabbing the kid and pulling him close. We're really high!

Nice, she says.

He watches as she puts the finishing touches to the margarita – and he knows this is why he could never be faithful to one woman, when there are women like this in the world. She pushes the two margaritas over the bar to them. He hands one to the kid, they cheers, he downs his in one, licks the salt from the rim, wipes his moustache with the back of his hand.

Jesus fucking Christ, he says. I love you! he calls to the woman, and he means it. She laughs.

The crocodiles, the kid is saying. Have you seen the crocodiles?

What's that?

Over there. The kid points, but there are people in the way and he cannot see.

What the –?

Would you like camarones? the beautiful woman is saying. To feed the crocodiles?

Mother*fucker*, he says. Yes please.

The woman is laughing again, bending and scooping a bowl-ful of dried shrimp from a bucket at her feet. The kid takes it, throws over a few pesos and they weave their way through several plastic tables to where there is a pit with a low picket fence around it, and in the pit are two crocodiles. They are each about six feet long.

Holy fuck.

They stand, the pair of them, for a long moment, staring in at the creatures, who are as still as though they are made from plaster.

He once saw an alligator kill a wild pig – it was in Florida, when he was at college; it was late at night and he was driving home from a party, and they stopped the car for a piss and in the moonlight he saw and heard it – the rolling and the rolling of the kill, the squeals and grunts and then the silence and the sounds of the swamp returning.

What do you think they think? he says. You think they look at us and see prey?

The kid bends to the bucket of shrimp and throws a handful in. The crocodiles turn towards him – twisting and snapping.

Jesus fucking Christ.

The kid stumbles a little and the singer reaches out to steady him. Sees how little it would take to unbalance him – the thrashing and the threshing and the blood and then the silence. The newspaper clipping being eaten along with his jeans.

He feels eyes on him – looks up. Sees through the cigarette smoke a table of drinkers. Gringos. Washed-up-looking, hunched over their beers. Staring his way.

C'mon, he says to the kid, let's go and sit down.

A band is setting up the stage on the other side of the room: sax, drums, trumpet. A microphone stand.

They make their way to a table in the corner where he pours out whiskies for the kid and himself. Knocks back a healthy one. They are still looking his way, the gringos. He raises his glass to them, and they look away.

He can feel the fear lacing the edge of things. The fizz in his blood. His jaw tensing – the motor of the speed. The pills and the peyote and the mescal and the beer and the margarita and the whisky now. He lights a cigarette and takes the smoke deep into his lungs, letting it out in a steady stream.

The kid's foot is tapping out a rhythm on the floor.

You feeling any better?

Yeah, says the kid.

See? Told you so. Blues. Works every time.

He pours another round.

The tables are full now – and there's a crowd at the bar. Over on the stage the musicians are warming up – the first set of the evening. He remembers that feeling: the London Fog, the Whisky, the clubs on the Strip. The first set, the bar would be empty. The first set the stakes were low. There were times, in the years before they were famous, when they played their best-ever sets to a room with only the owner and a teenage girl in the back, then you'd cross the road to the Beanery, have a couple of beers and a burger, maybe some whisky, maybe some LSD, before going back out to play again. By then the bar would be full – the dancers in their cages – ready to sway. And they would play.

Play.

The pure thing – to play – open-ended. No record contracts, no money-men, no producers asking you to go again go again a-fucking*gaingaingain* – no rules, just the rolling loop of it, like the best sex – the teasing, the teasing, the teasing, for hours, until, when the climax comes it's bigger and weirder and more soul-blowing than anything you could ever have imagined. The best thing about those nights was no one knew what the fuck to expect. *No rules.* You have rules and play becomes the Game. And the rules of the Game are rigged and you can never win. The band love the fucking Game though. They think they've won with their cars and their houses and their bank balances. They are wrong: play is where life is. The Game is death.

The trumpeter lifts his instrument and blasts out a note. The rest of the band come in – they are tight – the drummer high and tight on the snare – a sort of bossa nova rock – a cover of 'Satisfaction'.

You like them? The kid is grinning.

Sure I do. They're pretty fucking tight.

It's my uncle! he says. My uncle is the singer!

No way. He moves his chair so he can get a better view. The uncle is wearing a starched white shirt and flares.

Ahhh. Jesus, he says. *That's* why you wanted to get here so quick? To see your uncle play?

The kid nods – still grinning like it's Christmas morning.

You like them? The band?

Yeah, kid. I do.

He feels it all drop away. All the fear. The kid is a good kid after all. He never intended anything bad.

He looks at this kid, whose face looks carved in the low light. And he sees it now. He's a yellow-bronze god.

Hey, kid, he says. You're beautiful. You're the prince of fucking flowers.

The kid blushes, casts his eyes away.

He can see the girl working behind the bar – that blouse she's wearing, the flowers glowing in the low light.

I'm going to go get another beer, hombre, he says. You want one?

The kid shakes his head.

He's forgotten what speed can do for a man. The rainbow traces are gone, the seasickness is gone. He feels good. Better than good. He feels great. Sparks of golden light are shaking off the trumpeter's instrument as he pushes through the crowd over to the bar where the girl is serving someone else.

Hey, he says, leaning over the wood of the bar. What's your name?

Rosa, she says, over her shoulder.

Of course it is. You want to come with me, Rosa?

Where? She smiles, slow and sweet.

Anywhere. To Paris. To Huautla. Let's go see María Sabina. Let's go get healed.

He holds her gaze, and she smiles, but he can tell it's the sort of smile a beautiful woman gives to men she's serving on the other side of the bar fifty times a night. It's a smile without a hook in it. A smile with sides he slips back down from onto the ground, as she turns and serves someone else.

And then he hears it, a familiar riff – played on the trumpet, not the organ – his own song: the song that was number one for the whole summer of 1967, the song that made him and the band stars; the song that is probably still number one in Mexico now. And it sounds good, it sounds fucking great.

The crowd cheers. They start to sing along with the guy on the stage.

You like this one? he calls to Rosa.

Sure, she says. I love it.

He waits for her to join the dots. Wants her to recognize him. He wants to say – I wrote this! I wrote this motherfucking hit. It was number one for the whole summer of '67. Every time I turned on the radio it was being played. I heard it as I walked down the street, in every bar I went into, every club, every store. I jerked off to it. I fucked to it. You know how it feels to come to your song on the radio when your song is number one?

He wants to watch as she puts her hand to her mouth, stifles whatever noise wants to come out of there; he wants to know then whether she has a boyfriend or a husband or five hours left to go of her shift, he could suggest she comes with him and she would come – go wherever he wants, take a taxi back to the hotel, walk behind him up the concrete stairs to his room at the top, bend down and unbutton his jeans, knead his thighs with those slim fingers of hers, make him hard and put his dick in that beautiful mouth, take him into her slick heat.

She grins. And he grins and he can't help but watch the

crowd – and here it comes – a great rush of pure, unbounded joy – the pure hit of it. He wants to leap up and take the mike.

He's going to do it. He's going to take the mike and make this woman love him. Because there is only now now *now*. Because this might be his last night on this earth.

Just one more drink first.

Hey, he calls to Rosa. Can I get a beer?

Sure. She reaches below her, brings out a cold Pacífico.

I like your make-up, she says.

My what?

Your face.

Oh. He lifts his hands to his face. Feels the caked strip of dirt. He had forgotten all about it. Grins back at her. I'm Tezcatlipoca. You know him?

She shakes her head.

They're going to sacrifice me, in the morning. Cut out my heart with this. He takes out the knife. Puts it on the bar.

They both stare at it. He looks up at her, but she is not smiling. She looks troubled. As though with the blade's appearance they are in a different story now.

Hey. A heavy hand lands on his back.

He turns. Sees the gringo guys from the table on the other side of the room. Two of them. He squints to make sure. Definitely two. Although one of them has only one eye.

We were just talking. You sure do look like someone.

Oh yeah?

Yeah. Someone famous. The guy's grin reeks of shrimp and beer.

Oh, really? He makes his voice an almost-whisper, his accent bayou-thick. Ah get that ah lot. Wait . . . He reaches for his cigarettes. Either of you gentlemen got a light?

One-Eye flicks a Zippo. A singer, right?

The first drag steadies him a little.

He he he, naaaaw. He shakes his head. Ah'm just a regular guy on vacation. Jus' like you.

One-Eye's one eye narrows. I coulda sworn you're him.

There is a gun in a holster at the guy's waist. A Colt .45.

He can shoot a Colt. Those long afternoons out on the ranch up on Topanga, they'd smoke jimson weed and let rip at tin cans and stray dogs. Trying to feel real.

Oh him? Ah ain't *him*. He laughs, a high southern laugh. *He he he he.* Ah'm me! Now why don't you gentlemen just go and enjoy yourselves?

He touches One-Eye on the arm. For some reason he can't seem to shake this high purring, this Blanche DuBois. Whatever it is, it is freaking One-Eye out.

One thing he has learned in his life so far – if you're in trouble, get weird.

The band are coming to the end of the song, the singer hollering out the last lines of the chorus.

Take your hand offov me, One-Eye says.

Oh, ahm sorry, sir. I just – He rubs it up and down.

You think you're funny, mister? He sees One-Eye's hand move to his holster.

No sir. Not me, sir. Not funny. Not at all.

Hey. Hey. It is the kid, getting between them. He seems to have come from nowhere. This is my cousin, says the kid to One Eye. John.

Come on, John. We must go visit our family now.

Then the kid reaches in, takes the obsidian blade from the bar and pockets it.

Yes, says the singer. We must go visit our family now. One last stroke of the arm, he turns and tips his invisible hat to Rosa, and they move backwards out onto the street and start to run. And the pills must really be working now because he feels like he could run forever – run like this, with the kid – and his body is moving beneath him, and they are running running and the sweat is running down his back, one block, two blocks, three, until a pain in his left lung fells him and he has to stop, to bend over and cough.

Wait, he calls to the kid. Gimme a minute here.

He leans down, his hands on his knees, breath rasping. He hears the kid stop, come round the back of him, and then something sharp, right on his kidney.

Hey. He straightens up, feels the blade. They are in a dark street, no streetlights, no stores.

Aw, Jesus . . . he says. Really? C'mon.

No, says the kid. You come on. You are not the boss.

He puts up his hands. Okay, he says. Okay. I'm not the boss.

The kid pushes harder with the knife.

Hey. He yelps. Careful. You could hurt me.

I know. I want your money. I want it now.

You can have it. Here. He turns out his pockets. Hands over the hundred-dollar bill.

The other. The other hundred dollars.

I gave it to the woman on the square.

You're lying.

Sorry, kid.

I want more money.

Sure. How much?

One million dollars.

He laughs.

You think it's funny? The kid jabs him again. I want one. Million. Dollars.

Okay. Okay. He puts up his hands again. Sure. But the only way to get one million dollars is to wire our manager in LA.

He's asleep right now. But we can do it in the morning. I promise. I'll give you whatever you like.

I want it now.

Here, why don't we just go and get ourselves a little –

NO! I do not want a pinche fucking DRINK. And I am not
a fucking KID!

The kid slashes the knife against the singer's shirt. Perhaps
he means only to cut the shirt, but he cuts his arm, and blood
swells onto the white fabric. They both stare at it, and as they
stare it starts to flow, soaking into the white cotton.

Woah, the singer says. That's a lot of fucking blood.

It's bad, but could be worse. It doesn't hurt. Not yet at
least. But that's probably the speed.

The singer turns on the kid.

Give me the knife, he says.

The kid shakes his head.

Give me the knife, kid. It's my motherfucking knife.

The kid looks maimed somehow. Transfixed by blood. He
looks like he doesn't know whether to scream or cry or laugh
or piss himself.

The kid offers up the blade, his face a mess of tripping rictus
and alcohol blur.

See. That was easy, wasn't it? Huh? Now – He leans in, grabs
the kid, turns him so his left arm is against the kid's chest, his
right holding the blade to his neck. Now you walk that way, or
I'll cut your fucking throat.

The kid starts to whimper. The singer can smell piss.

Believe me, he says. I'll cut your fucking throat. I'm fucking
Bluebeard. You ever heard of me? I'm the Hunchback of fucking Notre-*Dame*. I'm Tezcatlifucking*poca*. I'll kill you. And I'll
eat you. And I'll like it. Now go.

He pushes the kid away.

The kid walks, then runs, half loping, weeping.

He stands there, not moving, his blood dripping through his shirt onto the ground. He can feel it now, the pain of the wound.

He takes off his shirt, tears off the sleeves. Takes the sleeve that is not soaked with blood and ties it as tight as he can over his arm. Then, shirtless, he turns and goes the other way, staying in the shadows, back towards the plaza, finds a bench away from the lights, and sits. His rasping breath. The sweat which has drenched him cooling. But everything is turning now – and he knows he is dangerously drunk – the great low spin of drunken worlds. He lumbers around his mind, tries to get a foothold.

Where was he going? Where was he heading? He was going to fly, wasn't he? Out of this country? Paris. He was heading to Paris. A room, high above the city. High above the clamour and the crowds. A place drenched in cold northern light. He blinks and it has gone and he is seasick – he turns around and vomits onto the bottom of a tree. He sits up and wipes his beard. He feels a little better. His eyes a little steadier.

A young girl is dancing not far from him. She is turning and turning and turning and she is like those astronauts, turning and turning, and he is seasick again watching her and he wants her to stop. But she is too beautiful to stop, wearing one of those skirts the Indian girls wear. She is beautiful, in a way he cannot name, made up of starlight and moonshine.

The girl starts to slow a little, her skirt stops ballooning, her arms come down.

She looks at him, and he looks back. Then she turns and walks slowly across the plaza. He stands and follows.

Her footsteps are deft and sure. Her bare feet make no sound. She picks her way along the cobbles as though she knows her way – there are dogs that sniff at her and then retreat, their ears back. She does not turn to check whether he follows her, but he knows she knows he does. That he has no choice. That he is grateful to have no choice.

He thinks he would follow her anywhere. He thinks this is what death might be like – perhaps this is what is happening, perhaps the knife went in, into the kidney. Perhaps he is slumped back there, his life bleeding out onto the stray-dog ground, and she is an angel come to lead him home.

They emerge and they are at the dockside – and there are boats – and the girl has gone, and he is alone again. Alone and bleeding. Shaking, cold.

Anyone could find him here. He can't go back to the hotel. Not the way he came. Not along that dark track.

He goes over the dock to where the boats bump. He recognizes the guy that rowed the Indians across, dozing in his skiff.

Hey, he says. Hey. Wake up.

The guy opens one eye. He looks frightened.

Take me to the rock, he says. The white rock. I'll pay you. I'll give you whatever you like.

Now?

Yeah, now. Right now.

In the morning is better.

No. Not the morning. Now. Let's do it now. C'mon c'mon c'mon. Please.

He is already climbing into a boat. He can see the guy does not want to ride with him, shirtless and bleeding as he is. He stands, gets his balance. How many ledges? How many times has he had the girls screaming as he does his human fly on the ledge? He looks out. There is no one there – for now. But they will find him soon, the kid and whoever he can drum up to help him. He does not have much time.

The guy laughs – shows teeth all limned with silver – revs up the motor and they are off, low and slow through the channel. The singer hunkers down, lying at the bottom of the boat, the engine throbbing through his throbbing body. He can smell the vomit from earlier, and his blood and his sweat. The boat bumps up against a small rocky beach. The skipper jumps out, tethers it to a tree. The singer hauls himself up to stand, climbs out onto the pebbled shore.

All is quiet – the night is thick – the moon is waning but still bright.

Gracias, he says. Gracias.

Veinte pesos.

Oh man, I'm sorry. I don't have money. He turns out his pockets. No tengo dinero. I'll bring it to you tomorrow. I promise. I'll bring you a hundred dollars. Cien dólares. Mañana. I promise, okay?

The guy looks dubious.

I *promise*, man. But please – you can't tell anyone I'm here. Por favor. He puts his finger to his mouth.

The guy curses in a low voice, untethers his boat, and starts to row back to shore.

Hey – he calls after him. Hey – wait – how'm I going to get back?

But the guy is already out of earshot, already wrapped back in the dark silk of the water.

He starts to think this was a terrible mistake. If they come to the dock and see the boat gone they will know he came over. If they come after him here, they can do what they want to him – shoot him and dig him a shallow grave.

The Indians, he has to find the Indians.

He moves a little inland, and finds a rock to sit on. He would like a cigarette – he still has his cigarettes but has no lighter. His

256

arm is hurting now – he takes off the sleeve, tries to probe the cut in the darkness. The knife has gone in a half-inch beneath the skin, and there seems to be a lot of blood.

There are rustlings in the darkness – animals, close by. The island smells of warm earth and salt water and stone. The dung of an animal by his foot. He knows he has to move from here, that this spot is too exposed, he knows he has to find the Indians or hide himself until the morning.

He starts to walk along a sandy, rocky path. Roots catch and rip at his jeans – a large one sends him sprawling, and when he rolls up to his knees he sees his jeans are ripped at the knee, his palms are skinned raw. He wants to cry out – cry out the way he did as a boy when he fell, when his mother would come and pick him up –

Suddenly he wants his mother – here kneeling on this rocky earth he is crying for her. She came to see him, came to see him play, and he did not let her come backstage – his mother and his brother. Why did he want to punish them? Lift me Mother, hold me Mother, please.

There should be no more punishment. No more pain. He has courted pain, sown it, lived amongst its bleak harvest for too long.

He curls into a ball, lies there, prone on the ground.

A sound, close by. A snapping of twigs – the fear courses through him. He is prey. He is bleeding. There may be creatures here: jaguars, come down from the jungle. They will scent him. Scent his blood. He must get up.

He brings himself to a stand, and walks on as silently as he can, the small rocks cutting his feet. It is pitch-dark here amongst the trees. The path gives out to an open space – there are the stars, and the light of the lighthouse above a cliff. The light strafes the island, illuminating the canyon, the cacti clinging to the sides of the cliff. For a long moment he stands, caught in its searchlight, exposed. But he sees the canyon is empty; there are no people here, no jaguars ready to pounce. The Indians have gone to their beds.

He makes his way to the far side, and finds a rock to lie on. He stretches out, and here he can see the stars, the great firmament above, and who he was is spindrift, spinning into this starlight, a man who was a singer who they called a star. He thought he was the alchemist, he thought he could turn himself into gold, but he was only ever base. Just a child, prancing the boards. He tried. But he is just an animal after all. He is Caliban. He is a pair of ragged claws. He is prey. Here is the real, the real he has been searching for.

Hurry up please, it's time.

He lifts his head – the sound of a low instrument, a voice, broken in all the right places. He stands, and makes his way over the rough ground, called by the singing. The music fades and then returns, louder than before. He comes to a small gate, which gives out onto scrub grass, a low thatched hut, a fire. There are people around the fire. The Indians. It is day, or it is night, he is not sure which. It is the place between. It is a real place. It is happening. It is a dream.

The family group is there – the younger men, the women, the older man. They look at him from within the circle of firelight and he knows what he must do – he drops to his knees, and crawls low-bellied over the ground towards them, and as he crawls he feels the roots clutch at him and tear his skin. He approaches the circle like this, prostrate, bare-chested, on hands and knees and then stops, puts his head on the ground.

The music stops, there is silence, the sounds of the fire, the pop and crackle of wood. He senses their shock at this ragged interloper, broken and bleeding and prone. And then footsteps – a hand on his shoulder, turning him – he sees the older man, the deer leaping on his trousers.

I have been searching, he says. All my life.

Or perhaps he thinks it only.

The man bends to him, feeling his body for injury. His hands are rough and welcome. Then the man leans in, puts feather-stick to his skin and sucks – as the singer twitches on the ground. The man spits into his hand. A black crystal, he holds it up to the firelight. Bends and sucks again – another – the same. And again. And again. Each time he twitches – each time the convulsions rack him. And then it is over. More hands pull him up from beneath his shoulders, pushing him towards the fire; the circle opens to receive him. He curls around himself.

And then, for a time, the world is dark.

He sleeps, or perhaps he does not. When he opens his eyes, the sky is navy blue and there is only one star left.

The old man is singing again, moving around the circle, brushing them with his feathers, holding them up to the sky, back to the fire. And he is singing to his cracks, singing to his wounds, binding them with starlight and song.

The song seems as though it will not end, and then he understands: it will not end until the sun has ended it, until the sun has risen in the sky. And he knows too that the sun's rising depends on this man's singing, on his singing it back into the world, praising it, calling it forth, loving it into the day.

The sky turns navy, then grey, then white and blue. He shivers, comes to sit as the family are all sitting, upright, facing the flames. Someone places a blanket over his chest.

It is dawn. The sun is here. The old man's song ceases. For a moment there is quiet, the sounds of a woman feeding her child. The men speak in low voices. There is everyday laughter.

The family stand, share fruit, they kick ash into the fire, gather their belongings. The colours are leached and yet full of life – the last embers of the fire, the grey-white ash. The orange the woman is feeding to her child. It is the first orange he has ever truly seen. She offers him a piece and he takes it, sucks it, and he has never felt so blessed.

The old man nods to him, beckons him to follow – he stands, walks on his bare feet on a sandy path, the scent of the ocean coming closer, and he emerges onto the beach. He watches them, the way they walk to the shore, offering their gourds and their candles. He remembers then the woven cross still in his back pocket – the eye of God – he places it into the sand, where it sits, its black diamond eye looking over to the west.

And then the family are packing up. They are quick in their movements.

They come to him, nod to him, speak to him. He gestures that he will stay here a while. And so they take their leave of him and he is alone with the dawn and the ocean and the rock and the offerings and the eye of God.

And then he understands what he must do.

He takes off his clothes and he folds them and he is naked. He walks towards the water. He is ankle-deep, waist-deep – he is swimming. He strikes out towards the rock, the water choppy, splashing in his face – salt in his nostrils, his moustache, salt in the slice of his wound. He feels the sting and the sting is welcome and good. And there are further stings, deeper wounds. He feels the ocean reach for them too, clean them with the salt of its tears.

He is headed for the rock, but he has no destination, not

really – he can dissolve, become liquid. Tell me, he whispers to the dawn. Teach me how to live. The sun is touching his skin.

Soon, sooner than he thought he would, he reaches the rock – smells its smell of crabs and piss and seawater and something ancient, troubling, beautiful. There are crabs all around the darkness where it meets the water. He wonders how deep it goes – how high the deeper rock of which this is only the tip. He can see the offerings left in its cracks: candles and gourds and hearts. He lifts his hands and climbs – hauling his great white body from the waves, the water pouring off him as he stands there, grappling for a moment, lifting his arms aloft to the sun, and then lets go – launching out again into the ocean, lying on his back. Beneath him the great swarming tides.

It is all back there on the shore: the pain and the complication and the battle and the hate and the love and the wounding and the choices and the profit and the loss, but here there is no life and no death, here in this liquid intimacy, this shattered silver – the water like mercury in the rising sun, rising and falling, rising and falling, here where the western night gives way to day. He is the sacrifice, he is the offering. The flutes are broken and he is ready for the reckoning. It is rich to give. Rich to offer – this is the simplest truth.

The Writer
2020

They help each other into the boat, steadying themselves as they find their seats on the wooden benches. When they are all settled, a complement of scruffy red life jackets is passed around, and they are encouraged to put them over their heads.

Her husband brings their daughter onto his knee as the pilot pulls on the outboard motor and they chug across the small stretch of quiet water. The sun is already low. They are late, later than they should be – she can see the frustration on the faces of the mara'akame and his son. They have been waiting for these lumbering westerners to put on their sun cream and their bug spray and their hats and their long sleeves and buy water and check their emails and their Facebook feeds, and they have a long way to drive back home before they sleep.

The pilgrims chatter about what they are going to do: whether they can find flights back to Germany and France and England. Whether there will be a scrabble at the airports. Whether the flights will be affordable. Whether the borders will close. The young French woman says she will stay – there is nothing for her to get back for, nothing urgent. The others nod, yes, great, why not?

The music producer is speaking to her husband, saying he can get a flight to Tijuana even if the US borders close – that's where he left his car – he can drive back to Joshua Tree from there. The woman can feel the static of her own anxiety increasing as they speak.

She thinks of those photos – the empty supermarket shelves.

If they manage to get a flight, and there is no food when they land, then what will they eat? She should go online – as soon as she can. Try to order a supermarket delivery. Wait in line for a slot.

Jesus. Am I really thinking this?

She can feel the slippage, the ordinary already cast in the light of a dream.

The Swedish man starts talking about the white rock, about how he plans to swim there – how he has heard it is not far – how desperate he is to get into the water. The Colombian man says he will join him.

Then – Wow, says the producer, suddenly. This is beautiful.

The writer looks up and out. He is right – the sun is low, lighting the Pacific in all its late-afternoon sleepy magnificence.

Where was the hotel? he says, turning to her. The one you were telling me about? The one in ruins, where he stayed in '69?

That way. The writer points south. Around the point, at the other end of the beach. You can walk there from the town. It takes about half an hour.

They are silent then, for the last minutes of the crossing – as though held between states – she can feel the currents tugging on them all: the clamorous world beyond, with its flights and its families and all its many fractured urgencies, the water beneath them, the island waiting ahead – and then they are on the other side, scraping against the rocks of a small grey beach, clambering out, leaving their life jackets behind, lifting their children over the water onto the land. The woman checks her daughter's legs for bites. The jejenes are already vicious – she can feel itching welts rising on her own calves. The granddaughter of the mara'akame is smiling at her daughter, wiggling her ears, grinning. She must be nine, the writer thinks, or thereabouts, wearing a version of her mother's clothes, a short blouse, a simple long skirt, her long hair loose – her teeth large when she smiles. Her own daughter is wearing a T-shirt with rainbows on it and blue shorts. Navy sandals. The writer asks the older girl her name. Tells her own. Introduces her daughter.

Hel-lo, the girl grins, wrapping her mouth around the English word. Then she giggles and waves and skips onwards to the front of the line to join her family again.

They walk down a shady track, where small trees curve over their heads, filtering the sunlight, and brittle leaves are scattered on the ground.

The writer holds her daughter's hand. She can feel the little girl's fatigue, her discomfort. Her feet slap the ground in her navy sandals.

Are you thirsty?

Her daughter shakes her head.

Hungry?

No Mumma.

Not long now, poppet, the woman says.

Her husband walks a few paces ahead, in a loose line with the mara'akame and the French woman. As they move through the dappled light the mara'akame flicks his head towards the French woman. Tu esposa? he says to the writer's husband.

No! both her husband and the French woman say quickly. No, no, says her husband. My wife is there. He gestures to where she walks, a few paces behind.

The mara'akame grunts. You should have more than one wife, he says, nodding at the young French woman. You should have two.

They all laugh: her husband, the mara'akame, the French woman. Only she – walking several paces behind, her daughter's hand in hers – does not.

267

She holds on tighter to her daughter's hand.

She puts her other hand in the woven bag, touching the gourd bowls. The warmth is making the beeswax melt.

The track emerges into a large open area where the grass is burned by the sun and buzzards swing lazy in the updraughts overhead. Ahead of them is a small rubbly hill, a lighthouse on top. The sun is fierce, and she can feel her skin tighten in its glare – the cracks and fissures in her desert-chapped lips.

The line of pilgrims moves quickly across the open ground, then passes through a gate in a low wooden fence and then into a field, where there is a palm-thatched cabin, the walls roughly made of stone and clay. A fireplace ringed by stones lies just outside the entrance door.

They burned it down, the Mexican man says, gesturing to the hut, whose sides are blackened by fire.

Who did? her husband says.

The mayor, they think, of the town. It's prime real estate. They want to turn it into a resort.

Jesus, says the woman's husband to the Mexican man, shaking his head.

The writer looks around her. It would be easy to think there is nothing here – just a hut and a cave and the buzzards, just some scrubby grass and biting insects. The hut, like so many of the sacred places they have visited on this journey, is surprisingly makeshift – it does not look as though it would withstand much in the way of weather. But she is learning that, for the Wixárika, this is how it is; that you do not emerge from five hundred years of attempts to destroy your culture by building basilicas that catch the sun. Their most holy places are hiding in plain sight – you must crouch to be near the fire, bend to enter the cave, climb to reach the top of the mountain.

The writer knows this is not the only one of their sacred

sites that is threatened in this way – El Quemado, the mountain in the north too; the place the Wixárika call the birthplace of the sun. They climbed it last week, some of them on foot, some on horses, a three-hour trek from an old silver-mining town to the peak. Her daughter had started on a horse with her father but hated it and cried to come down, and so they had climbed together, she and her three-year-old, side by side, as the air grew thinner, and the view became more and more magnificent. When they reached the summit, the pilgrims left the second of their three candles in the rocks, and then sat, looking out at the vast desert below – Wirikuta – the place where the sacred cactus grew. There were large beige acres patching the desert below. Tomato plantations, the Mexican man said. Many of them run by the cartels.

Then he told them about the Canadian mining company who had been granted a concession by the ex-president to mine the holy mountain for silver. A certain sort of mining, open-pit mining, that blasts the mountain open from above, rendering it unrecognizable. With the right sort of explosives, he said, you can crush a mountain in hours, but the leavings, the xanthates and the cyanide, would stay in the ground for years.

The woman hands her daughter to her husband and goes into the hut.

Inside, it is dense with darkness, and the smell of animals and sweat and candle wax and grease. She stays a moment, aware she wants to feel something – something which eludes her – has felt this often, on this trip, a sense that there is meaning here, but a meaning she cannot access, a language she cannot understand.

Through the narrow doorway, outside, in the hazy sun, she can see the mara'kame's daughter, waving again at her own.

The pilgrims swatting away the mosquitoes and jejenes. The son of the mara'akame is gathering twigs from the scrub around them now, stacking them in the firepit, lighting them. They catch immediately, and the pilgrims move towards the flames, gathering in a ragged circle around the fire.

She watches them, their faces growing pink and red in the heat. The mara'akame's family a little distance away.

She goes back out and takes her place by her family in the circle around the fire – glad of it, despite the heavy warmth of the afternoon – glad of the protection it offers, the biting insects kept at bay. The mara'akame moves quickly around them all, the feathers brushed once more against their cheeks, over their heads, their shoulders. She can feel the man's hurry now, the long journey ahead, seven hours back up the mountain and he has hardly slept and is no longer young.

He gestures towards a small cave, a little way above them on the hill, and they move away from the fire, forming a line to present their offerings. The writer stands between her husband and her daughter. As they approach, she sees the cave is small, no more than five feet high, and shallow, no more than two feet deep, and the rocks it is made from are jagged and burned by the smoke of many fires. It is littered with candles and gourds and pebbles and melted wax, and it is not clear what should be placed here – the candles? The gourds? The cross?

What do I do? the woman asks of her husband, panicked. Is this the place for a gourd? What do I put here?

Yes, her husband says. A gourd. Put one of the gourds here.

She plucks one of the gourds from her bag, hesitates again. It suddenly seems crucial that she get this right.

Her daughter looks up at her. Here, Mumma, she says, gently, pointing to a place where there is a little space. Put it here.

She does as her daughter suggests, bending and placing the gourd on the stone – there is no time to do otherwise, the next person is behind her, readying to place their own offering. The sun is setting, the insects are biting, and they walk quickly back down the little hill, towards the fire, the hut, and as they walk her daughter stumbles a little on the rocky ground. The writer gathers her up, holds her hand tighter as they follow the line of pilgrims back onto a path, more sand now than scrub, and you can hear it – the low crash of the waves – and then they are out, their feet steeped in sand and there is the wide beach and the white rock ahead of them and they move more quickly now, they take off their shoes and socks and feel the warm sand beneath their feet, the end, the rock, calling them forth.

Her daughter lets go of her hand and moves away, clambering up the small tipping hill ahead of her, then half running, half skipping to where the sand is hard-packed and the tide is out.

The writer stands on the beach, watching as her little girl crouches to the water – burrowing her hands into the sand. More and more of them are coming now, the pilgrims, moving like her daughter did towards the water – carrying the last of their offerings, their gourds and their candles, readying to plant them in the sand, to release them on the waves.

The Swedish man and the Colombian man have already let go of their offerings and are taking off their clothes, changing into their shorts, readying for the swim. The writer shades her eyes. It is not far to the rock, but neither is it close – a good three hundred metres or so, and the water out there is choppy, you could get in trouble easily, and there are no lifeguards here. She sees her husband is watching them too, standing a little further up the beach, close to their daughter. She knows what he is thinking. That he should swim too. That he would have done so: ten years ago, even five years ago it would have been his own slim torso bared to the sun. She watches him watch these younger men – caught here between his youth and his age, standing in the lee of these tumbled rocks that make a windbreak on the shore.

He used to say that they would grow old together – grow around each other like old trees. But they won't. Once they leave this beach, when they leave this country, they will no longer be a family in the way they have been until now. There will be no growing old together, no more growing around each other. There will be rupture and loss.

She wants to go to him, to cross this sand towards him, close the distance between them. To put her hand on his back and tell him that he is wrong, that they are wrong to do this, that they cannot part. How can they possibly part? They love each other too much for that. They love their daughter too much for that. She would like to say she is here for whatever is coming – that they will face it together, that they will walk each other home.

But she stays where she is.

The Swedish man and the Colombian man run, hollering into the waves, running, bending, then swimming to the rock. She watches her husband come back to himself, turn back to the sand, take out the last of the three candles from his shoulder bag. This one has a blue ribbon sewn on it. Blue for the ocean. Blue for the west. She sees its blue ribbon catch the sun. He looks over to her, acknowledges her with a nod – she nods back – and he walks to the water's edge, lifts the candle to the sun and plants it in the sand.

There, it is done.

When he stands he is different, his body looser, freer. He has finished. He has done what he came here to do. And when he has done it he does not move towards the writer, his wife, but walks instead towards where the men are – to where the other English man stands – lights a cigarette, shares a joke.

She knows it is her turn now.

She walks towards the water, towards her daughter. She kneels beside her. What are you doing, sweetheart?

Her daughter looks up, a slight frown of surprise on her face – surely, her expression seems to say, it is obvious. I am playing in the sand.

Her shorts are covered in sand. She hates wearing knickers, and so her shorts will be full of it. The writer feels a spasm of irritation, or exhaustion, as she thinks about how her daughter will be soaked, and her shorts full of sand, and she will have to negotiate the journey back to town, and her daughter will be uncomfortable with all the sand and all the grit, and as she thinks this she also knows that it does not matter, not at all – her daughter has been cooped up in the back of a hot van for hours. And she cannot truly understand it – this ugly part of herself, this need to control, this terror of what lies on the other side. Her daughter is three years old. She has been travelling for hours. She needs to play.

She watches as her daughter presses her hands into the sand – an impression is left and then the water swells back. She does this again, and again. And every time the water complies, erasing her handprint, plumping and glossing the sand, ready for her to press again.

Watching, the woman is assailed by a memory, of markings on the walls of a cave, of a journey to France the summer before.

They had gone there together: she, her husband and daughter, her father and mother. She had wanted to take her dad away. He could still walk then, just, with a stick. She had searched the internet for places, found one with grab bars and disabled toilets and showers. There was a pool in the garden and a room full of children's toys, but it rained all week and there was no one for her daughter to play with but her parents and her grandparents and it rained and rained and rained. They drove to supermarkets in the grey rain and bought cheese and wine and sweet things, then went home and ate them under the dripping tarpaulin. They told themselves the rain didn't matter but they all knew it did.

She did not know, not then, that the story she was living in was a fiction – that her husband carried secrets long-held, ready to detonate the grounds of their marriage – but the whole week was suffused with a strange atmosphere. Things unspoken. An unease.

They slept in separate rooms, she and her husband, she with her daughter on two singles in the attic bedroom, and her husband alone on the other side of the house. There was no way of hiding their sleeping arrangements, but her parents were too polite to mention it.

One day, in the driving rain, they set off together in the hire car, her husband at the wheel, her father in the front, she and her mother and daughter in the back. They drove for an hour through damp green lanes and past fields and low hills until they arrived at the mouth of a cave. They bought the last tickets of the morning for the tour. Her dad managed to walk with his stick to the little electric train, to clamber up into a seat. Her daughter sat between her and her husband, as they travelled more than two miles into the limestone, into the dark.

The guide pointed out the hollowed dens of cave bears, shone his torch to illuminate their scratches on the sides of the rock. Eventually, the train stopped at a low-ceilinged cavern, where they descended, walked a little way from the train on uneven ground. And there they were – all over the roof of the cave: rhino and ibex and bison and mammoth and horses, overlapping each other, as though the artist wanted to capture the crowded abundance of them.

This artist or artists would have had to have painted this ceiling lying down, the guide said – a prehistoric Sistine Chapel.

They stood, faces upturned, speechless. The ibex overlaying the horse, its generous horns against the mammoth's side, a frieze of mammoths, two mammoths facing each other, their tusks gently intertwined.

Around the pictures of the animals were other, different marks, snaking across the stone. These were made by fingers, the guide said. Children, many of them. Finger fluting, they were called, and many of them had been traced to the same three-year-old girl. The fourth finger, you see, he said, is shorter on a female.

The girl would have been held up by her parents, placed on her father's or mother's shoulders so she could reach out, dragging her fingers through the soft red clay, revealing the limestone, the moon-milk, below.

Moon-milk.

We do not know why these marks were made, said the guide, perhaps initiation rituals, or training of some kind, or, he smiled, simply something to pass the time.

The woman's husband gathered their daughter to him, lifting her onto his shoulders. Can you see, poppet? Can you see?

The woman stared up at the marks, the way they snaked and curved over the rock, imagined that little girl, her hands held out before her, the satisfying sensation as the clay gave way, her small hands mark-making in the torchlit dark.

She wanted them to mean something, to reveal their meaning to her, but perhaps they only meant what they meant – that thirteen thousand years ago, when the ice was melting all over Europe, at the beginning of the Holocene, a three-year-old girl was held up to make her marks in moon-milk, and thousands of years later, at the beginning of the Anthropocene, when the ice was melting at the poles, a three-year-old girl was held up on her father's shoulders to see.

Later that afternoon, back at the house, it was still raining. They sat in the living room. Her daughter watched *The Cat in the Hat* on the computer. Her husband marked exam papers. Her parents looked through the DVD collection and chose *Chariots of Fire*. She scrolled through her Twitter feed – that was her habit then, like pressing a bruise – counting up the bad news, the latest data from the latest climate scientists. She came across an article by a journalist who had written a book on ice. It stated, very clearly, that whatever anyone might say, there was simply too much carbon already baked into the atmosphere to keep warming to a level that would support much life. That the best thing we could do with our time would be to learn how to face the ending of things. To learn, in fact, how to die.

Reading it, the terror came upon her again. Terror for her daughter. The paralysis of it. She saw the futility of her recent arrest – understood it was just an attempt to bargain with the inevitable. Just a waypost in the stages of grief.

She must have made a sound of some kind, because her father looked up, asked her what she was reading. He looked troubled.

It's over, she said. This world. This world we thought we

knew. The tipping points have been breached. The ground is gone from beneath our feet. Do you know what it means? Do you know what two degrees of warming means? Three? Four? Do you know what it means for her? She gestured to where her daughter sat close by, clapping her hands at the Cat in the Hat.

What can we do? her father asked her. What can I do? He looked wild-eyed, terrified. Guilty.

Pray, she said to him. But she said it cruelly. It was not an invitation. It was a slap, and he flinched as though he had been hit. It was a word with which he'd had nothing to do all his life.

She should have been kinder. Could have been kinder. They were all as complicit as each other.

She thinks of her father now, in Manchester, in the chair in the corner of the room that he cannot leave. His own prow now set to the west. She knows how frightened, how terrified he is of the ending of things – how little his post-Irish post-Catholic default atheism has fitted him for this threshold. How nothing in his life has taught him to die.

She wishes she could give him something, something from this place, from this pilgrimage, something to ease the passage – a coin or two for the boatman, that shadowy figure, solicitous, practical, not unkind, preparing the small boat now, steadying the oars, readying for the crossing. What might help him on his way? Or any of them, come to that?

But all she really feels, standing here, on this beach, clutching this gourd, is confusion. Sadness. A vague sense of trespass. A portal closing. An overwhelming, crippling need for it to be over. A sense of having failed to measure up.

Still, the light in the west is beautiful.

They are all taking pictures of it, all the pilgrims, with their iPhones and their GoPros and their cameras. The producer has a small affair – a Leica or something similar, it looks like one of those '6os cameras, something one of those '6os photographers might have used – and they are all bending and framing their shots, trying to capture this extraordinary light.

The grandchildren of the mara'akame have broken away from their family now – the younger ones are taking off their clothes, the nine-year-old girl has chucked off her blouse and her skirt and is just in her knickers. Her brother is in his shorts. She comes leaping through the spray, kicking up the waves into wild spume. She bends to catch one of the candles left by the pilgrims and lifts it – hooking it overarm into the sea. Her brother does the same. The writer watches them – all these carefully placed candles, lifted and tossed into the waves. The children are laughing, screaming with laughter, their bodies shining with the water. She turns and looks at the mara'akame's family, wondering whether they will say something, whether this is okay – these kids just lifting and chucking these candles like this, but they, too, are smiling, laughing, not perturbed at all.

And now the young girl is going over to her own daughter, bending down to the sand, and her daughter is looking up to her – the magnetic attraction of child to child, kin to kin, their heads bent together as they press their hands into the sand, lifting and packing and shaping the sand, their figures merging in this hazy light, these shifting surfaces where the light bends and refracts. Shifting scale. Playing with them all.

She wanted to give her daughter certainty, firm ground, security, a future without fear. That was what she was trying to do, when she was arrested, that's what she told the judge – I did it for my daughter.

But what if her daughter needs something else to give her shelter? Jokes. Offerings. The responsibility of sacrifice.

Perhaps it is her daughter who can teach her how to

exist – how not to mind the sand in your knickers, the desert dirt all over your clothes, how to encounter it, to roll in it, allow it to enter you, change you. What if she already has many of the skills she needs for what is to come? The sense to hold this brief life as sweetly and as reverently as possible. To know where to place the gourd. To shape the sand with her wide-palmed hands. To play in this place where the water meets the shore.

Perhaps, she thinks, in the end, this is the love that is most holy – the love that animates most – not eros, not amor, not even agape – but ludus, the invitation to play.

They are all at it now – her daughter, the kids, the men who are boys – splashing back from the rock, laughing and shaking out their hair; the kids with their overarm throws and the mara'akame looking over them all, with his bad jokes and his half-smile. The trickster. The tongue in the cheek. The one whose job it is to take the holy piss. Showing her how to do it – not to grasp for the end of the story, but to surrender to this light on this sand, the way the waves make these patterns on the shore. To surrender the addiction to knowing how the story ends.

She needs to let go, she really needs to stop thinking now and let the fuck go – everyone else's coracle left their hands long ago.

She approaches the edge of the water, faces west, place of the ancestors. Place of the dead. Place of the white rock. Place of Tatéi Haramara, the mother of all. And maybe they are all there – in this shifting light, the ones who went before – the place of the dead, crowded with them all, waiting to receive her father; waiting for her in her time, all the many ancestors who did all they could with their troubles and their gifts, who bargained and worked and who prayed at night and negotiated with the gods for their children to survive.

Maybe they are all there with the ibex and the mammoths and the mastodons, waiting, across the water that we came from – the water we first crawled from to lie on the warm sand in the hot sun on the way to becoming what we are.

She looks down at the gourd in her palm; the deer now looks like nothing more than a blob and the people are melting too, losing their shapes, there again that spasm – she has not done well enough, not been careful enough, not made the deer face intricate enough or the corn look like corn enough or the figures of her family look strong enough, and perhaps when she releases it, it will be seen not to be worthy enough – the protection it might have afforded not strong enough to curry favour with the gods and to withstand whatever storms may come.

But it will have to do.

She bends down – can feel the pulse of herself in the cracked parts, the sting of the fissures in her lips. She would like to throw this coracle now, to rid herself of the responsibility of getting it right, chuck it overarm into the waves like these kids are doing, but she dare not – dare not be so free, so sure of herself, she has much to atone for, much to repent, and much, much for which she is grateful. And so, she bends, carefully, and places it gently on the waves, this wonky-shonky gourd with the corn and the deer and the family. It is all she has to give.

She watches as it bobs a little, is pulled back on the tide and then lifts and is jostled into shore where it lies beached for a long moment, held on its side at a jaunty angle, rocking gently back and forth, until the next wave lifts it and draws it back, sucking it away, finally – caught in currents she can never know, or control.

And there are memories now, rising from the water:

She is on a beach in Greece. She is very young, and she and the man who will become her husband have no money, and they cannot afford a hotel. So they are sleeping on the beach. And she is waking with the dawn. And she sits up and sees that she is enclosed, that framing her on the sand are concentric rings: a ring of bottle tops, then one of cigarette butts – thousands of them – then pebbles, then small pieces of driftwood, and then seaweed. They are arranged in the shape of a heart. Her husband is crouched at the far outer ring, putting the finishing touches to his offering. He has been awake all night, combing the beach, turning the flotsam to love.

Or – it is the day of her wedding. It is the point where afternoon is blurring into evening. Her dad is on stage. She can't remember how he got there – she is already hazy-drunk on too much wine and not enough food – but there he is, on stage in a damp tent, with a pianist accompanying him, and he is singing Simon and Garfunkel, 'The Boxer', the extra verse, the one her father told her that they only sang live.

He is flicking his hand out towards the audience as he sings, he has never done this, never sung like this on stage, in front of people, not in her memory, but they are loving it, the crowd, cheering him on. He is magnificent. He is absolutely free.

After changes upon changes we are more or less the same
After changes we are more or less the same.

Or – she is in a house in Mexico. The house belongs to an elderly German man. It is evening. There are photographs on the wall of a film director who stayed in this house fifteen years before – he is sitting behind his camera, looking into the distance, he is measuring, his hand held up to shade his eyes from the light – but she is sitting outside, in a shaded courtyard, and she is waiting for the man who will become her husband to come, waiting for him to arrive here, waiting for them to claim each other, there on the bright cusp of their love.

Soon, but not yet – not quite yet – the man who will become her husband will arrive, and their story will begin.

Or – she is in a jail cell in London. Somewhere near Victoria station. Outside it is warm – far too warm for an April day, but in here it is cool. There is a toilet in the corner. There is a camera up above. There is the number of a drug rehab unit sprayed on the ceiling. They have shut the door. She is alone.

Or – she is here, on the beach, with her daughter and her husband. The young men arriving back on the beach, wet from their swim, the children leaping – and all the ghosts of all the dead of all the souls in the west looking on. All the life that is to come looking on.

The white rock looking on.

Her husband looking on.

She sees he is watching her, and she raises her hand to him, waving across the distance between them. How much she has loved this man. How they have wound around each other, grown around each other, given each other.

She understands. She forgives him for all of it.

It was time.

It was time, after all, to get off. It was past time for her to get off the bus.

Her daughter though, her daughter should adore him beyond measure, this man, her father, what a beautiful word – *father*. Him with his wildness and his wide-palmed hands.

He turns back, her husband, back to the men, laughing at something one of them has said.

And here they come again, these children – barrelling across the beach, interrupting thought, the young girl is leaping, look at the way she is leaping! So high! The way her body moves in space. The writer remembers running like that – being a child like that, when your heart meets the air around you, and there is nothing in its way, your long hair whipping out behind.

And now her daughter is standing, and she is joining in. Trying to leap too. And the older girl is holding her hand, helping her leap higher. And the sun is low now in the sky – touching the bodies of these children, leaping above the water, the endless water, which glitters and shimmers at their feet.

Author's Note

Had my own fate and that of my family not taken me there, I might never have visited San Blas, a seemingly sleepy backwater on the coast of northern Nayarit, Mexico. Just prior to my first visit, however, and in the space of a brief internet search, I began to understand the astonishing history, strategic importance and ongoing ritual potency of the town and the white rock that lies a few hundred metres from its shore.

My own story touches the town and the white rock through my contact with the Wixárika people. For those wanting to learn more about the Wixárika, their culture and history, this is an excellent resource: https://wixarika.org.

The following article is a good introduction to the pilgrimage to the Pacific and the white rock: https://wixarika.org/what-draws-native-huichol-pacific-ocean.

For the Singer sections, I read all the usual biographies of Jim Morrison, but found the following books gave important insight into his creative and legal direction of travel in July 1969:

Burning the May Tree, the Sacrifice of Jim Morrison, Chris M. Balz, Bowker, 2019.

Jim Morrison, Friends Gathered Together, Frank Lisciandro, Vision Words & Wonder, 2014.

We Want the World: Jim Morrison, the Living Theatre, and the FBI, Daveth Milton, Bennion Kearney, 2012.

The Doors' time in Mexico is chronicled by Jerry Hopkins in the *Rolling Stone* article 'The Doors in Mexico'.

The most immediate and potent access points into Morrison's complex mind were, of course, his poetry and lyrics. These have been published in several previous editions, but now exist as an anthology:

The Collected Works of Jim Morrison: Poetry, Journals, Transcripts, and Lyrics, Harper Collins, 2021.

The Lieutenant is very loosely based on the character of Juan de Ayala, who took over the captaincy of the *San Carlos* in March 1775 from Don Manuel Manrique and, alongside his pilot, was the first European to sail into and chart the bay of San Francisco. Biographical details for Ayala are scant, and the Lieutenant of the book is entirely my own creation.

The following books and accounts were crucial in my research:

Flood Tide of Empire, Spain and the Pacific North West, 1543–1819, Warren Cook, Yale, 1977.

The Naval Department of San Blas, New Spain's Bastion for Alta California and Nootka, 1767 to 1798, Michael Thurman, The Arthur H. Clark Company, 1967.

For Honour and Country, The Diary of Bruno de Hezeta, ed. H. K. Beals, Western Imprints, 1985.

Juan Perez on the North West Coast, Six Documents of His Expedition in 1774, H. K. Beals, Oregon Historical Society, 1989.

Trafalgar and the Spanish Navy: The Spanish Experience of Sea Power, John D. Harbron, Naval Institute Press, 1988.

Including the voice of a Yoeme girl in this novel was always going to have the potential for cultural projection and appropriation.

Early in the writing process I came across the work of Gesturing Towards Decolonial Futures: https://decolonialfutures.net.

Their work includes a series of questions, challenges and provocations, which served as a guide and compass as I wrote.

During the editing process I was fortunate enough to engage the help of Dr David Delgado Shorter, Professor of World Arts and Cultures at UCLA, and Felipe Molina MFA, a leading Yoeme writer and educator. Both men read excerpts from the text, and the conversations and suggestions that arose from those readings were profound and decolonizing in themselves.

A note on naming: I took the decision, with guidance, to use the term Yoeme, not Yaqui. This choice follows the lead of many Indigenous communities to represent themselves in their own languages.

The following texts were vital in helping to gain an understanding of Yoeme history and culture:

Yaqui Deer Songs, Felipe Molina Larry Evers, University of Arizona Press, 1987.

We Will Dance Our Truth, Yaqui History in Yoeme Performance, David Delgado Shorter, University of Nebraska Press, 2009.

Yaqui Women: Contemporary Life Histories, Jane Holden Kelly, University of Nebraska Press, 1978.

The Tall Candle, The Personal Chronicle of a Yaqui Indian, Jane Holden Kelly, William Curry Holden and Rosalio Moises, University of Nebraska Press, 1971.

Throwing Fire at the Sun, Water at the Moon, Anita Endrezze, University of Arizona Press, 2000.

The Wixárika and Yoeme people are still fighting for their rights to their ancestral lands and water. In June 2020, two Indigenous Yoeme environmental campaigners, Tomás Rojo Valencia and Luis Orbano Domínguez were murdered in Mexico within the space of a week.

Global Witness work worldwide to end the attacks and killings of land and environmental defenders and to address the root causes of attacks against them: https://www.globalwitness.org/en/.

Please refer to the Resources page on my website for the most up-to-date information and campaigns: https://annahope.uk.

Acknowledgements

Thank you –

To my family, Pam, Dan, Emily and Sophie, for allowing me to use their words in the texts and emails of the Writer sections.

To Dr Allan Chapman for generously reading extracts from the book and for several fascinating phone calls on the subject of eighteenth-century methods of navigation.

To Felipe S. Molina for reading and commenting on the 1907 sections of the text, and for offering invaluable advice on Yoeme cultural and linguistic traditions.

To Dr David Shorter, who, over several months and some profoundly generative conversations helped me to transform the 1907 sections of the book.

In Mexico – thank you to Emilia Robinson who gave me some space to begin writing at ChacaLit, to Juan M. Gonzalez, to Rodrigo Barrera, and to Don Emilio, Mara'akame Niuwe Osaya and Don Eugenio, Mara'akame Uru Muile.

Thank you to my editor, Helen Garnons-Williams, for her insight, sound judgement and encouragement.

And to Caroline Wood, my agent, for her unswerving belief in and support for this book from the first.

To Bridie, for being the inspiration for this book, and for understanding where I go when I disappear into the cabin.

To Dave, for all of it (well, perhaps not *all* of it, but most of it).

And to my extraordinary, best beloved dad, Tony Hope, who died during the writing of this book – thank you.

He just wanted a decent book to read ...

Not too much to ask, is it? It was in 1935 when Allen Lane, Managing Director of Bodley Head Publishers, stood on a platform at Exeter railway station looking for something good to read on his journey back to London. His choice was limited to popular magazines and poor-quality paperbacks – the same choice faced every day by the vast majority of readers, few of whom could afford hardbacks. Lane's disappointment and subsequent anger at the range of books generally available led him to found a company – and change the world.

'We believed in the existence in this country of a vast reading public for intelligent books at a low price, and staked everything on it'
Sir Allen Lane, 1902–1970, founder of Penguin Books

The quality paperback had arrived – and not just in bookshops. Lane was adamant that his Penguins should appear in chain stores and tobacconists, and should cost no more than a packet of cigarettes.

Reading habits (and cigarette prices) have changed since 1935, but Penguin still believes in publishing the best books for everybody to enjoy. We still believe that good design costs no more than bad design, and we still believe that quality books published passionately and responsibly make the world a better place.

So wherever you see the little bird – whether it's on a piece of prize-winning literary fiction or a celebrity autobiography, political tour de force or historical masterpiece, a serial-killer thriller, reference book, world classic or a piece of pure escapism – you can bet that it represents the very best that the genre has to offer.

Whatever you like to read – trust Penguin.